Jeffrey Royer

The Mercy Project

This is a work of fiction. Any references to real people, or real places are used fictitiously. Names, characters, places, and incidents either are the product of the author's imagination or are used fictitiously, and any resemblance to actual events or places or persons, living or dead, is entirely coincidental.

Copyright © 2012 by Jeffrey Royer

All rights reserved.
No part of this book may be used or reproduced in any manner whatsoever without the permission in writing from the copyright owner.

ISBN: 0-9884-4010-5
ISBN-13: 9780988440104

JDR Global Press

For my wife, Dina—
Thank you for pushing me out of my comfort zone and helping me discover my passion for writing.

PROLOGUE

Daniel walked swiftly toward the exit; the sound of his dress shoes on the marble floors echoed off the walls. "Please don't let me be too late," he said to himself as he pushed the door open and stepped out into the bright sunlight. He instinctively reached into his suit coat pocket, pulled out his sunglasses, and fitted them onto his face. He quickened his pace, and his driver hopped out of the car and opened the door for him.

"Thanks, Tom," Daniel said.

"No problem, Senator. We're heading to your parents' place?"

"Yes, as quickly as possible."

Tom nodded his head and closed the door as soon as Daniel's leg cleared the door frame.

Daniel leaned back into his seat and said a silent prayer. Thoughts raced through his head. One part of him wanted it to be over, while the other part couldn't bear the thought of it. He dropped his head into his hands and tried to clear his thoughts. After a minute he sat up and looked out the car window as they raced across the city toward their destination. His mind was starting to wander toward the depressing thought again when his cell phone rang. He saw on the caller ID that it was his wife.

"Yes, Jane?" he asked, praying she wouldn't deliver the news.

"How far away are you?"

"We're just coming up to the bridge. We'll be there in a few minutes."

"All right. I wanted to let you know I didn't want to leave Henry home alone, so I brought him here. Are you all right with that? I think it's important for him to be here."

"Of course," he said, relieved.

"OK, then. I wasn't sure if that would upset you."

"Not at all. I'll be there in a minute."

"OK."

He ended the call and took a deep breath. She didn't say anything, and he didn't ask. He assumed that meant there wasn't any bad news yet. Or maybe she just wanted to tell him in person. He pushed his sunglasses up onto his forehead, put his head in his hands, and began to sob. It was a brief spell, and only lasted about twenty seconds. He got his breathing under control, pulled out his handkerchief, and wiped his eyes. It struck him as ironic that he carried around this old-fashioned handkerchief imagining he might give it to a crying lady, and here he was using it. He wondered if that made him chauvinist or sexist or some other -*ist*. The thought made him smile. He dropped his sunglasses back down as Tom swung the car into Daniel's parents' driveway.

Tom lowered his tinted window so the guard at the front gate could see him. The guard waved back, and the gates slowly opened as Tom closed his window. They sped up the long driveway. As soon as the car stopped, Daniel jumped out and nearly ran to the front door. The door opened before he could grasp the handle, and Jane looked at him with a frown.

"Am I too late?" he asked in desperation.

"No, come on. I think he's waiting for you."

They hugged, and then Daniel grabbed her hand and pulled her with him.

Jane pulled back a little. "Daniel, don't you want to be alone with him?"

"No, please come with me."

They walked through the grand foyer and then turned down the hallway toward his parents' bedroom. Henry was sitting on a chair outside the bedroom door. He suddenly looked much older to Daniel.

"How are you doing, big guy?" Daniel asked.

Henry didn't answer; he just nodded with his lower lip pushed out, fighting to stop himself from crying. He was trying so hard to act like a grown-up. Daniel bent down and hugged him.

"Do you want to come in with us?" Daniel asked. He could feel Henry shaking his head no. "All right. If you change your mind, just come in. I know Gampa would like to see you." Daniel felt him nod and felt the wetness on his chest; Henry had lost the battle not to cry. Daniel pushed back from him and patted his shoulder. Henry quickly wiped his eyes with his sleeves and looked away like he hadn't been crying.

Jane knelt down next to Henry. "Are you going to be OK, or do you want Mommy to stay with you?"

"You can go. Maybe I'll come in...in a little bit."

Daniel grabbed her hand and held it tight as she stood up. He pushed the door open, and they walked in.

His mother, Eleanor, looked up and smiled at him. Daniel didn't understand how she found the strength to be happy. She was dressed immaculately, and that kind of pissed him off. Here her husband lay on his deathbed, and she took the time to dress nicely and put on makeup. Now was not the time to say anything, but he knew at some point he would bring it up. He felt the tears roll down his cheeks as he walked to the bed, still holding Jane's hand.

Daniel looked at his father, Joseph Pendelton—the man some had called the greatest US senator of all time. He looked like a skin-covered skeleton lying on an enormous bed. At first all Daniel could do was smile at his father as the tears streamed down his face. He knew if he tried to talk he would break down in sobs. He let go of Jane's hand and took his father's into his. Here lay his father, literally on his deathbed, he thought. The idea that he wasn't going to get up out of that bed and recover was finally sinking in like darkness.

"What are you crying for?" his father asked.

Daniel was startled that his father's voice was so strong. He just shrugged his shoulders and looked into his father's eyes with a smile on his face.

"Don't be sad. If you knew the pain I'm in, you would be happy that I'm almost done with it."

"I know, Dad," he said, finally trusting his voice. "The last thing I want is for you to be in pain. I love you."

"I love you too," his father said and gave him a brief smile. Then his face twisted, and he made a loud grunting noise. Daniel felt a moment of panic. He looked to his mother as she sat on the bed and took his father's other hand in hers. He grunted a few more times, and his body contorted as if he were doing abdominal crunches in the bed. His face was turning red and the veins on his neck were starting to stick out. His eyes bulged so much that Daniel was mortified that they might pop out. He wondered in terror if that were a possibility. His father squeezed his hand with surprising strength. Daniel looked at the skin and bones of his father's arm, and he couldn't understand where the strength was coming from. Daniel looked at Jane; her hand covered her mouth as tears rolled down her face. Daniel felt his breath start to hitch, and he quietly whimpered as he watched his father.

"I'm here, Joe. You're OK," Eleanor said, still holding his hand and rubbing his shoulder. Daniel's father finally collapsed back onto his pillow and breathed heavily with his eyes half open. His skin was wet with sweat.

Daniel stood frozen, looking at his parents on the bed. His mother nodded toward the nightstand, and he realized she was asking for the small hand towel. He picked it up and handed it to her. She dabbed his father's face with it, wiping the sweat away.

"Joe?" she asked. She waited a few seconds and then asked again, "Joe?" He didn't respond. "I think he's sleeping."

"Where's Billy?" Daniel asked his mother in a voice a little louder than a whisper.

"He's in West Palm."

"Well, is he on his way?"

"I didn't call him."

"What do you mean you didn't call him?"

"You know how sensitive he is. I think it's best to just call him after...." She didn't finish her sentence. She just looked lovingly at his father.

Daniel looked toward Jane with an odd expression. He wondered if it was just him or whether it was strange that his father was lying here, literally dying, and his mother didn't want to bother his brother to let him know. Jane looked at him and slowly shook her head, as if she knew exactly what he was thinking and that now was not the time to say something. He understood now wasn't the time, but he couldn't help himself.

"Mom, what the hell? Billy should be here. Dad's goddamn dying, and you took the time to get all dressed up. You look like you're going out on the town."

His mother looked at him. "Daniel, I understand you're angry. I'm angry too. I don't want this to be happening either. If I could wish it all away, I would. I'm not calling Billy because I think that's the right thing to do. I'm dressed nicely and had my hair and makeup done so your father could remember me at my best. I'm sorry if that offends you or if you don't understand."

Daniel looked down at his shoes and wished he could take back what he had said. She somehow reduced him to feeling like a five-year-old in just a few seconds. "I'm sorry, Mom. Yes, I'm angry, and I have no right taking it out on you. I hate this feeling." He took a deep breath. "Where's Dr. Craig?"

"He's out on the patio having a cigarette."

He once again looked toward Jane with an *are you hearing this* expression on his face. She once again shook her head. "Should we let him know what just happened?" he asked.

"Why?"

"Because he's a doctor, and Dad's dying."

"Your father was very specific that he didn't want to be drugged. He wants to stay lucid until the end."

"Mom, you know how stubborn he can be. Maybe we should do what's best for him. He's clearly suffering. Just have the doctor give him some morphine or something to end the pain."

His mother didn't answer right away. She bit her lower lip and took a deep breath while staring at his father. It was as if she were hoping he would give the go-ahead to administer the morphine.

Daniel took her nonresponse as a yes. He released his father's hand and walked to the doors leading out to the patio. He opened the door and found Dr. Craig sitting with his feet up on the table, puffing away on a cigarette. He was looking down the lawn toward the Potomac that flowed gently below. The sunlight flickered off the water.

"Dr. Craig," Daniel said, "My mother wants you to give him some morphine or something for the pain."

He pulled his feet off the table and sat up. "You're father was very specific that he didn't want any drugs."

"Well, you can blame me if he gets upset."

The doctor squashed his cigarette into the ashtray, stood up, and strode toward the house shaking his head. Daniel followed him inside. The doctor stopped short of the bed and bowed his head. Daniel looked at him and wondered if he was praying. He went to walk around him and saw his mother openly sobbing and running her fingers through his father's hair. His father lay there with his head tilted to the side. His eyes were half open, and his mouth was dropped open against his chest.

The first thought that popped into Daniel's head was that his father looked like the guy in Edvard Munch's painting *The Scream*. He dropped his shoulders and his head and started to sob. Jane quickly came over and hugged him. The two of them went to the side of the bed.

His mother was quietly talking to his father. "I'm going to miss you, Joe. I love you. Now your parents have two Joes in heaven."

That comment made Daniel cry a little harder. His older brother Joe had died on his bicycle in a tunnel accident over twenty years ago.

He buried his head in his father's chest and cried as his own son had done to him earlier. "I love you, Dad. I love you. You've been such a good father."

His mother reached over and rubbed his back.

☙❧

The day of the wake, Daniel walked out onto the patio off his parents' great room and found Don Kepler talking with the US attorney general. Daniel looked down and saw people walking around the grounds, seemingly enjoying themselves. It took everything in him not to scream, *My father is dead, and you people are acting as if you're at a great dinner party!*

The attorney general stood up, patted Don on the shoulder, and made his way over to Daniel.

"Daniel, I'm truly sorry about your dad's passing."

"Thanks, I really appreciate that."

"If you or the family need anything, please don't hesitate to ask."

"Thank you. My father thought very highly of you, and he would be grateful for your benevolence."

He gave Daniel an awkward man hug and then went back into the house. Don motioned for Daniel to come over.

"Cigar?"

"Why not?"

"How's your mother doing, Daniel?"

"Surprisingly well."

A very attractive woman came over pushing a drink cart. "Would you gentleman care for a drink?"

Daniel looked at Don and indicated that he should order first.

"I'll have a Scotch on the rocks."

"Make that two," Daniel said.

She made their drinks and continued pushing the cart along the patio.

"I wouldn't mind tapping that, if you know what I mean," Don said.

"I'm sure you wouldn't, Don. She may mind, though," Daniel said laughing.

Don rolled his eyes, pulled a cigar out of his coat pocket, and handed it to Daniel.

"Is this a Cuban?" Daniel asked, sniffing the cigar.

"It's a special occasion; we're celebrating your father's life."

"It still gives me the creeps that he's laid out in the formal living room. My mother has this old-fashioned idea that funeral homes are for the poor."

"She kind of has a point there, Daniel."

"I still can't believe he's gone," Daniel said, looking down into his drink.

"I know. It's cliché to say, but at least he's no longer suffering."

"It's not just cliché—it's the truth. It would have been a blessing if one of his nurses slipped him a little drug cocktail six months ago and ended his suffering then."

"You could have done it."

"Well, yes and no. You get caught up in the emotions, and you never give up hope." He swirled his glass, and the ice clinked against the crystal as he lifted it up and took a drink. "The doctors knew months ago there was no hope. There should be some sort of program where the doctors could make an educated decision, do everyone a favor, and euthanize the terminally ill."

Don smiled and laughed a little, looking down toward the people on the lawn.

"I'm serious. The last couple days, I've been putting a lot of thought and research into it, and I wanted to bounce the idea off of you."

"The idea of a Kevorkian-like program?" Don asked, sitting up in his chair.

Daniel took a sip of his drink as if he needed it for courage. "For some reason, no one thinks twice about putting down a sick pet. You bring them to the vet, you and the vet assess the situation, and if there's no hope—only suffering—you euthanize them. And I know a lot of people who love their pets more than their families. I just think sometimes people don't know what's good for them. The government should start a program."

"You can't be serious," Don said, waving to General Mustin down on the lawn after he had waved up at him.

"I am serious, and like I said, I think the government should start such a program."

Don turned back toward Daniel. "I admire your 'thinking outside the box,' but I think you need to maybe lay off the hard stuff, if you know what I mean." He lifted his glass up and tilted it toward Daniel.

"Don, this is the first drink I've had today—I swear. I know the idea sounds out there, but I honestly think there is a need for this. As long as it's kept quiet, people would unknowingly be grateful. Isn't that what our government is here for? To look out for the greater good of the people?"

"I think your grief is clouding your judgment. Think of what you're saying, Daniel. How furious would you have been had you found out there were some secret program that euthanized your father?"

"I agree—*if* I found out. That's why one of the key components of the program would be keeping it secret. Either way, if they told me that some doctors made a decision and euthanized him, you're right—I would be furious. Initially. But hindsight is twenty-twenty, and knowing now what he went through for the last six months—hell, what we as a family went through the last six months—I would thank the doctors from the bottom of my heart. I'm not talking about being diagnosed with a terminal illness and being euthanized on the spot; I'm talking about when the doctors know there's no more hope. We could have Medicare or Medicaid require doctors to fill out some sort of form to alert them that there's no further treatment available. They would unwittingly make the decision, and then the government would do the job."

Don reached over with his lighter and lit Daniel's cigar. "I see your point, but there are two problems that immediately come to mind." Don took a drag off his cigar and blew the smoke up in the air.

"And they are?" Daniel prompted.

"First, don't doctors sign an oath not to do such a thing—like take a life?"

"Yes, the Hippocratic Oath," Daniel said, taking a drag off his cigar and blowing it into the air. "That's another component to the program. The person administering the drug cocktail doesn't have to be a doctor. Once Medicare or Medicaid is notified, then we could have military special-ops personnel who have been specially trained visit the patients and administer the doses. We could have them peppered throughout the country."

"You really have put a lot of thought into this. But, Daniel, this thing will never fly."

"After seeing what my father just suffered through, I'm going to do my best to make it fly. Now you said two problems. What's the other one?"

"Maybe I should have said this one first and saved us both a lot of meaningless conversation."

Daniel shook his head in frustration. He really needed Don on board if this program was to have a chance in hell of getting out of the gate.

"I know this is close to your heart with what you just went through. I'm just saying it's never going to happen. The government, as we both know, doesn't care about hastening someone's death just so people and their families won't suffer. This plan won't fly because it's going to cost the government money. The amount you'd have to pay the special ops alone to make sure the project actually stays quiet would cost a small fortune. And we both know no one in government is looking to spend money—they're looking to save money."

Daniel grinned and lifted his glass toward Don. "No truer words have been spoken. You're wrong, and that's exactly why this is going to work."

Don's eyes widened, he leaned back in his chair, and he looked at Daniel. It wasn't often that he was told he was wrong. "How so?"

"Do you have any idea how much the last six months have cost my mother in terms of medical bills?"

"Not a cent," Don replied. "He was a US senator; he had the best health insurance your taxpaying dollars could buy. You do too, Senator Pendelton."

"Don, you know my mother. Do you think she would let the American people pay for my father's medical bills? She wouldn't let the government pay anything, and it cost a small fortune, which led me to do a little research these past few days. Do you have any idea how much money is spent on Medicare and Medicaid?"

"A lot." Don said shaking his head.

"You're right. A lot—like billions of dollars. And a large percentage of that is spent on the last thirty days of the patient's life. So imagine we kill two birds with one stone. We expedite the process, ending a terminal patient's suffering and saving a vast amount of government money at the same time. It's a win-win, Don."

Don looked deep in thought. He looked over at Daniel then back down at the "partygoers." "I don't know, Daniel. Deciding who lives and who dies—"

"Don, we will have doctors filling out the forms letting us know who is suffering needlessly when there's no more that can be done. Let me ask you, have you ever put down a pet?"

"Yes."

"Well, so have I, and while it wasn't easy, I knew it was what was best for the pet. Watching Dad really opened my eyes to the fact that, while this may be a complex idea, the thought of ending just one other person's unnecessary pain is enough for me to move forward. If the government starts this project, it should more than pay for itself. And I promise you it will do exactly what this administration is looking to do; save a fortune in healthcare costs."

Throughout the conversation Don had been mostly humoring Daniel as he heard him flesh out his plan. But his last statement was like an epiphany. The wheels started turning in his mind as he thought of the amount of money that could be saved. This was exactly the kind of thing that could bolster his political career. "To be perfectly frank, I don't care about ending the suffering; the government savings is the way to sell it," Don said, his voice trailing off as he envisioned the possibilities. He nodded his head and took a drag from his cigar.

When Don said that, Daniel knew he had sold him on the idea.

☙❧

NINE YEARS LATER

I

In all of Eleanor Pendelton's eighty-four years on this earth, she had never been as pissed as she was at that moment. She finished putting her clothes into her suitcase and zipped it closed.

"The nerve of that man—putting his hands on me," she said to her empty room shaking her head. "I am the widow of one of the most beloved senators in US history. How dare he?"

It was unlike Eleanor to say such things. But after moving to Oak Tree Pointe just two weeks earlier, and after seeing the way the staff treated the residents, she'd finally had enough.

Before she called her driver to come pick her up, she needed to go and inform Alice of her decision. Alice and Eleanor had been friends since the third grade. Alice had moved into Oak Tree Pointe, a senior-living community, six weeks before. This was surprising considering Alice had very little money and the monthly charges started at $4,500. Alice had fallen and broken her hip, and she was just entering the early stages of dementia. During Alice's recovery in the hospital, the staff really came to like her. It was hard not to—she was a genuine, sweet old lady.

At the hospital she was assigned a caseworker, Susan Jenkins. Her nurses at the hospital begged Susan to try to find Alice a nice place for rehabilitation. They hated the thought of sending her to one of the usual Medicaid facilities where living conditions were usually deplorable. Susan contacted Oak Tree Pointe, which offered assisted living as well as nursing facilities with rehabilitation. It was the premier facility in the DC area where the rich and powerful came to convalesce or live out their remaining days.

If a person off the street called Oak Tree Pointe and asked if they accepted Medicaid, the answer would be no. Susan knew, however, they had to admit a small percentage of Medicaid patients. In order for Oak Tree Pointe to accept Medicaid funds—which they did once they depleted a resident's funds—they had to set aside a certain number of beds for Medicaid-only patients. Susan pulled some strings and worked on Alice's behalf with admissions at Oak Tree Pointe. Fortunately she got Alice one of the coveted Medicaid slots.

Since Eleanor's husband had passed away, she had lived by herself in her family home—a century-old mansion. She had staff that cooked, cleaned, and took her where she wanted to go, but she was lonely. Her children were grown and had lives of their own. She wished they would visit more often, but she would never guilt them into a visit. Her youngest son, William, was unmarried and stayed at her home when he was in town, but unfortunately for Eleanor that wasn't very often. The parties she used to throw were becoming much less frequent, and her old friends were dropping like flies.

After visiting Alice on a daily basis, Eleanor decided it might be nice to move into Oak Tree Pointe. The residents played cards and watched movies; they even had a cocktail hour. Plus she would have people to talk to other than paid staff, and it would be nice to be around people her own age. So she moved in a few weeks after Alice. She decided to give herself a few months to test it out, and if it didn't work, she could always move back home. She kept the staff on at her home just in case she wanted to move back, but she told people the staff was kept on for William when he was in town.

What Eleanor did not anticipate was that while Oak Tree Pointe seemed fun and entertaining, after a while it became more depressing than fun. It seemed that almost every day another resident was dying or being taken to the hospital. Playing cards wasn't much fun when half of the people couldn't remember what game they were playing a few minutes into the game (or where they were, for that matter). There was also the fact that the staff was usually nice during the day when visitors were around, but at night some of them could be downright mean.

The previous night Eleanor left her room and walked toward the cafeteria to see if she could get a late-night snack. The cafeteria staff was always nice to her and said she could stop by anytime. On the way there, she bumped into Bob, a night aide.

"Where do you think you are going?" he asked.

"I'm just going down to the cafeteria to get a snack," Eleanor replied. She wasn't used to having to answer to people.

"I'm going to get a snack," Bob said in a mocking tone. "How 'bout instead we get on back to our room there, dearie?"

"I beg your pardon?"

"You can beg my pardon all you want. You heard me. You can't just be wandering the halls. Now get back to your room." He grabbed Eleanor's shoulder, squeezed it, and spun her around to the direction she had come from.

"Don't you dare put your hands on me."

"I'll put my hands on you whenever I like." He put both hands on her back, up by her shoulders, and pushed her back down the hall. "Now get moving before you have an accident. Wouldn't want you to fall and break a hip now."

Eleanor was seething. She knew better than to argue with this ass. She sucked up her pride and walked back to her room. Then and there she decided to move back home the next day. She felt like calling her driver to pick her up right then, but she didn't want to bother him late at night. She decided she would have her son Daniel, a US senator, have this place investigated. Rarely did Eleanor try to use her influence, but she had been keeping a journal on the mistreatment she witnessed at the facility.

She checked the bathroom medicine cabinet to make sure she wasn't leaving anything behind. She then went back into the room and slowly got down on her knees and peeked under the bed to see if she was forgetting anything under there. Not finding anything, she looked in the mirror to make sure she was presentable then left to go find Alice.

She checked the dining room where they were serving breakfast and didn't find Alice there, so she continued down the hallway toward

Alice's room. When she reached the room, she found Alice's door ajar. She knocked lightly on the door.

"Alice? Alice, are you here?" she called out. She pushed the door open and looked into the room. It appeared empty. The bed was neatly made, and the only other piece of furniture in the modest room was a small dresser with a television on it, which was turned off. The door to the bathroom was open, and Eleanor could clearly see Alice was not in there.

Eleanor stood in the doorway pondering her next move. She was tired from the walk and had no energy to traverse the maze of halls in search of Alice. She had a fleeting thought about how getting old sucks. Her exhaustion made the decision, and she went in and sat down on Alice's bed.

As she sat on the bed, she thought of how she would present her idea to Alice. She'd tell Alice to join her and move into her home. She would have physical therapists come to the house for Alice's rehabilitation. She knew Alice would put up a fight over the cost, but Eleanor wouldn't take no for an answer. They both knew Eleanor was very well off and could easily afford it. As she sat on the bed waiting, she caught herself starting to fall asleep. Eleanor decided to lie down. She slowly drifted off, inadvertently making the biggest mistake of her life.

2

Marcus Landon walked through the main entrance of Oak Tree Pointe. He went to the table where there was an open book and a sign that read *All Guests Must Sign In*. He signed the name *Max Jacobs* and walked toward the elevators. He found that every adult home was pretty much the same. No one really cared who came in; they were only concerned that the residents couldn't get out.

He knew exactly where he was going. He had memorized the layout of Oak Tree Pointe, including all exits and storage areas—places to either hide or get away if the need arose. Of course he knew he would most likely never have to do either of those things, but as a specially trained former operative in the army, he also knew you could never leave room for failure.

He was technically a visitor at Oak Tree Pointe, but the person he was going to visit had never met him before. He was actually employed by a company called Black Rock, and he was there to do a job. Official government records showed Marcus was honorably discharged from the US Army. Unofficially he was moved to a different sector and made an employee of Black Rock, which was secretly funded with government money. Marcus knew Black Rock wasn't a real company, and he honestly didn't care. All he cared about was the enormous paycheck that was regularly deposited into a secret bank account in the British Virgin Islands.

The way his job worked was that his handler would text him a number. He would then log on to a secure database on his laptop and enter the number. A name, picture, and location would come up. He would memorize the information and then log out. After each job was finished, he would text the number back to his handler, indicating the job was complete. He would then wait for another number to come his way.

Today was Alice Andrews's day. Marcus walked down the hall, making his way to her room, 718. There was an old guy pushing a walker toward him farther down the hall. Marcus assessed the situation and decided this resident shouldn't be a problem; the robe the man was wearing was not tightly closed, and he apparently forgot to put anything else on. It was safe to assume that walker man would not remember the stranger going into Alice's room.

He reached room 718 and found the door open. He slipped in quietly and closed the door. She was lying in her day clothes on top of her bed. Her face was pointed toward the wall, and he was grateful for that. He didn't care to look her in the face. He walked toward the bed, and at first glance he thought maybe she had beaten him to it—and that would have been fine with him. On more than one occasion, his subject had expired before he had to do his job. He stared at her a few moments to see if she was still alive and breathing. He finally noticed her chest lightly moving up and down with each breath.

He reached into his pocket and pulled out the syringe containing the fluid that would end her suffering. The fluid was a formula that was stolen from the Chinese and was completely undetectable after a couple of hours in the body, which was crucial in case there was an autopsy. Although not too many people questioned the cause of death for someone in the end stages of life. He waited a moment and watched her as she lay there breathing. Although he had killed more people than he cared to remember in the military—and he was very good at it—he still didn't like ending someone's life. In the service he only killed people who were either a direct threat to him or a threat to innocent people. His unease wasn't a religious thing—he was agnostic. He just had a core belief of live and let live, which he knew was a paradox considering what he was about to do.

He took the job because they sold it to him as a way to help end a person's suffering. Most of the other guys who did the same job—in other parts of the country—didn't need to be sold on it. The money was incentive enough.

He tried to give them the shot in an inconspicuous place. Taking a deep breath, he started to gently pull her pants down a little in the back, which was simple since they had an elastic waistband. She started to stir.

"What's this?" she murmured.

3

Alice shuffled down the hallway with her walker, returning to her room after visiting with her friend Rose, who had just lost her husband. She accidentally turned into the doorway right before her room. At first she was startled when she found Margie Peters sitting in her room on her bed, but then it dawned on her that she had, once again, accidentally walked into Margie's room and not her own. She tried to pretend she had intentionally come in.

"Hello, Margie, I just thought I would see how you're doing."

Margie would have no part of it. "What I'm doing, Alice, is wondering how many times you're going to *accidentally* come into my room thinking it's yours and pretend you're concerned for my welfare," she said laughing.

Alice stood there with her face flushed. "You know that's not true, Margie. You're my next-door neighbor, and I was concerned about you. I didn't see you at breakfast this morning." Alice wasn't sure where she came up with that one, but fortunately for her, Margie actually didn't make it to breakfast that day since her stomach was feeling a little off.

"Well, I'm doing fine, Alice. Thanks for checking on me. I'm not sure what I would do without such a concerned neighbor. How lucky am I?" she asked, rolling her eyes.

Alice could tell she was being condescending, but at least she believed she had fooled her into thinking she had intentionally come in to check on her. She wasn't sure why she was so embarrassed of becoming more forgetful each day or why she felt the need to pretend she wasn't forgetful. She could hear her friend Eleanor in her head saying, *Alice, we're in our eighties. We have the right to forget whatever we want.* That always made Alice feel better.

"All right, Margie, no need to thank me. I'm right next door if you need me." With that, Margie gave her a nice sneer, and Alice turned and went back out into the hallway, shuffling along behind her walker.

As she came out of Margie's room, she saw Glen what's-his-name coming toward her pushing his own walker. As usual Glen was wearing just his robe, which was untied and hanging open, with nothing on underneath it. He looked at her and made a big grin. She knew that Glen intentionally walked around like that for the world to see his business and that he pretended not to realize what he was doing. This was evident by the now-enormous grin fixed on Glen's face. He moved to the side of the walker so Alice could get the full view. He waved his arm at her.

"Hello, Alice!" he called out.

"Put some clothes on for Christ's sake, Glen!" she said to him, shaking her head. "No one wants to see your business!" She pushed her door open with her walker and made her way into her room.

As Alice walked through the door, she didn't understand what she was seeing. First, she had walked into Margie's room by accident, and then she saw more than she cared to see of Glen what's-his-name. Now there was a man bending over her friend Eleanor, who was lying on her bed. The man looked over, and Alice could tell by the look of shock on his face that she had startled him. He had Eleanor's pants pulled down a little in the back with one hand, and he was holding something else in the other.

She walked toward them trying to see what he was hiding. Although the man tried to block Alice's view, she saw that he was pulling a hypodermic needle from Eleanor's buttocks.

"What's the meaning of this?" Alice nearly shouted. "What are you doing to Eleanor?"

He looked at her as he palmed the needle, hiding it from her view. He grabbed the cap from between his clenched teeth, put it on the needle, and slipped it back into his pocket.

"You're in the wrong room, dear," he said. "This is Alice Andrews. She fainted, and I was helping her into her bed." He looked at Alice thinking she must have dementia or that "old-timers" disease. He smiled and tried to reassure her. "Stay with her, and I'll go get the nurse."

"That's not Alice. I'm Alice Andrews, and that's my friend Eleanor. What were you doing to her?"

Eleanor had a confused look on her face. "What happened?"

He smiled at her and then stood looking at Alice. It took a few seconds for what Alice had just said to register. He didn't want to believe her. He had never killed the wrong person before. The realization of his error crashed into him like a freight train. The job had been so easy for him that he had gotten comfortable and sloppy; breaking the cardinal rule and assuming that it was his target in the bed.

Trying to push the chaos out of his mind, he evaluated the situation. He quickly surmised that if the woman in the bed wasn't Alice, then he should finish the job and take the now-confirmed Alice out. It made sense, he thought. She was apparently the one who was actually suffering. He couldn't undo what he had just done to this Eleanor woman. He would wrestle with that problem later. The staff would think the real Alice came into her room and found her friend dead, and such a shock gave her a heart attack. It worked for him. He started toward Alice. "Now listen," he said, walking toward her, pulling another needle from his pocket.

"Are you OK, Alice?" Glen asked, standing at the door. "I heard shouting," he said. He pulled his robe closed when he spotted Marcus.

"Glen," Alice called out in relief. It was the first time she was actually glad to see the old flasher.

A flash of anger hit Marcus. Everything was rapidly going south. He was pissed at the real Alice for not being in her own goddamn bed, and this flasher guy Glen was completely messing it all up. He took a deep breath, and his years of training kicked in.

He suppressed his anger and realized that three heart attacks would be a little suspicious. In addition he only had one more needle, and there were two old farts to take down. The best thing to do was just get out of there before he messed things up any further. He dropped the needle back in his pocket and pushed past Alice. "I'll get the nurse." He brushed past Glen as he left the room. "Get out of the way, Glen, and get back to your room," he growled, poking Glen hard in the chest with his finger.

Glen quickly turned and headed back toward his room. He didn't want any trouble. Marcus hurried down the hallway just short of a run. As a trained assassin he was always calm during his maneuvers, but this thrust him into unchartered territory. He had never felt his heart beat this hard. *What are you doing to Eleanor? I'm Alice Andrews* kept running over and over in his head. He went quickly out the entrance of Oak Tree Pointe and hurried toward the parking lot. He couldn't get to his car fast enough. *Get in the car and get out of here* was the mantra he now repeated to himself.

He started his car and raced out of the parking lot. A short while later, when he felt he was far enough away, he pulled into a grocery store parking lot. "What do I do? What the fuck do I do?" he yelled in his car. He wondered whether he should alert his handler to the mistake, or whether he should just text the number back to him and pretend he got rid of Alice Andrews. Chances were his handler would never find out, but Marcus knew what would happen if he did. He screamed a primal scream in frustration.

He took a deep breath and picked up his phone. He scrolled to the text that was sent to him earlier with Alice's number. He pressed *reply* and typed the number, indicating Alice Andrews was taken care of. He stared at the screen for a minute trying to decide if he should send it. He let out a deep breath and pressed *send*. Relief came over him. He put the car into drive and pulled out of the parking lot into traffic.

4

Alice tried to help Eleanor up into a sitting position but quickly realized that Eleanor was not doing well. Her face was flushed, and she was starting to sweat profusely.

"I don't feel so well," Eleanor said, rubbing her chest with her hand.

"I know, Ellie. That man said you fainted and he helped you into my bed. He's gone to get help, so sit tight—you're going to be all right. What are you doing in here in my bed?"

Eleanor looked puzzled. "What am I doing in here?" she asked herself. Then a look of understanding came over her face. "I came to tell you I'm moving back into my home…and I want you to come with me, but you weren't here," she said, starting to look confused again. She shook her head and started to slowly speak again. "So I sat on your bed to wait for you…and I must have dozed off. What was that man doing to me?" And then Eleanor grabbed her chest with both hands and cried out. After a few moments of labored breathing, she looked at Alice. "Please call Daniel, and tell him to come."

Alice could hardly think straight. Where was the nurse? Why were they taking so long? She held onto Eleanor and promised she would call Daniel as soon as the nurse got there. Unfortunately, what Alice and Eleanor didn't know was that the nurse wasn't coming since Marcus never actually went for one.

After a few minutes, Eleanor closed her eyes. She was biting her lower lip, and she started to moan softly.

"Where is the goddamn nurse?" Alice muttered under her breath so she wouldn't frighten Eleanor. After a few more minutes, Eleanor lost consciousness. Her breath was so shallow Alice could hardly hear it. Alice had had enough. She gently laid Eleanor down on the bed and quickly threw open her door. She hurried down the hall pushing off the wall, not noticing she had forgotten her walker. "Nurse! Nurse! Help! Eleanor needs help! Something has happened. Oh, dear. Help!" she called out. "Help!"

Nurse Karen Gurkin was sitting in the lounge watching her favorite soap opera with some residents when she heard someone yelling for help. She hopped up and went out into the hallway. There was Alice Andrews rushing down the hallway without her walker, clearly panicking about something.

"What's the matter, Alice? Slow down and breathe. Where's your walker? Your hip isn't completely healed."

"Eleanor is sick! Where have you people been? That man said he was going to get a nurse and we've been waiting."

"Calm down, Alice. What happened to Eleanor? Where is she?"

"In my room. Please hurry—she doesn't look good."

They rushed down the hall toward Alice's room. Karen took one look at Eleanor and pulled the panic cord on the wall. A buzzer went off in the hallway, and a light flashed outside the room. She grabbed her radio and shouted, "Code blue—room seven eighteen! It's Eleanor Pendelton. We need an ambulance."

Tisha Piplin was covering the front desk that afternoon. She heard Karen shouting into the radio, and her heart sank when she heard the name. *Any other resident,* Tisha thought, *not Eleanor Pendelton, the Moby Dick of the residents.* That's what the administrator called Eleanor. She was the late senator Joseph Pendelton's wife, and she had more money than all the other residents combined. Code blue meant two things: call 9-1-1, and call the contact person in the resident's file. Tisha called 9-1-1, and while waiting for them to answer, she pulled up the file on Eleanor to get her son Daniel's phone number.

5

Senator Daniel Pendelton was sitting in a meeting with the president's chief of staff Donald Kepler and two four-star generals, General David Mustin and General Len Krytzer. Daniel always thought the stars were silly. It was like you were a fourth grader—your teacher gave you a star, and you put it on your shoulder to show off to your friends. He wisely kept that thought to himself.

Don was on one of his rants. He had been going off for twenty minutes now with no signs of slowing. Daniel was starting to drift off when Don's secretary, Janet, came in without buzzing or knocking first, which was not like her. She interrupted Don, which Daniel was pretty sure was grounds for termination. He hoped for Janet's sake that this was a true emergency.

"Excuse me, sir," she said to Don. Then she looked at Daniel. "Senator Pendelton, there's been an emergency. You have a call on line two."

Daniel's mind, which five seconds ago was close to sleep, was now racing a hundred miles per hour. When she said there had been an emergency, his heart jumped in his chest. He stood up and walked toward the phone. "Thank you, Janet," he said, reaching for the phone and pressing line two.

"Hello, this is Daniel."

"Senator Pendelton, this is Tisha Piplin at Oak Tree Pointe. It's your mother. She's…well, I've called nine-one-one, and they're on their way. We think she's having a heart attack."

"I'll head that way right now. Please call my cell phone if they take her to the hospital before I get there." He started to rattle off his number, and Tisha confirmed it was already on file. He hung up and turned back to the three men staring at him. "It's my mother. They think she's having a heart attack. I'm very sorry, but I need to go." He walked back to the conference table and gathered his things.

"Call for a car, and have it ready downstairs, Janet," Don instructed. "Let me know if there's anything we can do, Daniel."

"Thanks, Don. I'll give you a call as soon as I know what's going on. Gentleman," he nodded toward the two generals, "please excuse me." And with that he hurried out the door toward the elevator.

6

After seemingly taking hours to get there—in reality twelve minutes after the call—paramedics reached Eleanor. Just by looking at her when he entered the room, the first paramedic could tell it was too late. Her skin was grayish white, and her lips were light blue. Her eyes were fixed open.

"Hurry, hurry!" Alice cried through her tears, although even she knew it was too late.

Karen informed them there was a do-not-resuscitate order in her file. One of the paramedics checked for a pulse and shook his head indicating she was gone. This sent Alice into deep sobs, while Karen tried to console her. The paramedic reached his hand over Eleanor's face and closed her eyes.

"Does she have any family?" he asked.

"Her son is on his way," Karen responded.

He and the other paramedic tried to position Eleanor the best they could to make her presentable for her son.

❦

Daniel arrived at Oak Tree Pointe fifteen minutes after the paramedics. Tisha greeted him in the lobby and quickly ushered him toward Alice's room.

"What happened?" he asked as they hurried down the hallway.

"Her friend Alice yelled for help, and when the nurse went in, your mother was already unconscious. Paramedics got here about fifteen minutes ago."

They turned the corner in the hallway, and there were two paramedics standing outside the door with their workbags on the floor. The looks on their faces told Daniel he was too late.

He walked into Alice's room and saw his mother laid out on the bed as if asleep. Alice sat next to Eleanor on the edge of the bed, gently petting her arm while softly crying. Daniel could feel a lump forming in the back of his throat as he went over to his mother. He didn't want to cry in front of the nurse or paramedics, but to his surprise he couldn't hold back the tears. Trying to hold them back caused him to make a strange wheezing noise.

Alice looked up. "Oh, Daniel, what are we going to do?" she managed to blurt out.

She wrapped her arms around his waist and cried into his chest. Daniel had one arm around Alice while the other gently rubbed his mother's arm, just like Alice had been doing when he had walked in. His mother's arm was still warm. He could feel the tears running down his cheeks, and he was embarrassed because they were dropping onto Alice's head.

They stayed that way for a few minutes until Alice pulled away from him. "I think we could both use a tissue, dear," she said, motioning with her hand.

Daniel looked in the direction she was motioning and saw a box of Kleenex on the nightstand next to the bed. He grabbed a couple and handed them to Alice, then grabbed more for himself.

"What happened?" he asked her.

"I don't know, Daniel. I just came back from lunch, and some man was standing over her on my bed. It looked like he gave her a shot in her rear. I don't know how that was supposed to help her," she said, looking down shaking her head. She looked back up at Daniel. "I asked him what he was doing, and he said your mother had fallen, but he called her by my name. Isn't that strange? I corrected him and told him I was Alice and that she was Eleanor. Then he said he was going to get a nurse, and he left, but he never did get the nurse." She looked puzzled as she remembered the events.

Daniel could feel the blood rushing to his face and his heart racing uncontrollably.

"Are you all right, dear?" Alice asked.

Apparently consumed in thought, Daniel gazed off into space.

"Daniel, are you all right?" she asked again, shaking him gently.

Daniel regained his composure. "I'm all right; it's just hitting me that Mother is gone," he said.

Alice looked at him with her mouth turned down in sorrow. "It's all right, dear; it's all God's plan. She's with your father now."

His mind kept trying to go down the path he knew he couldn't let it go to. All he wanted was to quickly get home and get to his computer to make sure what had happened to his mother was indeed part of God's plan.

Daniel waited until the man from the funeral home rolled the stretcher into Alice's room. He kissed his mother's now-cool lips and went out in the hallway to say goodbye to Alice. "I'll let you know about the arrangements."

"Thank you, Daniel. Now remember that you made your mother very proud, and she loved you very much. Right before we lost her, she said to tell you how proud she was of you." That was partially true. Eleanor had told Alice to call her son, but Alice thought that little embellishment would make him feel better—and it did.

"Thanks, Aunt Alice," Daniel said. Although she wasn't really his aunt, she had been around the family for so long that everyone called her Aunt Alice. Daniel knew how much it meant to her to be part of the family. He didn't want her to think that since his mother was gone she was no longer a part of it.

"Have you told William yet?" she asked.

"I tried his cell phone, but it went straight to voice mail," he said.

By William she meant Billy, Daniel's kid brother. Daniel was sure Billy was in Rio or the Cayman Islands or some other jet-set place. He was always off somewhere on a "goodwill" mission. This meant donating the family money to some charity that had outposts in beautiful locations where the women were scantily clad. He kissed Alice and hugged her good-bye. He then made his way to the car waiting for him outside.

7

It was a warm fall day, and the sun was shining. Daniel wished it was raining so when he got home he wouldn't feel guilty for wanting to just crawl into bed and go to sleep. Unfortunately the last thing he could do now was sleep. It was just after three, and he figured his wife, Jane, must have landed by now. She and two girlfriends had flown down to a spa in Clearwater, Florida, for a couple days. He had tried her earlier on the way to Oak Tree Pointe, but it went straight to voice mail. He dialed her cell now, and she answered on the first ring.

"Hi, Danny," she said.

"Hi, Jane. How was your flight?" he asked.

"It was a little bumpy and quite turbulent toward the end. Nothing a few glasses of wine couldn't cure—though Sharon apparently had a few too many since she spilled some wine on the front of her blouse."

Daniel could hear Sharon in the background yelling, "I went to take a drink right when we hit a bump. You make me sound like a drunk!"

"But you are a drunk," Jane's other friend Lucy yelled in the background. The ladies all erupted in laughter.

Daniel smirked to himself with tears rolling down his face. He knew he was about to turn her mood around, and he felt bad for doing it.

"What's up, honey?" Jane asked.

"Jane, I have some bad news."

"What's wrong?"

"It's my mother. She passed away."

"Oh my God, honey, I'm so sorry. What happened? I was just there visiting her yesterday, and she seemed to be doing so well. She was in a great mood." Daniel could hear Sharon and Lucy in the background asking what happened.

"They believe she had a massive heart attack," Daniel said.

"Oh, Daniel," Jane said. Then he heard her tell the girls his mother had passed away; he could hear them offering condolences in the background.

"Tell them I said thanks," Daniel said.

"Let me call Steve and tell him we need to fly back. I'll be there as soon as I can," Jane said. Steve was the pilot for their family jet.

"No, Jane. Stay there. It's all right. There's nothing you can do here. We'll have the service in a few days. Relax and come back when you planned. I'll be all right. I'm on my way back to the house. The funeral home has already taken her—" and he started to choke up.

"Oh, honey. She lived a long, wonderful life. She's at peace now. I'm so sorry. I'm going to come home. I'm calling Steve now. I don't want you to be alone."

"No, Jane, seriously—I'm all right. I know you three have been looking forward to this trip for a while. Mother would want you to enjoy yourself. Have a martini in her honor. Esther can make me a nice native dish that will 'make my spirit happy.'" Their housekeeper Esther was originally from Ecuador. She didn't have a good grasp of the English language, and "my spirit happy" sounded like something she would say. Daniel and Jane got a welcome little laugh out of that one, and it broke some of the tension.

"Are you all right to drive?" Jane asked.

"Don had a driver take me, so I'm just having him take me home. I'll get my car tomorrow."

"Have you called Henry yet?"

"I tried him earlier and left a voice mail to give me a call," he said.

"Well, I won't rush back tonight if you insist, but I'm coming back tomorrow. I don't want you to have to make all the arrangements alone, even if you do have Esther to take my place."

He chuckled a little at the Esther comment.

"That's really not necessary. I'll call you this evening," he said.

"All right, honey, I'm so sorry. I love you."

"I love you too," he said and ended the call.

The driver pulled up to the large gates at the start of the driveway. He rolled Daniel's window down so he could enter the gate code. He entered the code, and the gates slowly rolled open. Daniel rolled his window back up as the driver proceeded up the long tree-lined driveway to the three-story, brick-and-stone Georgian mansion. Every time Daniel went up his driveway, he really appreciated what a beautiful home they had. Carl pulled to the front entranceway and stopped the car.

"Thanks very much, Carl."

"Would you like me to wait, Senator? Mr. Kepler told me to be at your disposal until you no longer needed me."

"I won't be going anywhere else tonight, Carl. Thank you though."

"Not a problem, Senator. I know it's none of my business, but I'm really sorry about your mother. I never met her, but I used to see her in the news with your dad. Everyone always had nice things to say about your mom and dad. She was a class act. And your dad was—I'd have to say—the best senator this country ever had."

"Thanks, Carl. I really appreciate that."

He closed the car door and went up the front sidewalk into the house as Carl pulled away.

He went straight to his office and started his laptop. While it booted up, he went to the wet bar and poured a glass of Basil Hayden's. He downed it in two gulps and then poured another. He settled into his leather chair and waited for the laptop to start. Once it was ready, he logged in through six different security screens, each with its own password, until he came to the data page he was looking for.

He typed in his mother's name. After a few seconds, it came back with the message *no match*. He then typed *Alice Andrews* and hit *Enter*. A few seconds passed, then Alice's name and statistics popped up with the status *completed*. It didn't say *pending*; it said *completed*. Daniel rubbed his eyes and looked again at the screen. Nothing had changed; the screen still displayed *Alice Andrews—completed*. Alice Andrews was supposedly dead. He could feel the blood rushing to his head.

He reached into his desk drawer and fumbled toward the back. He felt around with his fingers until he finally found a small case shaped like a capsule. He pulled it out. He got it at a trade show a while ago, and it contained a small flash drive encased in a capsule. It was a promo from some pharmaceutical company. While he was pulling it out, he also spotted an old pack of cigarettes he had hidden long before quitting. A pack of matches was shoved into the cellophane. He grabbed these as well.

He pulled apart the capsule and popped the flash drive into the USB port. He minimized the windows to see the desktop. He right-clicked the icon that said *Health-Care Initiative* and copied it to *E:*, the port where the flash drive was located. A warning box with a password field opened, indicating the data was classified. He typed his password and hesitated. He then thought of his mother's face as she lay dead on Alice Andrew's bed and pressed *Enter*. A box opened up on the top-left side of his screen indicating the files were copying.

He went back to the screen where he had found Alice's name and pulled up the master-list file of names. He sorted them by *pending* and then *completed* in alphabetical order. He right-clicked, chose *Save As*, and titled the file *Patient names*. He clicked on the file tab, clicked *Send To*, and selected the *E:* drive—again for the flash drive. Another warning box opened indicating the data was classified. He reentered his password and pressed *Enter*. The box cleared, and an hourglass popped up indicating it was processing.

He knew if he wanted to end this thing, he would need proof that the project even existed—hence the flash drive. He had contemplated uploading the information to a server or e-mailing it to himself as an added precaution, but he knew that either could easily be hacked and deleted. Once he tried to stop it, if the committee didn't agree to end it, he knew they would invalidate his passwords and deny him access to the project. The project would continue, and if Daniel tried to expose it, they would make him look like he was crazy. He could imagine the leaked reports: *Senator Pendelton has been under a lot of stress, especially since the loss of his mother*. They would supply witnesses to discredit Daniel and offer bizarre stories showing he was heading toward a breakdown. He had seen it happen before to other government employees who didn't go with the flow. He copied the files to the external drive as a little insurance policy.

After a minute a bell sounded and the message popped up: *file transfer complete*. He pulled out the flash drive and put it back in the capsule. He now had his safety net. He just hoped the committee would realize one accidental death was reason enough to shut down the project. He didn't want to have to threaten to go public. He pushed back in his chair and stood up, placing the capsule in his pocket. He grabbed his drink and his pack of smokes and headed out the French doors to the patio off of his office.

He sat in a chair on the patio, put his drink on the side table, and tapped a cigarette out of the pack. *Jane would not approve of this whole smoking again*, he thought. He struck a match and inhaled it into the tip of the cigarette. He looked out over the expansive grounds toward the slow-moving Potomac below. He blew the smoke out then breathed in. "Oh my God, Mother, what have I done?" he said to the empty patio. He leaned forward, put his head into his hands, and softly sobbed over the realization of what had happened today—and how he was responsible.

8

Henry Pendelton startled awake covered in sweat from a nightmare he was having. He dreamed a guy was chasing him through the woods in his parents' backyard next to the Potomac River. Every time he turned around, the guy was much closer, no matter how fast Henry ran. He didn't know why he was being chased, but somehow he knew if this guy caught him, he would kill him. He went to jump into the river, and as soon as he hit the water, he woke up.

It took him a second to remember where he was. The week before, he had gone back to college, and he was in his bed in the town house his parents had bought for him. After their sophomore year, students could move out of the dorms and off campus. Dorm life just wasn't what it was cracked up to be. He tried it but had no interest in sharing a communal bathroom or having an RA who had it out for you. So his parents bought this place "as an investment," they would say. But Henry knew they could easily afford to purchase it—they just didn't want anyone to think he was spoiled. He had two roommates who paid him rent—occasionally—but that added to the college experience.

He looked over, and lying next to him was his girlfriend, Jessica. They had met in Europe over the summer. Henry first saw her sitting alone in a café. At first he thought she was French. Once he sat down, he quickly discovered that not only was she not French, but they were both from the DC area, and they attended the same college. They ended up traveling across Europe together over the summer and had been dating ever since.

She lay on her back with her breasts exposed. Her arms were crossed over her head, shielding her eyes from the light seeping in around the window shades. He reached over and softly caressed her breasts. Whenever he woke up with a hangover, he was always incredibly horny. This time was no exception. He slid toward her to spoon her. She moaned, and without opening her eyes, she pulled the covers over her chest, knocking Henry's arm away in the process. She rolled away from him. The thought crossed his mind that maybe she just wanted it from behind, and that was why she had rolled over, but he knew he was only kidding himself. *A guy can dream, can't he?* he thought. He understood he wasn't getting any right now. He lifted the sheet up and saw that they both were naked. He couldn't remember if he had gotten lucky the night before. He didn't think it would be a great idea to ask her, so he kept that question to himself.

He pushed himself into a sitting position on his side of the bed and placed his feet on the floor trying to determine if he could actually stand up. His head lightly ached. Not bad considering the amount of alcohol he had abused himself with the night before. He figured he was still drunk. He reached for the bottle of Fiji water on his nightstand and poured the little that was left down his parched throat. He waited a little bit then eased himself up. *So far, so good*, he thought. First things first—he had to take a piss.

He stood in front of the toilet draining his bladder for a good two minutes. He chuckled to himself wondering if this was the piss that would never end. When he finished he made his way out of the bathroom and over to his pile of clothes on the floor. He grabbed his boxers and slipped them on.

He went to the kitchen and started a fresh pot of coffee. Everyone else was apparently still sleeping. He turned the television to channel ten's all-day DC news. They were talking about a gang shooting in a shady part of town. The reporter was interviewing the mother of one of the victims. The woman was flanked by two people trying to hold her up while she wailed into the camera, "Why did they kill my son?" Henry said to the television, "Lady, what you should be asking is why your friends are letting you go on television at a time like this." He shook his head and went back into the kitchen to check on his coffee.

He poured a cup of black coffee. He thought of the movie *Airplane* where the little boy asks the little girl if she wants cream in her coffee, and she says, "No thank you. I take it black—like my men." He chuckled to himself. He was decidedly still drunk and goofy. It was already one thirty in the afternoon. He had missed all of his classes that day. The last time he had checked his watch it was 5:00 a.m., and he and Jessica were at an after-hours party. He figured they must have finally crashed around six or seven that morning.

He went back to the bathroom and hopped in the shower. He soaped up, rinsed, and then sat on the bench in the shower, letting the hot water hit his back, trying to wash away his hangover. After a while he stood and started to rinse off. He felt a hand brush against his back. He was still wound up from the nightmare, so he jumped and quickly swung around to see who touched him.

It was Jessica standing in the shower doorway naked. "Hey, didn't mean to scare you. Hangover jitters?" she asked.

"Oh my God! You almost gave me a heart attack, Jess," he sighed and then smiled.

"I'm sorry, sweetie. Thanks for making coffee," she said with a smile. She placed her coffee on the vanity counter. "I thought I'd join you."

"I'd like that," Henry said. He grabbed her around the waist and sat down on the bench, pulling her on top of him.

After a while the water started to run cold. They rinsed off, got out, and toweled off.

"That was nice," Jessica said and kissed him.

"It was. We need a bigger hot-water tank so we can stay in there longer."

She kissed him again. "You get right on that," she said, wrapping a towel around her body. "In the meantime would you mind grabbing me some more coffee while I dry my hair?"

"I can do that," he replied. He wrapped a towel around his waist and headed toward the kitchen with both of their mugs.

He poured the coffee and went back to the bathroom. He gave Jessica her mug. "Are you hungry, Jess?" Henry asked.

"Starving."

"I'll go see if I can find something for us to eat."

"Good. Mama's hungry," she said, rubbing her belly.

"You're such a freak," Henry said laughing. He left the bathroom and went to scrounge the refrigerator for something to eat.

"Jackpot!" he said to the empty kitchen. He found two whole subs they must have gotten at some point in the morning before they came home. Thankfully they hadn't eaten them. Better yet they had put them in the fridge instead of leaving them on the counter.

He grabbed half of the ham-and-cheese sub and started to devour it over the kitchen sink. He thought he heard someone on television say "Pendelton." He looked up, and the story had finished; now they were talking about a panda cub that was just born at the Washington Zoo. He grabbed the remote and rewound the news. While it was rewinding, he saw a picture of his grandparents come up; then as it continued to rewind, it showed the newscaster.

He pressed *Play* and watched the newscaster Diane Thomas. "We are just getting word and have very sad news to report. Eleanor Pendelton, the widow of the late senator Joseph Pendelton, has apparently passed away. Mrs. Pendelton was a socialite and heir to the Henderson family fortune. We're waiting for further details and will pass them along as soon as we receive them. Mrs. Pendelton was eighty-four years old." They showed photos of Henry's grandparents while Diane was talking. Now they went back to a shot of Diane and her co-anchor, Tom Bussley, at the news desk.

"That's really sad news, Diane," Tom said. "Senator Pendelton was a true gentleman and great senator, and Eleanor was the epitome of a classy lady. She was known for her generosity. She will be missed."

Henry stood staring at the television. Were they serious? Gammy was dead? He went back to his room to find his cell phone. He put the half-eaten sub on top of the dresser and dug through his clothes for the phone. He pulled it out and looked at the screen—three missed calls. He checked his voice mail and found he had three new messages. The first was from his roommate Paul.

"Hey, loser. Where did you and Jess go? We're heading over to Ella and Sam's Diner on M Street. Meet us there."

The automated voice came on: "To save this message in archives, press one." Henry pressed four to delete. The next message came on.

"Hi, Henry, it's Dad. Give me a call when you get a chance."

Henry pressed four again. The third message came on.

"Henry, it's Mom. Give me a call as soon as you get this message."

He pressed *End* then called his mother.

"Henry?"

"Hi, Mom, I just saw the news. Is it true about Gammy?"

"Oh, honey, I'm sorry you had to find out on the news. Yes, your father called me earlier. They think she had a heart attack this afternoon, and as you know, she didn't make it."

"That sucks," Henry replied. He could feel his lower lip pushing up and was surprised that he was going to cry.

"Honey, what sucks is the fact that I just landed in Florida, and your father is insisting that I don't come back early."

"Listen to Dad, Mom. He would tell you if he wanted you to come home early. I'll head over and see him in a little bit." Henry wiped a tear that fell down his cheek.

"You know he'll just try to talk you out of it," she said.

"I won't call first; I'll just show up. He's not going to make me leave once I'm there."

"Good thinking, Henry. See, all of this schooling is actually paying off."

"Right, Mom."

"Sweetie, I'm really sorry that Gammy has passed away."

"I know, Mom. Thanks. I'll call you when I get to the house."

"All right, Henry. I love you."

"I love you too, Mom," he said and ended the call.

The hairdryer stopped, and Jessica came out of the bathroom and into the bedroom still wearing her towel. "Did you find anything to eat?" she asked. "I wasn't kidding—I'm starving." She was brushing her hair looking toward Henry who was also still in his towel sitting on the edge of the bed looking toward the floor.

Henry looked up, and Jessica could see he was crying.

"Henry, what's the matter?" she asked, looking very maternal all of a sudden.

"I just found out my grandmother died," Henry said.

"Oh, Henry, I'm so sorry." She came over and sat next to him on the bed.

"Thanks, Jess."

She pulled him over and hugged him.

"I'm all right, Jess." He wiped his eyes. "I think I'm just still a little drunk from last night and feeling a little sappy."

"It's perfectly normal to cry when you lose a loved one. It doesn't make you any less of a man, Henry."

"I know, Jess. I'm a manly crying man." He smirked and leaned over and kissed her. He wiped his eyes again. "Listen, I need to get dressed and head over to my parents' house. My mom's down in Florida, and my dad's all alone—it was his mother."

"Of course, Henry. What can I do?"

"Nothing. Thanks though, Jess. I'll call you later and let you know when the service will be. You will come be with me, won't you?"

"You know I will. Just let me know if there's anything else I can do."

"I will, thanks," he said. "Will you let Paul and Chad know about my grandmother? And tell them just because I'm not here that doesn't mean have a keg party and trash the place. At least not when I'm not here to enjoy it."

"I'll take care of it. Don't worry about anything."

Henry got dressed and packed a small bag to take with him. He sent e-mails to his professors letting them know he would be absent due to a death in the family. He hugged and kissed Jessica goodbye, then went out, got in his BMW, and headed toward home.

9

"Hello, Daniel," Don said. He was in the house standing in the doorway of the office, looking out toward Daniel sitting on the patio.

"Hey, Don, what are you doing here?" he said, looking up in surprise.

"Didn't mean to startle you. Esther let me in. I heard your mother didn't make it, and I wanted to stop over to let you know how sorry I am."

"Thank you, Don."

"Can I get you anything?" Don asked, motioning with his hand indicating a drink. "Or do you mind if I make myself one?"

"Help yourself. And if you don't mind, will you bring me the bottle of bourbon that's out on the bar?"

"Not a problem," Don said. He disappeared from the doorway, and Daniel looked back out toward the Potomac.

Don came back with a drink in his hand and the bottle of bourbon. He sat down across from Daniel. He reached over and poured some bourbon into Daniel's glass, put the bottle down on the table, and then tapped his glass against Daniel's.

"To Eleanor Pendelton, may she rest in peace," Don said.

Daniel looked down shaking his head with his mouth turned downward as if he were about to cry. "We killed her, Don. Do you realize that?"

Now it was Don's turn to look startled. "What are you talking about, Daniel?"

"What I'm talking about is that it wasn't a heart attack, Don. It was us. Our little project," he said, waving his finger between the two of them. "The 'Health-Care Initiative.' My mother's friend Alice told me when I got there," he said, shaking his head.

"Told you what?" Don asked.

Daniel lifted his glass and took a drink. "She said some aide was pulling my mother's pants down and giving her a shot when she walked in." He gave Don a disgusted look and continued: "Then my mother had this 'heart attack.' For some reason my mother was in her friend Alice's bed when an 'aide' must have mistaken her for Alice."

"Daniel, you've been under a lot of stress. You're not thinking straight. I'm sure this Alice was mistaken."

"No, Don, I've never thought more clearly, and I'm not mistaken. What in the world were we thinking? We should have never gone though with this project." He seemed to mumble toward the end with tears rolling down his face.

"Daniel, get a hold of yourself. I assure you this has nothing to do with the project."

"No, Don, you're wrong. I already looked into the system when I got home. My mother's name was not on the list, of course, because as we both know, our family members are exempt. However, when I look up her friend Alice—the one whose bed my mother just happened to be in—guess what the system showed then, Don? You want to guess?" Daniel was practically shouting now. Don sat still with no emotion on his face. Daniel continued. "No guess, Don? All right, let me end the suspense for you. Alice's name is not only on the list, but it shows that her case was completed as of today. And I assure you, Don, Alice is not completed; she is very much alive, and my mother is very much dead. I'm thinking maybe the 'aide' needs a little reprimand for making this little mistake, especially since Alice said she told him it was my mother in her bed. What do you think, Don? So he made a little mistake and took one old lady out when he was supposed to take another, and then he entered Alice into the system as completed. What's the big deal? Huh, Don?" he asked sarcastically, wiping the tears from his face. "So you tell me—how we are not responsible?"

Daniel pushed back from the table. "I need the restroom," he said. He got up and walked back toward the door. He went into the house and walked over to the wet bar in his office, putting some fresh ice in his glass.

"Are you sure you should be having another drink, Daniel?" Don asked.

"Look at you, Don—you have already filled my mother's shoes," he said, glaring at him.

"Daniel, you need to listen to me. I'm sure once this all shakes out, you'll see that you're jumping to conclusions. For all we know, the 'aide' was supposed to help Alice end her pain, and you're mother coincidentally had a heart attack. Stranger things have happened. Let's just not do anything rash."

"You're unbelievable, Don. What Kool-Aid have you been drinking? Or should I say, what Kool-Aid do you think I've been drinking? We both know that this was a job because of the project. But the worst part is that Alice doesn't even come close to the parameters for the project. This wasn't going to be a mercy killing or euthanasia. Alice is on the mend. Another month or two of physical therapy and she'll be out of there. So when did the parameters change, Don?" Daniel asked.

Don looked at him and sighed. "Daniel—we both know this started as a way to end suffering and, shall we say, help the patient while reducing government costs. And as you know, at first the committee would decide on a case-by-case basis using the questionnaires that we required hospitals and nursing homes to fill out. That was fine in the beginning. Then as time proceeded, the budget-management office pointed out that the cost of the mercenaries was starting to exceed the patient savings, so the project was close to being scrapped. I adjusted the system so that instead of just deciding case by case, we could also have the system choose candidates based on the codes that were being billed to Medicaid. Clearly we're going to have to review the data and adjust the criteria to warn us of possible patient recovery."

Daniel's mouth hung open, and he stood frozen with his drink in his hand looking at Don. "Please tell me you're joking about using a system based on the Medicaid codes. This is lunacy. I was on board for euthanasia or mercy killings—whatever you want to call it. Hell, we know it was my idea after watching my father suffer so badly at the end. If my elderly dog was in pain, and the outcome was most certain death, I would put him down. Why not do the same for elderly people? I was doing it for compassion, remember? But as you pointed out, the only way I could sell it was by showing it would also save money. Now, though, you've twisted it—we're not doing it for compassion anymore but just for money. Don, this has to end."

Don looked at Daniel and shook his head. "It's not going to end, Daniel. The decision has already been made. The administration is looking at all options to cut expenses. Do you think it was just my idea to push it forward to keep the project alive? Use your head, Daniel. The administration wants lower health-care costs. Think about this. Do you really think they're going to end a program that is saving this much money?"

"I don't care how much it saves, Don. This isn't compassion—it's flat-out murder. I'm putting an end to it."

"An end to it?" Don said with a laugh. "Pandora's box is already open, Daniel. You have no idea what you started, do you?" He laughed harder. "Once the project started saving real money, another committee was formed to look into other areas of Medicaid and Medicare expenses to save even more money. They're looking into all terminal-disease expenses like chemotherapy and radiation for cancer patients. Hell, they have already opened the project to pediatrics. I had no idea how much money the government kicks in to save premature babies. Did you, Daniel?"

Daniel once again found his mouth hanging open. "This is madness, Don. Babies? Really? To save money? If you think that would stop me, you've just lit the fire under my ass to really put an end to this," he said with disgust.

"Where's the flash drive, Daniel?" Don asked.

Daniel looked at Don. Thoughts raced through his head. How could Don possibly know that he copied the files to the flash drive?

"Daniel, I realize this has been a stressful day, and I truly am sorry about Eleanor, but please—just stop acting crazy. You've expressed your concerns, and we will discuss them, but do you actually think this is something you alone can put an end to? You have no idea how much money the government has saved since we put in the new parameters. You can't stop this, Daniel, so just give me the flash drive and stop trying to be the hero."

"Get the fuck out of my house, Don!" Daniel yelled at him. He turned and headed toward the bathroom.

"I'm not going to ask you again," Don said, walking over toward Daniel.

Daniel stopped and turned around. "What are you going to do, Don?" he asked. "Search me? Get out of my office," he said, pointing toward the doorway. "And while you're at it, get the fuck out of my house."

Don came toward him and slammed his hands into his chest. Daniel stumbled back but caught his balance. He now wished he hadn't had so many drinks. He tried to think about how many he'd had when Don slammed him again from the side. This time Daniel went down hitting his side into his office chair, knocking the breath out of him.

"This doesn't have to be like this, Daniel. Where is the fucking flash drive?"

"I don't know what you're talking about," Daniel sputtered out.

Don grabbed Daniel by the shoulders and pulled him in close. "You fucking moron. As soon as you tried to copy the project onto the flash drive, the system alerted us. Why do you think I'm here? You think I came just to offer my condolences? Did you think we wouldn't know what you're doing? This was your idea, and now there's blood on all of our hands. I'm not letting you drag us all down. Do you understand? The project is not going to be stopped. If you try to expose it, not only would it spell the end of our political careers, but quite possibly indictments and prison time. Do you hear me, Daniel? Prison. Don't you understand there's no stopping it?"

Don leaned down and started patting Daniel's pockets. Daniel grabbed Don's wrist, twisted it with all of his strength, and tried to roll out of his grip. Don cried out in pain.

The look in Don's eyes said it all. Daniel knew this was not going to end well. Don's hair hung down in front of his eyes, and sweat poured down his face. He put Daniel in a headlock.

"It didn't have to end this way, Daniel," Don said. He reached inside his suit coat and pulled out a syringe that, unfortunately for Daniel, contained the same fluid that his mother received just hours earlier.

10

Henry turned off the street into his parents' driveway and stopped at the gates. He entered the code, and the gates swung open. He drove up the driveway toward the house. As he approached the house, he noticed a town car parked out front under the porte cochere at the main entrance. There was a driver behind the wheel and some big guy sitting in the back looking over his shoulder toward Henry. Henry veered right where the driveway split off and drove around to the side of the house. He pulled into the garage and got out of the car.

He went in the house and walked down the hallway toward the kitchen. Esther, his parents' housekeeper, was standing at the counter chopping vegetables.

"Hi, Esther," he said.

"Henry, what you doing here, sweetie?" Esther responded in her Ecuadoran accent. She came over and hugged him.

"Mom called and said she didn't want Dad to be alone."

"He'll be happy to see you. I'm big sorry for you about your Gammy," she said, rubbing his shoulder.

"Thanks, Esther, I appreciate that. Dad's here? I didn't see his car in the garage."

"He get ride home because driver take him having to go to Gammy's. He's in office. Your Uncle Don is with him." Don Kepler was an old family friend who Henry grew up calling Uncle Don.

"I wondered whose car that was out front. Thanks, Esther. What time's dinner?"

"In about an hour. I hope you brought you hungry. I making pot roast. Good hearty food to help you sad."

Henry knew what she meant.

"You're a good egg, Esther. We're lucky to have you," he said, patting her on the shoulder.

"I no egg, Henry. And I lucky to be with you family," she said.

He smiled and gave a little laugh. "I'm going to go see Dad," he said, leaving the kitchen.

Henry walked down the corridor toward the main entrance. His father's office was past the main entrance and down another corridor. When he crossed the foyer, he could hear his father and Don talking in loud voices. It almost sounded like they were arguing. Henry couldn't figure out why they would be arguing after what had happened to his grandmother. He walked quietly to the doorway to see what was up. When he looked in, he couldn't believe his eyes. Don was bending over his father and had him in a headlock. He was pressing down the plunger on a hypodermic needle that he had in his father's neck.

Daniel saw Henry appear in the doorway to his office. He looked toward his son with a look of shock.

"Dad!" Henry called out.

"Henry! He's having a heart attack," Don blurted out, quickly standing up and pocketing the syringe.

"Dad," Henry called again, and then finally freed himself from the shock he was in and quickly went over to his father.

Don stood back making room for Henry. "He was so upset about your grandmother. He...he.... It's his heart, Henry."

"What did you do to him?" Henry asked, looking up at Don. "Call for help!"

"It's his heart, Henry," Don kept repeating, stepping back from the two of them.

"Jesus, Uncle Don, what was in that syringe? What did you do to my dad?"

Don's face lost its remaining color. He was hoping Henry hadn't caught sight of the syringe, but clearly he had. He stepped away from Daniel and Henry, walked toward the French doors, and pulled out his phone.

Henry knelt on the floor and pulled his father's head onto his lap. "You're going to be all right, Dad. Hang in there."

Daniel fumbled his hand into his pocket and pulled it out with something clutched in his fist. He reached his hand up and pushed it into Henry's hand. Henry looked down and saw it was a small plastic capsule.

"Take this and get out of here. You have to run, Henry." Daniel was whispering so Don couldn't hear. "I'm so sorry this is happening. You have to expose what the government is doing. It's all on here. Go take it to Uncle Billy. He'll help you figure out what to do." Daniel couldn't believe his son was now going to depend on his little brother Billy to help him get the truth out and shut the project down. Unfortunately he had no other idea, and his heart was racing uncontrollably.

In the reflection in the glass of the French door, Don saw Daniel give Henry something. He knew it must be the flash drive. Don dialed a number on his phone and both Daniel and Henry overheard him. "We have a problem, Jack. Get in here." Then he ended the call and looked out the doors with his back to Daniel and Henry.

Apparently he wasn't calling nine-one-one, Henry thought. Daniel was breathing hard now.

"Go, Henry. Find Uncle Billy. I'm so sorry; it wasn't supposed to be Gammy," he said with tears rolling down his face. "It was supposed to be Alice. Alice not Gammy. Please forgive me. I love you. Tell Mom I love her too. Now go!"

"Oh, Dad," Henry said, trying hard not to cry, but for the second time that day he lost the battle. Tears fell down his cheeks as he kissed his father on the forehead and then gently laid him down on the oriental rug. "I love you too."

"Go!" Daniel urged.

Henry quietly stood up and moved quickly to the door. He headed back toward the kitchen to grab Esther and get the hell out of there. Just as he was coming up to the entrance, the front door opened, and a large guy wearing a jogging suit walked in. Henry realized it was the guy who had been waiting in the car.

Don called out from his father's office behind him. "Henry, where are you going? Help me with your father. He's calling for you."

Henry didn't turn around because Don was clearly lying. The big guy now started walking toward Henry. *Unfortunately Esther's on her own*, Henry thought and darted left through the formal dining room.

"Get him, Jack," Henry heard Don yell.

Henry turned left again after the dining room into the two-story great room. There was a wall of French doors with equal-sized windows above them showcasing the dramatic view of the Potomac below. He headed toward the right side of the doors to get outside. If he could get outside, then he could go around the back of the house to the garage and get his car. Halfway through the great room, Henry turned to see how close the big guy—apparently named Jack—was, and surprisingly he was only about fifteen feet behind him and curving around Henry's right to intersect him at the doors. Henry banked left and turned on the speed, jumping over a tan leather couch and knocking over a vase on the table next to it. "Mom's not going to be happy about that," Henry said to himself. He reached the far-left set of doors, grabbed the handle, and flung the door open, practically diving out onto the terrace.

Jack came flying out one of the doors on the right and started heading toward Henry. Henry figured he could just go the long way and loop around the front of the house toward the garage as long as Don didn't get in the way. Just as that thought crossed his mind, he heard Jack yell out.

"He's coming around front."

Henry looked back and saw that although Jack was holding a phone to his ear, he was somehow gaining ground on him. Henry came around the corner of the house and slammed into Don. Fortunately Henry's momentum bounced him off Don, and he veered down the slope toward the Potomac.

Henry navigated down toward the banks of the river, glancing back at Jack and Don close behind. He angled to the right where there was a wooded section downstream. As soon as he entered the woods, he started weaving through the trees. The woods formed a small peninsula out into the river, and when he glanced back, he realized his mistake. He could see Jack following him into the woods, but Don was going around to the right, forcing him further out onto the peninsula. Instead of the woods slowing them down, they had trapped him.

He had a moment of déjà vu and remembered the nightmare he'd had that morning. He felt like he was going to vomit, and his lungs were burning. He ran full force to the end of the woods realizing there was no option but to dive into the Potomac. He dove off the bank, trying to make it as shallow of a dive as possible. He knew from many years playing down on these banks that there were large sharp rocks just under the surface in places. Unfortunately for Henry, this time when he hit the water he didn't wake up from a bad dream.

II

When he left the grocery store parking lot, Marcus had decided to drive around after the incident at Oak Tree Pointe. He knew if he went home he would drive himself crazy thinking about the innocent life he had just taken. Unlike most people, driving calmed him down. After driving aimlessly for a while, Marcus found himself in the area near his sister's house. She and her husband were out of town, and Marcus had told her he would stop by occasionally to check on things. He decided since he was close, he would stop over now to try to distract himself from his thoughts.

As he pulled up the driveway, he noticed the pile of newspapers on the front porch. He drove up and parked by the garage. He opened the side door to the house and the alarm started beeping. An automated woman's voice spoke, alerting him to enter the code to disarm the system. He closed the door, went over to the keypad, and quickly entered the code. The beeping ceased, and there was complete silence.

Marcus closed his eyes for a second and stood in the silent house. At first his mind was refreshingly blank, but that lasted only a few moments. His brain kicked in, and before he could stop it, he thought of the woman, Eleanor, and the permanent silence he inflicted on her today. He pressed his hands against his head and bent into a crouched position. "Fuck me, what did I do?" he moaned to the quiet house. He sat down on the floor, ducking his head down between his bent knees, and covered the back of his head with his hands. He sat that way for a while trying to clear his thoughts.

He finally got ahold of himself and stood up, looking around the house. He remembered the pile of newspapers on the porch. *No better way to let would-be burglars know you're out of town than newspapers piling up,* he thought. He walked to the main entrance and opened the front door. He went out and scooped up the newspapers. He counted nine of them.

You would think the paper-delivery person would have noticed them not being taken in, he thought. He took the papers out to the garage and dumped all but one into the recycling bin.

He went back into the house and went to the kitchen. He pulled the newspaper out of the plastic sleeve and flipped through it on the countertop, looking for the customer-service number. He found it and called customer service. Pretending he was his brother-in-law, he had them put delivery on hold until further notice. He hung up the phone and looked out at the backyard. It was a beautiful sunny day. He went over to the refrigerator, grabbed a beer, and walked around the quiet house.

In the family room, he found a book—*Already Dead* by Charlie Huston—on the end table next to his brother-in-law's chair. He picked it up, went out to the patio, and sat in one of the lounge chairs. He opened the book, and before he knew it he was almost halfway through it. He pried himself up from the comfortable lounge chair and went back into the house. He went to the bathroom and then grabbed another beer from the kitchen before returning to the patio and settling back into the lounge chair.

He tried to read, but he couldn't stop thinking about what happened earlier in the day. The vision of Alice coming to the room and the shocked look on her face…why the hell wasn't she in her room when he came? He couldn't help thinking Alice was partly responsible for the death of the woman, Eleanor, who was sleeping in her bed. He went around in circles, blaming himself, blaming Alice, blaming Eleanor. He took a long drink of beer and then looked up at the sky.

He thought back to when he first enlisted in the military at his father's insistence. He remembered the conversation he and his father had that night he came home from the recruitment office. Marcus had been sulking in his bedroom when his father came in and sat next to him on the bed.

"If I kill someone, I'll be a murderer, Dad. Will that make you happy?"

"No, that will not make me happy. And that's nonsense, Marcus. If you kill someone in combat, that's not murder—that's your job."

"So as long as someone instructs me to kill someone, then that's all right?"

"Yes."

"Then I instruct you to go kill Denis Brandon. I hate that kid. I think his parents mixed up his name, and the *D* should have been a *P*—Penis Brandon."

"Don't be a smartass, Marcus. No one is killing Denis, even though you're right—that kid is a little piss head. I guess Penis would have been an appropriate name after all," he chuckled.

Marcus laughed a little too. "I thought you said as long as someone instructs you to do it, then it's not murder. Come on, Dad, kill Penis."

"Marcus, why do you always have to pull shit like this? You know what I'm saying, and yet you're being intentionally obtuse."

"You're not the first person to call me that, Dad. Maybe you should have named me Intentionally Obtuse instead of Marcus.

His father just looked at him. After a few minutes, he got up and walked to the window. "Did I ever tell you the story about the man in my grandfather's village and the poisonous snake?"

"Oh no—here we go with a feel-good great-grandpa story."

Marcus's father reached across the bed and smacked him upside the head. "This is exactly why I made you enlist. You need discipline. Now shut your mouth and listen. There was a man in my grandfather's village who found a poisonous snake in his garden."

Marcus rolled his eyes at his father and heaved a loud sigh.

His father looked at him and shook his head. "Anyway, the man's wife came out and saw him just staring at the snake in the garden. 'Well, aren't you going to kill it?' she asked. The man shook his head no. 'It's not doing us any harm, so just leave it be,' he replied. Well, the man's wife shook her head and went back into the house unhappy."

"Honestly?" Marcus asked. "Did a man come by and offer to sell him some magical beans too?"

"I'm warning you, Marcus," his father said and then continued with the story. "So a few days go by, and now the man is out chopping wood to prepare for winter. He hears his wife start screaming and runs up to the house to find out why. When he goes into the house, he sees his wife sobbing and holding their only child, a boy, and his skin is a pale-blue color. She looked at him and screamed, 'You did this—you killed our boy!'"

"What, the father murdered the boy with the ax? Or did someone instruct him to do it, so it wasn't murder?" he asked with a smirk on his face.

"Any doubts I had about you going into the military have been erased, smartass," his father said. "The father didn't murder the boy—the poisonous snake bit and poisoned the boy. The point is, had the father killed the snake when he first discovered it, his boy wouldn't have died. In other words if you kill someone in combat, you are killing the snake before the snake kills you or an innocent person."

Marcus sat quietly looking down at his hands. His father put his hand on his shoulder.

"Listen, Marcus. It's all right to be afraid. If you have to take another person's life, as long as it's to stop that person from harming someone else—or to protect yourself—you're good. OK?" he asked.

Marcus just nodded his head.

He looked out at his sister's yard trying to reason the death of the woman named Eleanor. He took another drink of his beer and reopened the book on his lap. He didn't think he would be able to concentrate, but before he knew it, he was immersed in the book again.

He heard a twig snap and branches rustle, prompting him to jump up out of the chair. He leaned down and brought his foot up so he could pull his gun from his ankle holster, keeping his eyes trained on the bushes. His mind raced: There was no way his handlers could figure out so quickly that he'd messed up, was there? Did they have his car tagged so they knew where he was? He wouldn't be surprised. He brought his gun up with both hands in a shooting stance and slowly backed toward the house.

There was a fence hidden by a wall of bushes that lined the perimeter of the property. Marcus scanned the hedgerow, looking for additional movement. Then there was louder rustling in the bushes. A gate swung open and a small man rolling what looked like a luggage cart came barreling through the gate. He looked at Marcus and froze. He quickly raised his arms like he was being robbed. Marcus immediately dropped his arms down and put his gun back into the holster.

"It's OK, sorry. You can put your hands down. Sorry," Marcus said, holding up his hands and showing him they were empty. "Can I help you?" he asked the man with the cart.

"We're supposed to pick up the patio furniture and put it in storage for the winter."

"OK, that's OK. I wasn't expecting anyone. Sorry again. Go right ahead," Marcus said. He gave a little wave and embarrassed smile to the man, picked up his book and almost empty beer, and went into the house.

He walked over to the side door, looked out into the driveway, and saw a large box van with Booker's Moving and Storage stenciled on the side. He waited until they finished packing up the patio furniture and then locked up, activated the alarm, and decided to head home.

12

It had been a long, hot summer, so the Potomac wasn't that cold, although it still took Henry's breath away when he hit the water. He tried to stay under as long as he could before surfacing. He kept his head buried in his arms and scrunched his shoulders up in an effort to shield himself from the sharp rocks in the water. When his lungs were burning and he couldn't stand it anymore, he finally pushed up and surfaced, gasping for air. He quickly looked behind him to see where they were.

At the same time that Henry looked back, Jack locked eyes with him. He raised his arm pointing at Henry. Then a flash of light came from the end of Jack's hand. Apparently he wasn't just pointing his finger—he was pointing a gun. Henry slipped back underwater and resumed kicking and shielding his head. He didn't feel any pain so the bullet must have missed. *Holy shit*, he thought, *they're not just trying to catch me; they're trying to kill me.*

Because he was swimming downstream in a fast current, when Henry resurfaced he saw that he had traveled a considerable distance. He angled himself and swam toward the bank. He grabbed onto a tree that had fallen, its branches touching the water. Henry thanked God for the tree because once he started to climb out, he realized it would have been nearly impossible without it since the rocky banks were covered with a slimy, moss-like film.

He lay on his back on the steep bank catching his breath while his mind raced a million miles an hour. Gammy was dead, and now his dad may be dead. He couldn't let his mind go there. He reached into his pocket and pulled out his cell phone. It was soaked and wouldn't turn on. Suddenly remembering the capsule his dad had given him, he reached into his pocket and pulled it out. He pulled the two ends apart and a flash drive fell out onto his stomach. Fortunately it was still dry. Thank God for the little case it came in. He popped it back in the case and shoved it down into his pocket. He propped himself up on his elbows and surveyed the scene.

After sitting there for a minute, he pushed himself up and navigated his way through the underbrush along the river. He had an idea where he was, but he wasn't 100 percent sure. He knew if he kept going downstream, he could make it to Gammy's house, which was a couple miles from his parents' house, down on the banks of the river. Even though she had moved into the retirement home, he knew she had kept the house open in case she wanted to move back. Dad called it her safety blanket.

About half an hour later, a military helicopter flew down the river just a few feet above the water. Henry scrambled and ducked into the undergrowth, lying down on his stomach. It didn't seem to notice him and kept going downstream. Twenty minutes later he heard it coming back upstream, and once again he dropped on his stomach and waited it out.

Forty-five minutes later he finally made it to the banks that led up to Gammy's house. He could see that some interior lights were on. Henry thought Uncle Billy must be in residence. Billy didn't own a home; he just traveled and stayed in one of the several properties Gammy owned throughout the world. He was the epitome of a trust-fund kid. Fortunately for Billy, he was Gammy's favorite, and since Gampy died there was really no need for him to get a job. He just donated family money to the needy and got laid in the process. He was good at that.

Henry came straight up the back lawn toward the back of the house. He made his way to the door off the kitchen, and to his surprise the door was unlocked. He walked in, and standing by the island in the kitchen was Uncle Billy. He gave Henry an odd look.

"Uncle Billy."

"Henry, what's up? What the hell happened to you?" he asked, shaking his head. "Want a beer?"

Henry looked at him. "A beer would be great. Any chance I could bum some dry clothes from you? I fell into the river at Mom and Dad's and wound up a little downstream, so I figured instead of trying to make it back upstream, I would come here."

"Only you could fall into the Potomac, Henry," he said, shaking his head. He went to the refrigerator and grabbed a beer. "Here's the beer, and why don't you go hit the shower in your room, and I'll bring you some clothes. God only knows what disease you may have caught in that river. It's a virtual toilet."

Henry had tried not to think about that. He grabbed the beer and went to his room. Pretty much everyone in the immediate family had a room at Gammy's house. There were more than enough of them. On the way to the room, he was trying to decide if he should involve Uncle Billy in all of this. He knew his father had told him to, but his gut was telling him to keep him out of it. He went to the bathroom off his bedroom, started the shower to warm it up, stripped off his wet clothes, and stepped into the hot spray of water. He lathered up and rinsed off, and then pressed his hands against the wall in front of him, leaning forward and letting the water beat down on his head and back. He stood there for a while in shock thinking about all that had just happened. Even in his wildest dreams, he wouldn't have imagined the series of events that transpired that day. He finally pushed back from the wall and turned off the water. He was toweling off when he heard Billy in his room.

"I put some clean clothes on the chair in here," Billy called to him.

"Thanks, Uncle Billy," Henry said, wrapping the towel around his waist and heading into his room. Billy was looking out the window that had a view of the front lawn. Henry looked out to see what he was looking at. There was a car coming up the front drive pretty quickly.

"Who's that? Are you expecting someone?" Henry asked.

The car came up to the porte cochere off the front entrance.

"Is that Uncle Don?" Henry asked, his heart starting to jackhammer in his chest.

"Henry, Don called and told me about the fight you had with your father. He said we can work this out and that he saw the whole thing—that it was an accident and that your father hit his head. You're not in any trouble."

Henry looked at Billy thinking this had to be a nightmare. "Uncle Billy, what are you talking about? Uncle Don injected something into Dad's neck that apparently gave him a heart attack. Then Don and some big guy chased me out of the house, and I dove into the Potomac to get away from them."

"Henry, listen—I forgive you for what you did. Don said he walked in and heard you fighting with your Dad about your inheritance since your grandmother died. He said he saw you push your way past your dad, and he slipped and fell back hitting his head on the hearth of the fireplace. He said it wasn't your fault, but you panicked and said you were going to kill yourself, and you ran out and jumped in the river. Now relax. He said if I saw you to call him, and he would help you understand that it wasn't your fault and that everything is going to be all right."

"Are you fucking insane, Uncle Billy? I didn't push past Dad—I walked in on Uncle Don fighting with Dad and injecting something into his neck." Henry grabbed the clothes that Billy put out for him on the chair. It was a black jogging suit, and he quickly put it on. He grabbed his clothes from the bathroom and transferred the contents of his pockets from his wet clothes into his borrowed clothes. He was terrified.

"Fuck! Fuck! Fuck!" Henry practically screamed. "Don's here because you called him. This is unreal. He doesn't want to help me. Don wants to kill me for some flash drive Dad gave me to try to expose some cover up."

"Henry, he said you would try to blame him to cover for yourself," Billy said, now sounding unsure of himself.

Henry grabbed Billy by the shoulders. "Listen, Uncle Billy. You have to believe me. Even if he's telling the truth, just humor me and stall him. Tell him I'm still in the shower." Henry darted into the bathroom and turned on the shower. He came back out and looked at his uncle. "Please just stall him, and give me a head start. You have to believe me. Are Gammy's keys to her Bentley on the hook by the garage door?" Henry asked. He looked pleadingly at Billy.

"Yes, Henry, just...please don't try to hurt yourself," Billy said, grabbing Henry's arm. "No matter what is really going on here, suicide is not the answer. Please be careful. Use the back stairs and I'll hold him off as long as I can." He gave Henry a concerned look. "I'm sorry if I fucked things up for you." He let go of Henry's arm.

"Not your fault, Uncle Billy. Is Dad...?" Henry couldn't finish the question; he just looked down at his feet.

Billy nodded his head slowly, "Yes."

Henry didn't want to believe that his father was actually dead. He shook his head and bolted down the hallway toward the back staircase.

13

The front gate started opening as Don's driver turned into the Pendelton estate. The driver slowed, and Don rolled his window down.

The guard slid the glass window open. "Good afternoon, Mr. Kepler. Mr. Pendelton is expecting you."

"Thanks, Walt," Don replied, rolling his window back up. The driver went up the long drive and pulled the car up to the main entrance. As soon as the car stopped, Don and Jack both got out. "Go around back in case this pinhead gets another idea to run," Don said to Jack.

Don and Jack were shocked that Henry wasn't hit while he swam downstream. Jack was one of the best, and he was almost certain that he had hit Henry just before he disappeared from the surface of the Potomac for the last time. They already had their story figured out for when Henry's body was found downriver. They would say that after he attacked Daniel, he had attacked Don and Jack for trying to stop him. Unfortunately he was shot in the scuffle, and he then ran off and jumped into the river.

Don had figured that if he wasn't hit, he would probably make his way downriver to his grandma's house. So he had called the house to find out that Daniel's brother William was there and told him the story about Henry jumping into the river. Then they got the phone call from William saying that Henry was coming up toward the house. Don was hoping that the luck that had apparently been on Henry's side was about to run out.

Jack walked toward the back of the house, while Don walked toward the entranceway thinking how pissed he was that it had come to this. He couldn't believe what had happened with Daniel. He and Daniel were like brothers. Why did Daniel have to pull this shit and try to be the hero? Don understood that he was pissed about his mother—and rightfully so. But Daniel knew there was no way they were going to shut down the program just because the wrong old lady was accidentally terminated—even if it was Eleanor Pendelton. *Tough shit*, Don thought, already forgiving himself for getting rid of Daniel and reasoning that offing William and Henry was just cleaning up Daniel's mess.

Don tried the door, and fortunately it was unlocked. He walked through the elaborate front entrance that was the size of a small home. Don had been here several times for dinner as well as formal occasions. The entrance always reminded him of a hotel lobby.

He went down the back hallway that led into the great room in the back of the house. "Great room" was an understatement. The room was enormous. Don thought you could probably comfortably seat seventy-five people with all of the couches and chairs arranged throughout the room. William was standing at the bar making a drink.

"William, how are you?" Don asked.

William jumped a little and looked over at Don. Don could see there were tears in his eyes.

"Hey, Don. What a day, huh? Un-fucking-believable. First Mom and now Daniel," he said, shaking his head.

"I know, William. I'm sorry," Don said, glancing around the room trying to figure out where Henry was. "Where is he, William?"

"Poor kid—he's upstairs in his room taking a shower. He told me he fell in the river and the current swept him down. He didn't mention anything about the fight with my brother, so I didn't say anything to him. I didn't want to scare him off."

"Where are the clothes he was wearing?"

"I'd imagine in the clothes hamper in his bathroom. Why?" William was starting to think he'd made a mistake by calling Don.

"I just want to make sure there isn't any blood on them from your brother," Don quickly replied, trying to cover the fact he was looking for the flash drive. "I didn't want to say it earlier, William, but it wasn't exactly an accident. When the investigation starts, if you don't want to see Henry spend the rest of his life in prison, I need to start covering some things up."

William realized his mouth was hanging open and slowly closed it. He was thoroughly confused. "He'll be down in a minute, and then we'll get his clothes. Here, have a drink." William handed Don a glass of Crown on the rocks. He didn't know if he should believe Henry or Don.

14

Henry came down the back stairs into the hallway that led to the garage. He caught sight of Don heading down the hallway toward the great room. The sight of Don made his racing heart beat even faster. When he reached the door that went out to the garage, he realized he had been holding his breath since he saw Don. He exhaled, grabbed the car key off the ring, and quietly opened the door.

He got into the light-blue Bentley convertible and slid behind the wheel. The car still smelled new. He turned the key, and the engine started. Henry was relieved at how quiet the engine was. He pressed the garage-door opener on the visor and put the car in reverse. He watched the rearview mirror praying no one would show up at the garage, and thankfully it looked like the coast was clear. Fortunately for Henry, Jack had already made his way to the back of the house.

He cautiously backed out of the garage. Pressing the button on the visor, he closed the garage door and then put the car in drive and made his way down the driveway. The gates swung open on his approach, and he gave a wave to Walt. Walt looked surprised when he saw it was Henry, but Henry didn't slow down—he just kept driving.

As soon as he exited the driveway, he opened up the engine. He was impressed—but not surprised—by the amount of power the Bentley had. Before he realized it, he was going eighty-five down the curvy road. He let off the gas and slowed to a more reasonable speed. He reached for his cell phone only to find that it still wouldn't power up. He kicked himself for not remembering to ask Uncle Billy to borrow his phone, but then he thought maybe he should give himself a break since it was his first time on the run.

His first thoughts were to go to his place in Georgetown, but he figured Don would surely have the place watched or have someone there waiting for him. He hoped Jessica and his roommates weren't in any danger. He needed to call them. He looked around for a pay phone, which would have been easy to find ten years ago, but now you could hardly find one. While he drove and looked for a pay phone, he started to formulate a plan.

He needed a place to hide. He decided he, Jess, and the roommates could hole up at the Ritz-Carlton in Georgetown. Jessica's parents always stayed there when they came into the city, and who would expect them to hide out in such an expensive place. He would have Jessica put it on her credit card in case they were monitoring his. He drove into the city and finally found a pay phone at a gas station. He looked in the console between the front seats and found some change.

He put some coins into the phone and called Jessica.

"Hello?" she said after several rings.

"Jess, it's me, Henry."

"Henry—I didn't recognize the number."

"My phone doesn't work, so I had to find a pay phone. I'm in the city. Listen, Jess, is anyone there with you?"

"Just Paul and Chad. Henry, what's going on?"

"You have no idea. When I got to my parents' house, I walked in on my uncle Don arguing with my dad. Then they struggled, and he gave my dad a shot of something in his neck that caused him to have what I think was a heart attack. And...and he's dead, Jess. My dad is dead."

"What? Are you joking, Henry?" Jessica asked.

"No, I wish I was, Jess."

"Oh my God, Henry, why would your uncle do something like that?"

It took Henry a second to understand her question, and then it dawned on him. "Don's not really my uncle. He's just an old family friend that we've always called uncle, and I have no idea why he did it. He and my dad were arguing about something."

"Oh, Henry."

"Either way, Jess, my dad gave me a flash drive before he died that apparently has some government secret on it. He said he wanted me to expose the information on it. Now Don is chasing me. I don't know if it's because he saw Dad give me the flash drive and he wants it back, or if it's just because I saw him give my dad the shot that killed him. Who the fuck knows. What matters now is that they're chasing me. They shot at me, and I'm not sure what they will do to try and find me. You guys need to get out of there immediately. I imagine they'll come there looking for me."

"Henry, are you OK? Did you get shot?"

"No, they missed."

"This is surreal."

"You have no idea. He tracked me to my grandmother's house and told my uncle Billy that I argued with my dad and pushed him, and that my dad hit his head and that's how he died. So not only did I see him kill my dad, but now he's trying to make it out that I killed my dad and that now I'm on the run. I'll tell you more when I see you." He stopped, took in a deep breath, and then exhaled. "Please just get out of there. I don't know what these people are capable of. Just grab Paul and Chad and tell them there's an emergency and I need you guys. Can you meet me at the Ritz-Carlton? The one your parents stay at?"

"The one they converted out of the old incinerator?" she asked.

"Yes."

"Of course. You really don't think it's safe here?"

"I don't know, Jess, but I'd rather not take the chance. Will you do me a favor and grab my laptop and bring that with you too? I want to see what's on the flash drive."

"Sure. Anything else?"

"No, I'll meet you in the lobby of the Ritz. We'll get a room where we can figure out what to do."

"We'll be there as soon as we can. I love you, Henry."

"I love you too, Jess. Please be careful."

"You too," she said, hanging up.

Henry held the phone to his ear for a few seconds after she had hung up. He wondered whether he should have just kept Jess and his roommates out of it. He finally placed the phone back on the receiver. He hoped that by having them with him, he could somehow keep them out of danger. It seemed like an oxymoron since he was the one Don was after, but he felt they were in more danger if Don tried to use them to get to him. He just hoped he was right.

He put more change into the phone and dialed his mother. He dreaded this call. It rang only a couple times before she answered.

"Hello?"

"Mom, it's me, Henry."

"Oh, Henry. My God, what happened?" He could tell she was crying.

"Who told you, Mom?" Henry asked.

"Don called and told me."

"Of course he did."

"He said that he walked in on you arguing with your father. He said you two struggled and your father fell back and hit his head on the fireplace hearth. Then you ran off. Where are you?"

Henry was silent.

"Henry, are you there?"

"Yes, Mom." He closed his eyes tight and leaned his head against the side of the pay phone.

"What were you arguing about?"

He didn't want to bring his mother into any of this. He struggled with his thoughts; not knowing what to say. He was terrified that if he told her the truth, she too could be in danger. He decided it didn't hurt to let his mother believe the lie Don had spun. Soon enough the truth would come out.

"Mom, I didn't mean for him to fall." This was technically correct. It was misleading, but at least he wasn't lying to her.

Her heart sank when he said that to her.

"What happened?" she asked.

"Mom, can we please just discuss this in person when you get back. I think I'm going to be sick."

She didn't know what to say. "I'm flying back as soon as they finish refueling the plane. Please just go back to the house and wait for me. We'll figure everything out. Don will help us figure it out."

At that last sentence, Henry now felt he was actually going to be sick.

"I'm so sorry, Mom. I can't believe this is happening."

"We'll get through this."

"I hope so. I love you, Mom."

"I love you too, Henry. I'll see you when I get home."

Henry pressed down the receiver and ended the call.

He got in the car and headed toward the hotel. On the way there, he spotted his bank and pulled up to the ATM drive-through. He knew he needed to stop using his credit cards or he would leave an electronic trail for Don. So he needed to get some cash. He put his card in, entered his code, and withdrew $500. He first tried $1,000, but it wouldn't let him—not for lack of funds, but because it exceeded his daily limit. He put the cash in his wallet and continued toward the hotel.

He drove around looking for a spot a few blocks from the hotel. He finally found an open spot on a side street and parked. It was farther away than he cared for, but he didn't want to point Don in the direction of where he was staying. Using the valet at the hotel was out of the question in case the police were looking for the car. He grabbed some change out of the console for the meter but put it back deciding there was no point. He wasn't going to trot back out here every couple hours to feed the meter, and he didn't think Gammy would care now if she got a ticket. That thought brought a wave of sadness. He fought back the tears, trying not to think of Gammy or his dad.

He walked toward the hotel and cut through The Shops at Georgetown Park, thinking it would be a good way to pass the time waiting for Jessica and his roommates to get there. He passed people happily shopping and enjoying themselves. Unfortunately it just made him feel more isolated. He went into one of the small gift shops and bought a baseball hat—to try to disguise himself—and a copy of *The Washington Post*. He left the store and then exited the mall. He crossed a footbridge over a canal and then went down Wisconsin Avenue toward the Ritz-Carlton.

He walked into the lobby, and there was no sign of Jessica, Paul, or Chad. He sat on one of the couches off to the side to wait for them. He pulled the tags off his new hat and shaped a curve into its flat bill. He pulled it down low on his head and opened the paper. He tried to read it in an attempt to distract himself from the day's events.

15

Don looked at his watch and realized he'd been making small talk with William for over twenty minutes. He decided the kid had showered long enough. He got up and walked toward the stairway leading to the second floor. William quickly stood up.

"Where are you going, Don?"

"I don't have all day here, William. We are impeding an investigation. I'm going to get Henry."

"He told me he'd come down when he finished."

"Like I said, I don't have time, William," Don said, starting up the stairs.

William didn't know what to do. Don was going to find out Henry wasn't in the shower, and frankly Don scared him, and he wasn't sure what he would do when he found that Henry wasn't there. He followed Don up the stairs.

"Where's his room, William?"

"Right down here." He walked past Don toward Henry's room. He reached out and knocked on the door. "Henry, it's Uncle Billy."

There was no answer. He knocked again, this time a little louder.

"Henry." Once again there was no answer. He turned to Don, "He must still be in the shower. The kid's obviously had a rough day."

Don pushed past William and tried the door. The door swung open and revealed that Henry was not there. Light emitted from the bottom of the closed door that must be the bathroom, and they could hear the shower running. Don walked toward the bathroom door and looked back at William.

William shrugged. "Why don't you let the kid finish showering?" he asked.

Don turned the knob on the bathroom door and pushed it open. The shower had a glass enclosure, and he could clearly see no one was in there even though the water was running.

"Where the fuck is he, William?" Don yelled. The fury that showed in Don's eyes made William's heart skip a beat.

"He told me he was going to take a shower," William squeaked out.

Don picked up Henry's wet clothes and went through the pockets. It didn't take him long to figure out the flash drive wasn't in any of the pockets.

"Don't fuck around with me, William. Where is he?" Don asked, stepping toward him.

That was when William made a critical mistake. He tried the honest route with Don. Later he would realize that he would have done much better had he pretended that he didn't know anything.

"Listen, Don. He saw you come up the driveway, and he freaked out. He tried to convince me that you injected something into Daniel that killed him and that there is some big conspiracy going on," he said, waving his hands in the air like Henry was crazy. "He's not going to kill himself. Let the kid go. What's the harm? Like you said, Don, it was an accident. Let him calm down and he'll come back."

"An injection? Is that what Henry said?" Don asked.

William knew he had done the right thing. Don was smiling. He laughed warmly and patted William's shoulder. William's heart started to beat closer to normal. Don kept his hand on William's shoulder and walked toward the doorway with him.

"Oh, William," Don said reassuringly. "That's what Henry said? An injection?"

William started laughing. Although he didn't really know why—it wasn't really funny.

"I know, right?" William said.

Don reached his arm around William's neck and pulled him toward him. At first William thought he was pulling him in for a hug.

Then before he knew what was happening, Don forced him down and got him in a headlock.

William felt a sharp pain in his neck. Then Don released him and stood up. William rolled onto his back and looked up at Don. He put his hand to his neck where the pain was.

"Where did he go, William?" Don asked.

William just stared at him. He was terrified. Was he really going to die? *Apparently Henry was telling the truth*, he thought.

"Where did he go, William? There's still time left for me to make this very painful. Now work with me here. Where did he go?" Don asked.

"I don't know. He saw you and took off. I tried to stop him." Don looked at him, and he believed him. William's face was flushed and he was covered in sweat. Sweat stains started to appear on his clothes.

Don looked down at him. "I'm really sorry, William. I liked you. Actually, you might say, out of this whole family I liked you best. You were smart enough to sit back and reap the benefits of being a Pendelton. You didn't try to be the hero like your brother. I'm truly sorry, William."

The pain in William's chest was now crushing. He fumbled for the phone in his pocket to call for help, but the pain was too great.

Don straightened his clothes and went over to the fireplace. He grabbed the poker and came back, bending down and patting William's head. William just stared at him and was now starting to gasp for air.

"I'm sorry, William," Don said.

Don waited by William's side until he went unconscious. He stood, wound up the poker like a golf club, and swung it at William's head. He tried to stand back out of the path of splattering blood. Then he went to the bathroom, grabbed Henry's clothes, and wiped down the handle of the poker. He took out his phone and called Jack.

"He already got away. Come inside the front entrance."

He went downstairs and walked through the house to the intercom by the front entranceway. There was a button marked *gate house*. He pushed it, then Walt came on the speaker.

"Guard house."

"Walt, there's been an incident. There should be an ambulance and the police coming soon. So you may want to leave the gate open."

"Is everything all right?"

"I hope so, Walt. We found William pretty badly hurt upstairs."

"Do you need my assistance?"

"No thanks, Walt. Listen, have you seen Henry this evening?"

"He just left here shortly after you arrived," Walt said.

"Did you notice what car he was driving?"

"He was in Mrs. Pendelton's Bentley."

"Thanks, Walt.

"Is there anything else I can do?" Walt asked.

"Just say a prayer for the Pendelton family. Today doesn't seem to be their day," Don said.

Jack came in the front door. "What happened?" he asked.

"Apparently Henry also attacked his uncle," Don said. "It seems like he's trying to get as much inheritance as he can."

Jack smirked. "Where is William?"

"Hold on." Don held up a finger motioning for Jack to be quiet while holding the phone to his ear.

"Nine-one-one emergency. How can I help you?"

"I need an ambulance—there's been a man attacked," Don said. He gave the address. He explained that he was a government official trying to investigate the incident, so he couldn't stay on the phone. He hung up and turned to Jack.

"Now I need to sell this inheritance thing to Tom Laurel," he said. He stood in the foyer piecing the story together in his head. He took a deep breath and called Tom Laurel, the director of the CIA.

"Don, what can I do for you?"

"Tom, there's been a developing incident regarding the Pendelton family."

"I know," he said. "I heard about Eleanor and Daniel. What a shame."

"Well, now you can add her other son, William, to the list."

"What?"

"We have a major problem. I went over earlier to offer my condolences to Daniel. When I was walking toward his home office, I heard his son Henry arguing with him. I heard Daniel say something about the fact that he and his brother William were the sole beneficiaries to Eleanor's estate. Then I heard Henry say that was bullshit and something to the effect that he wasn't going to wait forever. When I looked in the office, I saw Henry shove Daniel backward." Don paused for effect and took a deep breath. "Well, Daniel tripped, fell back, and hit his head on the fireplace hearth. When Henry saw me in the doorway, he freaked out and ran out the back of the house. Last we saw of him, he jumped into the Potomac."

"Have they recovered a body?"

"Well, that's the thing. I had called William Pendelton to let him know what had happened and found out he was in town staying at Eleanor's residence. I told him if Henry showed up there to alert me. I figured since Eleanor's estate is downriver, he may show up there. Well, I was right. William called and told me Henry did in fact show up and told him he had fallen into the river. So when Henry went to shower and change into dry clothes, William called me. I told him to wait outside and we would be there immediately. Apparently William didn't listen. He must have thought he could reason with Henry. Unfortunately sometime after the shower, Henry decided to get rid of the other heir to the Pendelton fortune."

"Is William dead?"

"Not yet, but I don't think he's going to make it. The ambulance hasn't gotten here yet. So, Tom, here's the thing. We need to put out an all-points bulletin on Eleanor's convertible Bentley."

"Why?"

"The guard at the end of the driveway just told me he saw Henry leaving here in it. And obviously I'm going to need an APB put out for Henry. With Daniel's death we could have gone with accidental to save face for the family, but with William we're not going to be able to explain it away."

"Where's Jane Pendelton? Is she secure? Wouldn't she be the next in line if Daniel and William are out of the picture?"

"Good point, Director." Don was having a hard time keeping up with the tale he was spinning. *Of course,* he thought, *if the kid was actually killing for inheritance, he would naturally go after the mother.* He continued, "I would imagine Jane would be the next in line. I called her to inform her about Daniel, and fortunately she's currently on the family jet coming back from Florida. Henry hasn't been able to get to her yet. I'll make sure we're there when she lands."

"I'll call the chief of police and make sure there is an APB put out for Henry as well as the Bentley."

"Thanks, Director. Have them contact me as soon as either is found. I don't want anyone trying to take him down. I want to be the one that gets Henry. Just have them find him for me. This is personal. The Pendeltons have been like family to me."

"Got it, Don."

Don ended the call.

"Why didn't you just tell Tom what really happened?" Jack asked.

"Because, Jack, if I can get my hands on that little bastard and get rid of him before he can contradict me, then no one needs to know I took out Daniel and we get the drive back," Don said, as if explaining something to an idiot.

Don ran his fingers through his hair and then went back upstairs to check on William. Don had to make sure William didn't survive the brutal attack Henry had supposedly delivered by the time the ambulance arrived. As luck would have it for Don, William had died.

16

Chad had never seen Jessica freak out like this. She was always the most mature of all of them. But to see her completely freaked out in turn freaked Chad out. She told them they needed to get out of there immediately because someone was coming to look for Henry. Chad kept thinking about what a bad idea it had been to wake up and smoke a joint. *Wake and bake* was the first thing that popped into his head that morning. *Why not?* he had thought. Now he realized why not. First, Jessica told him about Henry's grandmother, which was a bummer but not the end of Chad's world. Then Henry called, and all hell broke loose.

Chad grabbed his things and followed Jessica out the door. Paul was taking his time, which made Jessica freak out even more. Jessica leaned her head back in the door and tried to whisper loudly.

"Paul, could you please hurry? This isn't a joke. Henry said people are looking for him and are coming here to try to find out where he is. Since we know where he is, he thinks we are in danger."

Paul was walking around the house with the house phone to his ear.

"For God's sake, Paul, who are you calling?" Jessica asked. "We have to go."

"I'm calling myself," he replied.

"What?"

"Relax, Jessica. I'm coming. Here it is," Paul said, pulling his now-ringing cell phone from between the couch cushions. He hung up the house phone and dropped it on the end table.

"I'm not going anywhere without my phone," he said, holding it up and waving it at her.

He followed Jessica out the door toward her car that was parked at the curb. Chad was leaning against the car looking up and down the road for anything or anyone suspicious, which in turn made him look suspicious.

"Hey, guys," came a voice from next door. Jessica and Paul both jumped and looked over.

It was Patricia Maso, the neighbor, standing on her front porch holding shopping bags. She lived there with her husband Jim, a professor.

"Hello, Patti," Jessica said and gave a little wave, never slowing from her fast pace to the car.

"Hi, Patti," Chad said.

"Hey, Patti," Paul said, stopping and facing her with a big smile on his face. He inhaled trying to pump up his chest to appear more muscular. "Don't you look beautiful today?"

"Hello, Paul," Patti said, returning the smile.

Paul had had a crush on her since he first met her. She was in her early thirties, and Paul thought she was incredibly hot. Patti was the older woman Paul wanted to conquer.

Jessica grabbed him by the collar. "Would you come on?" she said. "Sorry, Patti, we're in a rush."

"No problem, Jessica. I won't keep you. Please tell Henry we're so sorry for the loss of his grandmother."

"Thanks, Patti, I will."

The three of them piled into Jessica's Audi and quickly drove away.

"You do realize Patti is married? Right, Paul?" Jessica asked.

"She wants me, Jess."

"She's married, Paul."

"Her husband shouldn't leave her home alone so much. I'm sure that makes her lonely."

"The man has to work, Paul. Did it ever occur to you that someday someone may be simple enough to marry you, and you just might have to go to work and leave her home alone? And some horny college kid is going to try to get in her pants?"

"No woman I'm with is going to want to cheat on me, Jess. Come on—have you looked at me?"

"Payback's a bitch, Paul. In this scenario you're a lot older than you are now, and some hot college kid is going to snag your wife as payback."

"Jess, you're assuming I'm not always going to be this devilishly handsome. Come on," Paul said.

"Would you two shut up?" Chad piped up from the backseat. "Patti is hot for me. I bet you money I'm going to bang her first."

"You two thoroughly disgust me. She is a married woman. Her husband is a great guy and better looking than either of you goofs. He would beat the living daylights out of both of you if he heard you talking this way about his wife."

"Uh oh, I think Jessica is hot for Professor Maso," Paul said. "I think we need to alert Henry to this impending affair."

They all went quiet after Paul mentioned Henry. Their nervous chatter seemed unimportant all of the sudden.

"So what did Henry say again?" Paul asked.

"He said there are people who are after him," Jessica said. The thoughts that had been nagging her as to whether there was a remote chance that Henry was lying to her crept up again.

"Are you sure he wasn't smoking some of Chad's stash, and he's just experiencing a little paranoia?" Paul said.

"No, he was not high. He was terrified," She said, once again flipping over to the thought that he was telling her the truth. Although they had only been together for a short time, she truly believed she knew Henry down to his soul.

"Terrified of what?"

Jessica deliberated for a moment. She figured that at this point they were in it as much as she was. "He said he walked in on his uncle Don killing his dad."

"His uncle killed his dad? Holy shit, that's crazy," Paul said.

"He's not actually his uncle. He's an old family friend that Henry calls 'uncle.' Henry said he's not sure if this guy Don is after him because he saw him kill his dad or because he may know that Henry has some flash drive that Don doesn't want made public. He just doesn't want us at his place in case Don comes looking for him."

The seriousness of the conversation shut both guys up. They reached the hotel, and Jessica turned into the parking area. She drove down the aisles looking for a spot, found one, and parked the car. They all got out and headed toward the hotel.

Paul held the door for Jessica that led from the parking area into the hallway that entered the lobby. Chad followed behind and kept looking over his shoulder to see if anyone was following them. He had full-fledged marijuana paranoia going on, and for once in his life, he actually had very good reason for it.

They walked into the lobby and looked for Henry. Jessica spotted him first, sitting off to the side on a sofa reading the newspaper.

"There he is," she said. She quickly walked over to him, and Paul and Chad followed.

"Henry," she called to him.

He dropped the paper on the table, stood up, and hugged her. "Jess, I'm so sorry." He kissed her.

"What are you sorry for?" she asked.

"For dragging you into this shit. Hey, guys," he said, holding onto Jessica with one arm. He shook hands with Paul and Chad. "I was just telling Jess I'm so sorry to drag you guys into this shit."

"Your shit is our shit, Henry," Paul said.

"Yeah," Chad said. It was all he could come up with. His mouth was bone dry and all he wanted was something to drink. He looked around for a vending machine but didn't spot one.

"Jess, I don't want to use my credit card because I don't want to leave an electronic trail," Henry said. "I'd imagine Don has my cards flagged. I'm pretty sure it will take a while for them to connect you with me. By that time—if and when they do—we won't still be here. Do you mind getting a room, and we'll meet you over by the elevators?"

"Not a problem," she said.

Once she checked in, she met them by the elevators. They piled into the elevator and Jessica pushed the button for their floor. Everyone was silent until the elevator doors closed. Once they were closed, Chad broke the silence.

"I'm starving."

"Of course you are, stoner," Paul said.

Henry started laughing and Jessica joined in.

"You have no idea how good it feels to be with you guys," Henry said. "So far, today sucks."

No one knew what to say, so they kept quiet.

"You remembered the laptop, Jess?"

"Right here." She patted her bag.

"Thanks."

The elevator stopped at their floor, and the doors slid open. They followed the hallway until they reached a set of double doors at the end. Jessica slid the card through the reader on the side of the door. The red light turned green, they heard a click, and a green light displayed by the reader. She pushed the door open.

There was a small foyer area that led to a large family room with a wall of windows overlooking the Potomac. To the right was a large kitchen and to the left a hallway with several doors.

"I thought if we're going to be on the run, we may as well do it in style. This, gentlemen, is the presidential suite," Jessica said.

"Jess, your dad is not going to be happy when he gets your credit card bill," Henry said.

"Holy shit!" Paul said. "If you guys are ever on the run again, please make sure you include me."

"When I explain to my father the shit day you had, I'm sure he will understand," Jessica said.

"Where's the room service menu?" Chad asked.

"You're too much, Chad. Thanks, Jess," Henry said, kissing her.

"No problem, Henry. Let's find that menu. I'm starving too."

17

Don waited until the DC police arrived. He gave a brief statement and told them he had to leave to continue the investigation involving Henry. He and Jack left the Pendelton estate and headed over to Henry's townhome in Georgetown. On the way there, Don called Jim Tanner, his government contact in electronic investigation.

"Jim, it's Don Kepler, could you do me a favor?"

"Sure, Don. What's up?"

"I need whatever you can get on Daniel Pendelton's son Henry. I need any current credit card activity. I also need you to look into his cell phone records."

"What's going on, Don? Does Daniel know you're doing this?" Jim asked.

"Jim, Daniel's dead. That's why I'm asking you to do this."

"Oh my God. What happened?"

"I'm sorry—I can't get into it right now. Just know it's very important that I get this information as quickly as possible. Henry's credit card and cell phone records, please. I'm looking for any current activity."

"Got it. I'll call you as soon as I get anything."

"Thanks a lot, Jim. I owe you for this, and I won't forget it."

Don hung up the phone as they continued to Henry's townhome.

The driver pulled up and parked in front of Henry's. Don and Jack walked up to the door, and Don rang the doorbell. They waited a few seconds, and then Don rang it again. After a minute passed and still no response, Don asked Jack to open it. Jack pulled out a small plastic pouch from inside his coat pocket that contained a lock pick and bent down to work on the lock. Less than a minute later, Jack stood up, turned the knob, and swung the door open. He motioned for Don to enter first.

"Good job, Jack." Don said and walked in. "Hello? Anybody home?" he called out into the town house.

There was no answer.

"Check upstairs. I'll check down here," Don said.

After checking both floors, it was apparent no one was home. Don looked through a pile of mail on the counter. Most of the mail was addressed to Henry, but he found one piece of mail from a bank addressed to Paul Mayer and another piece from the university addressed to Chad Turner. He called Jim, gave him the two new names, and requested he do the same check he was conducting on Henry.

Don called for a couple of his men to come and conduct surveillance on Henry's townhouse in case Henry or the roommates returned, even though he didn't think they would. He checked with the neighbors on both sides to see if they had heard or seen anything. He had Jack go wait in the car since he wasn't dressed for the part in his tracksuit. He checked the townhouse to the right first, and no one answered when he rang the doorbell. He then checked the neighbor on the left. He rang the bell and heard someone on the other side.

"Hold on, I'm coming." The door opened and there stood an attractive woman in her mid-thirties. "May I help you?"

"Hello, I'm Don Kepler with the US government." He pulled out his identification and showed it to her. "We're looking for your next door neighbors." He motioned toward Henry's place.

"I know who you are. You're the president's chief of staff. Is everything all right?" Patti asked.

"We're conducting an investigation Ms.—"

"It's Patti." Patti extended her hand to Don.

"All right, Patti, have you seen Mr. Pendelton today?"

"Mr. Pendelton sounds so formal. No, I just saw Jessica a little while ago, but I haven't seen Henry today."

"Jessica?" Don asked.

"Henry's girlfriend, Jessica."

"Do you know Jessica's last name?"

"I'm sorry, I don't."

"Where did you see her?"

"I saw her and Henry's two roommates leaving earlier."

"Do you by chance know the roommates names?" he asked, trying to confirm the information he obtained from the mail on the counter.

"Chad and Paul, but I'm sorry, I don't know their last names either."

"Do you know where they were going?"

"I didn't ask. Is this about Henry's grandmother? I saw that she passed away today."

"I'm sorry, Patti—I can't divulge information regarding this investigation. Do you know what kind of car they were driving?"

"Yes, they took Jessica's Audi."

"Is it a two-door or four-door?"

"Four."

"Color?"

"Silver."

"Do you know if it's a newer car or older."

"I think it's the newer model. Is there something I should be aware of? Are they in danger? You're starting to scare me with all of these questions." Patti crossed her arms and gave Don a small grin.

"Once again I'm sorry, but I can't divulge any information regarding the investigation."

Patti was getting a little pissed giving all this information and not receiving any in return.

"Is this normal practice for the president's chief of staff to be out searching for a person?" she asked.

"It is when it's the son of a senator," Don replied. He made a mental note to contact his friend at the IRS to make sure this woman Patti spent the rest of her life accounting for every penny she's ever spent for questioning him.

He was pissed at the fact that—yes indeed—he was the chief of staff, and yes he was out schlepping around trying to get his hands on this little prick. The only satisfaction he had was the knowledge that when he found him, he was going to strangle the life out of young Mr. Pendelton.

Don pulled out his card and handed it to Patti. "If you see Henry, or any of his group, please call me at this number," he said dryly. "I also have to ask you not to alert them that we are looking for them—if or when you see them. Just contact me. And I have to remind you that it's against the law to impede an investigation."

Patti looked down at the card and then at Don with a now-serious expression on her face.

"All right, I will."

"Thanks for your time." Don reached out and shook Patti's hand, resisting the urge to pull her in close and head butt her.

She closed the door, and Don headed over to the car to wait for his men to come and relieve them for surveillance.

On the way back to the car, Don remembered Jane Pendelton. He reached the car and tapped on the driver's window. The driver rolled down the window.

"Yes, sir?" he asked.

"Will you notify the car service to send a limo here to pick us up? We need to go to the airport to pick up Senator Pendelton's wife and her guests, so we'll need a bigger car with more room."

"Of course, sir. I'll call it in now," the driver responded.

Don walked toward the back of the car, and the driver rolled up his window. He leaned against the trunk so he could make some phone calls without the driver overhearing him. He called Jim Tanner first. Jim answered on the first ring.

"Hey, Jim, it's Don."

"I'm sorry, Don, I don't have anything yet."

"That's all right. I just wanted to give you another name," he said. "Henry's girlfriend's name is Jessica. I'm sorry; I don't have a last name. Could you cross reference any numbers he's called or that have called him in the last few days, and see if any of the numbers belong to a Jessica?"

"Sure."

"All right, then once you get her last name, could you also check to see any credit or cell phone activity for her as well?"

"Sure."

"Plus—I'm sorry to be asking for so much—but I know she drives a silver Audi. I need a tag number. Is that something you can do, or should I call my guy at the DMV?"

"I can get it, Don."

"Once again I owe you, pal. Thanks in advance."

"Not a problem. I'll call you as soon as I get anything."

Don scrolled through the address book on his phone for General David Mustin's number. General Mustin was in charge of the mercenaries for the project. He found the number and placed the call.

"What can I do for you, Don?" the general asked, answering his phone.

"General, we have a problem. Do you remember earlier when Senator Pendelton had to leave our meeting because of his mother?" he asked.

"Of course, Don, and I heard she didn't make it. That's a shame. She was a great lady."

"That she was, General, but like I said we have a problem."

"What's the problem, Don?"

"Well, it turns out that Eleanor Pendelton just happened to lay down on her friend's bed at the assisted living home she moved into, and that friend just so happened to be one that was targeted by our project."

"You don't say," he said, pausing before he spoke. "Now what the hell was Eleanor Pendelton doing in an assisted living facility? The woman had more money than God. Why didn't she just have a live-in nurse? For Christ's sake, she could have afforded to have an entire staff of live-in doctors for that matter."

"Who knows, General. Maybe she was starting to lose it mentally. Either way here's the real problem. Not only did one of your guys target the wrong person—that being Eleanor Pendelton—but he entered into the system that the correct person was euthanized."

"How do you know that my guy knew he euthanized the wrong person?" the general asked.

"Because Eleanor Pendelton's friend—the one who was the actual target—told Daniel when he got there that she walked into her room and caught some man giving Eleanor the shot. And," Don said, taking a pause, "she said she told him the woman he gave the shot to was Eleanor."

"No shit," the general said.

"Yes shit, General. Now I want you to find out which one of your little psychos did this," Don said, coming just short of yelling.

"Don, we've got over fifteen hundred 'psychos,' as you call them, out in the field. You know the protocol. I'm not supposed to access who does what. That intentional darkness is supposed to be like the hood of an executioner. Don, you know all of this. You were in on all of the meetings."

"I don't give a shit. Remove the goddamn hood," he shouted into the phone. "And find out which one of them did this. I want him taken out for all of the collateral damage I'm dealing with here."

"What collateral damage?"

"It's a long story, General," he said, distracted by his thoughts.

"What exactly do you mean by taking him out?"

"Do I have to spell everything out for you?" Don asked. "What do you think it means? This jackass has put the whole project in jeopardy. He euthanized Eleanor Pendelton for Christ's sake. What more do you need? Just get another one of your little killing machines to do their jobs and get rid of this idiot. Or—"

"Or what, Don? Don't you threaten me. Do you understand? I am a goddamn four-star general, not one of your little minions you're used to bossing around. You don't tell me what to do. I'll take care of matters the way I see fit," he said, taking his turn shouting into the phone.

Don tilted his head back and looked up at the canopy of trees he was standing under. He took a deep breath.

"General, I apologize if I offended you. I will let the president know that you are taking care of this, and I trust you will handle the matter appropriately," he said with a grin on his face. Don knew by mentioning the president that the general—four stars and all—would do what he had asked and eliminate Eleanor's killer.

"I always handle matters appropriately, Don. Is there anything else I can do for you?" the general asked, sounding thoroughly pissed off.

"No. Thank you, General," Don said, ending the call.

Don got into the back of the car and looked at Jack. "Now we wait," he said.

Don settled back in his seat and leaned over to Jack so the driver couldn't hear him. "I'm going to strangle that little fucker Henry when I get my hands on him."

Jack shook his head and gave a little chuckle.

18

Jessica called room service and ordered the food. Chad flipped the television on and turned on the national news with Diane Sawyer.

"I want to bang Diane Sawyer," Paul said.

"Me too," Chad chimed in.

"Honestly?" Jessica asked. "Is that all you think about? She could be your grandmother."

Paul just smiled and nodded.

"I can't believe this is happening," Henry said. He sat down on one of the couches and dropped his head in his hands. Jessica sat down beside him and rubbed his back.

"What exactly did happen, Henry?" Paul asked.

"Well, I woke up this morning and saw on the news that my grandmother passed away. So I called my mom, and she confirmed it. She and some girlfriends had just landed in Florida for a spa trip, so my dad told her not to come back right away. He told them to stay a couple days and enjoy the trip. He didn't want to ruin their trip. So I told my mom to stay there and that I'd go be with him. So I just showed in on him. I knew if I called him he would just

knock at the door. "Room service," a man said from

the door.

Look through the peephole to see that it's actually him.

It was a guy in a hotel uniform with a cart full of food, and he rolled in the cart.

"Thanks."

"Bring it in and set it out for you," he said.

"No, really—here is fine," Jessica said, insisting.

"Well OK then." He handed her a bill and she signed it and handed it back with a generous tip.

"Thank you very much," he said.

"No problem. Thank you."

After he walked out, Jessica put the *do not disturb* tag on the door handle and closed the door, engaging the dead bolt.

She left out a beer for each of them and put the rest of the case of beer they had ordered in the refrigerator. She pushed the cart into the living room, and Henry continued with his story.

"So I got to my parents' house, and when I walk into my dad's office, I see this guy Don—an old family friend—on top of my dad pulling a needle out of his neck. I freaked and went over to my dad. Don said he was trying to help him and stood up and moved back. He pretended to call nine-one-one—the asshole—but instead he was apparently calling his goon outside to come in and take care of me because of what I had just witnessed." He paused and took a drink of beer. "Either way, I knelt down by my dad, and he pulled me in close. He handed me a flash drive and told me he was sorry, but I had to get out of there, and he wanted me to go find my uncle and have him help me expose whatever it is that's on the drive. I looked over and Don was looking out the window, so I tried to quietly sneak out. I was halfway to the main entrance when Don called out to me to tell me that my dad was calling for me, which I knew was bullshit—he probably wasn't even still conscious at that point."

"Major asshole," Paul said.

"Then the goon—this big thug guy apparently named Jack—walks in the front door. He was the asshole that Don called and told to come in while my dad was giving me the flash drive. When I wouldn't stop for Don, he told Jack to get me. So I started to run, and he chased me through the house. Once I got outside, I tried to make it around back to the garage to get my car, but Jack came around my side and blocked my way."

"Here, Henry." Jessica handed him a fresh Heineken and also gave one to Paul and Chad.

She went to hand him one of the covered platters with a cheeseburger and fries, but he waved it away.

"Not yet. Thanks though, Jess."

She gave containers to Paul and Chad, and then took hers and sat next to Henry.

Henry continued: "So I tried to go the other way around the front of the house, and fucking Don collided with me. Honestly it was like a bad movie. So I ran away from them down toward the backyard, and I ended up getting trapped on the peninsula out in the Potomac. Once again, cue the bad-movie music. So I jumped into the river to get away." He took a long drink of his beer, finished it, and went to the fridge to get another. "Anyone, beer?"

"Yes," Paul and Chad answered in unison.

"I'm all right," Jessica replied. "But, Henry, you're drinking like a fish. Maybe you should slow down."

Henry rolled his eyes at her. "Jess, I'm a big boy. Thanks for your concern though," he said genuinely. He continued to the kitchen, grabbed the beers, and went back to the living room. He gave Paul and Chad their beers.

"So after I jumped in the river, I tried to stay down as long as I could. When I finally couldn't take it anymore, I surfaced and looked back—and fucking Jack was standing on the bank of the river, and he looked right at me. At first I thought he was pointing me out to Don, but the asshole wasn't pointing at me—he was aiming at me."

"Oh shit," Paul uttered.

Chad just stared wide-eyed at Henry like he was watching a scary movie.

Henry continued: "He fired a shot at me, so I dove back under and swam until I thought I was going to pass out. Fortunately I was swimming with the flow, so the next time I looked up, I was way downstream and didn't see anyone." He took another long drink from his beer. "I climbed out and realized I must be close to my grandmother's house. It's a little way down the river from my parents' house, so I made my way there. A couple times a helicopter flew over, and I hid in the underbrush."

"Do you think whoever was in it was looking for you?" Jessica asked.

"I would imagine so. It was flying really low over the Potomac—first upstream and then back downstream. Both slow and low. It could just be a coincidence, but my gut says they were looking for me. So I get up to my grandmother's house—soaking wet from the river and filthy from the brush I crawled through—and I went in the back entrance by the kitchen. My uncle Billy was standing there in the kitchen."

They all knew of Uncle Billy.

"I didn't know what I should tell him," Henry said. "I was just expecting to find maybe some of my grandmother's staff there when I found the door unlocked. So I told him I fell in the river at my parents' place and ended up swept downstream to there. Now that I look back on it, I should have known something was up when he didn't act too surprised to see me. I think if I were him, I would have had a lot more questions had my nephew shown up in the condition I was in."

Chad stood up and walked toward the kitchen. "Beer?" he called to them.

Everyone said yes this time, including Jessica.

Henry continued: "Uncle Billy tells me to go take a shower and he'll bring me up some of his clothes to borrow."

"I wondered whose those were," Jessica said, rubbing his shoulder.

Chad came back and handed out the beers.

"So I take a shower, and when I finish, Uncle Billy yells to me that he's putting the dry clothes on the chair in the bedroom for me. So as I walk out from the bathroom to the bedroom, I pass a window that looks out on the front lawn, and I can see a car coming up the driveway. So I ask Uncle Billy if he's expecting someone, and he says yes—it's Uncle Don."

"Get out!" Paul exclaimed.

"How did he know you were there?" Jessica asked.

"Well, that's the best part," Henry said sarcastically. "Uncle Billy told me that Don called just before I got there. Don told him he had stopped by my parents' house to see my dad and found us arguing. He told Billy he saw me push my dad, which resulted in him falling back and hitting his head on the hearth of the fireplace. Then he said I freaked out and tried to kill myself by jumping into the river. He told Billy to call if I showed up at my grandmother's house, and he would come over and let me know I wasn't to blame. So Uncle Billy called fucking Don when I went upstairs to take a shower."

"Look!" Jessica said pointing to the television.

A picture of Henry's grandparents came up on the television screen, and you could hear Diane Sawyer talking. Paul grabbed the remote and turned it up.

"And this story continues to unfold in Washington, DC, this evening," she said. "Several members of the well-known Pendelton family have been found dead today, and another family member is being sought for questioning. Let's go to David Muir covering the story in DC."

"Good evening, Diane. It's either a very strange coincidence or one of the Pendelton family members is in a lot of trouble this evening. Officials are telling us that first, Eleanor Pendelton passed away at a nursing home earlier today. She was ninety." A picture of Daniel Pendelton flashed on the screen. "Then officials say her son, Senator Daniel Pendelton, was in some sort of argument with his son Henry Pendelton, a student at Georgetown University." Henry's picture from a benefit he went to with his grandmother came up on the screen. "Apparently during the argument, the senator was hurt and subsequently died this afternoon. Then to make the story even stranger, a friend of the family stopped by to offer condolences to Eleanor's other son, the infamous bachelor William Pendelton."

Henry put his hand across his open mouth. "Oh no."

A picture of his uncle Billy posing with a beautiful blond displayed on the screen.

David Muir continued: "Apparently William Pendelton was found dead this evening at the home of Eleanor Pendelton. Now officials are saying that Henry Pendelton is a person of interest. Some sources have said these deaths may be a result of who stands to inherit Eleanor Pendelton's vast fortune. Diane."

The screen went back to Diane Sawyer with a picture of Henry displayed in the corner. "David Muir in Washington, DC," Diane said. "Thank you, David. We'll be sure to post further developments on our website. Now on a much lighter note, there was a new arrival at the Washington, DC, zoo today." Henry's picture was replaced with the picture of a baby panda bear.

Paul turned the volume down on the television, and they all looked at Henry. No one knew what to say.

"Please tell me Ashton Kutcher is going to jump out and tell me I've been punked," Henry said. "This honestly can't be happening." Henry dropped his head in his hands. "That fuck killed Uncle Billy, and now he's trying to make it look like I killed my dad *and* uncle to get to my grandmother's inheritance. What an asshole," Henry said as tears rolled down his face. "So if we're to believe this theory—that I'm supposed to be working my way through the family to get their share of an inheritance—the only other person I could hurt now would be my mother," Henry said.

"You don't think he would really hurt your mom, do you, Henry?" Jessica asked.

"I wouldn't put it past him. Where's your phone? I've got to call her."

"Here," Jessica handed him the phone.

Henry quickly dialed his mother's number. Her phone went straight to voice mail.

"She must still be in the air," he said. He left a message. "Mom, it's Henry. Listen, you have to stay away from Uncle Don. I didn't want to say anything to you earlier because I didn't want to get you involved. I didn't fight with Dad. I walked in on Uncle Don and Dad fighting, and I saw him inject something into Dad's neck with a needle. He killed him, Mom. Now he's trying to set me up as if I did it. Before Dad died he gave me a flash drive and he said he wanted me to expose what's on it. I think Don's after me and trying to set me up because I saw him kill Dad, but he could also somehow know I have this flash drive. Just please stay away from Uncle Don. I'm not sure if he'll try to hurt you as well and try to pin it on me. Please be careful. Call me on Jessica's phone as soon as you land. I love you," he ended the call.

19

The Pendelton family jet touched down on a private airfield just outside of Washington, DC, then taxied over to the waiting limousine. Don was standing outside the limo waiting for Jane to exit the aircraft. The door opened, and the stairs unfolded. Jane appeared and started coming down the stairs. Don could see her eyes were puffy and red from crying, but even with the puffy eyes, Don was still impressed at just how beautiful she was. Don couldn't suppress the thought that now she was a widow and available. She was about ten years younger than Daniel, and even younger than Don, but maybe his powerful position could win her over.

"Thank you so much for being here, Don," Jane said and hugged him.

"Daniel would want me here to comfort you, Jane."

She pushed away from him, holding his shoulders with her hands. "You were like an older brother to him, Don."

"I know," he said and pulled her in and hugged her again. *God she smells like heaven*, he thought. After a few moments, Don pushed back and held Jane's shoulders with his hands. "I'm so sorry, Jane."

"I know, Don. Thank you."

"Jane, I'm afraid I have more bad news."

Jane's eyes grew big. "What is it, Don? Did something happen to Henry?"

"Well, there's no easy way to put this. William is dead, and the last person seen with him was Henry."

"What? You don't actually think Henry did anything to him, do you?"

"Listen, Jane. Clearly Henry isn't thinking rationally. Do you think he may be on drugs or something?"

"I can't believe you're saying this, Don. You know Henry. I don't think there could be a more level-headed young man on this earth. He would never hurt William, and no, sir, my son does not do drugs."

She pushed away from Don and walked toward the limousine. The driver opened the door for her, and she got in. Her friends Sharon and Lucy, who were standing off to the side trying to give Jane and Don some privacy, now followed Jane into the back of the car. When they got in, they saw Jane was crying again.

Jane pulled her phone from her purse and looked at the screen. "Sixty-two new messages," she said, shaking her head. She dialed her voice mail. *You have sixty-two new messages*, the automated voice stated. *First message: Jane, it's Zoe. I just heard the news about Daniel*—Jane pressed the number seven to skip the message. Her voice mail continued: *Hi, Jane, it's Gabriella Jacob. I just heard about Daniel. I'm so, so sorry. Whatever I can*—Jane pressed seven again. *Hello, Jane, it's Ally Nicholas. I heard about Daniel and*—Jane gave up, disconnected from the voice mail, and called Henry's phone. She was frustrated that one of the first few messages wasn't from Henry, and more than likely the rest of the messages were from friends who had heard the news. The call connected and went straight to Henry's voice mail. She left a message. "Henry, it's Mom. Please call me as soon as you get this message. I'm very worried. Why aren't you answering your phone? Please, Henry, I'm serious—call me. We just landed, and we're heading to the house. Please call me. I love you." She disconnected the call.

She was praying that Henry was waiting at the house for her as she had asked. She looked around to see what the holdup was and why they weren't moving yet. She saw that Don was standing outside the car toward the back overseeing the driver placing their luggage into the trunk.

"What did Don do that upset you?" Sharon asked.

"Don just told me Daniel's brother William was found dead."

"What?" Sharon asked.

"Oh my God, Jane, I'm so sorry," Lucy said.

Don got into the car and sat opposite Jane. "I'm sorry, Jane. I didn't mean to upset you." He put his hand on her leg.

"I know, Don. Just please," she pushed his hand away. "I don't want to think about anything right now. Could you please just take me home? Please?"

"Of course." Don picked up the phone that was connected to the driver up front.

"Yes, sir?" the driver asked.

"Take us to Mrs. Pendelton's residence, please," Don said. He hung up the phone, and the driver pulled away.

20

Henry pulled himself together and got his laptop. He came back to the couch and powered it up. He waited for it to boot up and then pulled the flash drive from his pocket and popped it into the USB port. Jessica leaned over trying to see the screen. Paul and Chad looked at Henry.

"Well?" Paul said.

"Hold on," Henry replied. He double-clicked the drive the flash drive was plugged into. A window popped up. There were two folders; one showed *Health-Care Initiative*, and the other showed *Patient names*. Henry double-clicked the folder *Health-Care Initiative* and started to read the file.

"The mission statement says something about a program to both show mercy to the sick while saving the government money. Now if I can just find the section that says 'kill people who find out about it,'" Henry tried to joke. "Do you mind snagging me another beer, Jess?"

"You really need to eat something, Henry. Eat some of your burger, and I'll grab you a beer."

"OK, Mom," Henry replied sarcastically.

Jessica gave him a look and handed him the container with his food. "Eat, Henry. You don't want to get sloppy."

"I know. I'm sorry, Jess."

He opened the container and mindlessly ate while he read through the file.

Wheel of Fortune had come on television after the news. Chad and Paul were playing along trying to solve the puzzles. Jessica was half watching the TV and half peeking over at Henry's laptop. The current puzzle's clue was *person*. There were a few letters shown on the puzzle.

"Famous welder Stephen Kong!" Chad called out.

"Seriously?" Jessica said. "Famous welder Stephen Kong?"

"There could be a famous welder named Stephen Kong," Chad replied.

The player called for a *t*, and Pat said, "Yes, there are two *t*'s." Vanna showed the letters in the puzzle.

After a couple seconds, Jessica said, "Famous writer Stephen King?" She looked at Chad. "Famous welder?" she asked laughing. "Chad, you've got to lay off smoking so much pot, my friend."

They all laughed except Henry. He was still scrolling through the file on the laptop and didn't seem to hear them.

As Henry read on, he caught parts of the file talking about Medicare and Medicaid costs. There were graphs showing illnesses and costs. He kept scrolling. Finally he came to a section of the report titled "End-of-Life Measures." Henry read through it. "I think I found something," he said.

They all looked over at him.

"It talks about Medicare and Medicaid costs. There are graphs showing how much it costs for patients living in nursing homes or hospitals—what types of injuries cost the most, what ailments cost the most. There's a quality-of-life assessment questionnaire. Now I just found a section that talks about a committee that would decide if a patient's life should be ended. It says, and I quote, 'Ending their suffering will not only benefit the individual, but will also result in a direct cost savings to the federal government.'"

The room was silent.

"Do you guys understand?" Henry said. "They have a committee that is killing people to save the government money."

"What does that have to do with your father?" Jessica asked.

"I don't know—maybe he was on the committee."

Henry minimized the screen and double-clicked the *Patient names* file.

"I just remembered something. When my dad handed me the flash drive, he kept telling me he was sorry and to please forgive him. He said, 'It wasn't supposed to be Gammy; it was supposed to be Alice.'"

"Who's Alice?" Jessica asked.

"Who's Gammy?" Paul asked.

"Gammy is what I call…." He paused and looked down. "Or I guess now it's what I *used* to call my grandmother. And Alice…that's the thing. At first I thought he was delirious, but now I remember my grandmother's childhood friend Alice. She was the reason my grandmother moved into Oak Tree Pointe."

"What's Oak Tree Pointe?" Paul asked.

"It's really expensive housing for old rich people, and it's also kind of a nursing home. There's a list here on the flash drive that says 'Patient names.' I'm trying to see if Alice's name is on the list."

Henry scrolled through the names, which seemed to be filed in alphabetical order. "She's not here," he said.

Jessica looked at the screen. "What does 'pending' mean?" Next to each name and location, it displayed *pending*.

"I would imagine it means pending saving the government money," he said. He scrolled down through the list. "Look at all of these names. The government is going to kill all of these people to save money. Unfucking-believable. Wait a second…." At the end of the *pending* list there was a space and then another list of names with *completed* in place of where the other list displayed *pending*.

"Here she is," Henry said. "Alice Andrews. It has today's date, and it says 'completed.'"

"Completed as in they killed her today?" Paul asked.

"Well that wouldn't make sense. Why would my dad say it was supposed to be Alice if Alice is dead?"

"Maybe she isn't," Jessica said. "Maybe that's it. They were supposed to get rid of Alice and instead got rid of…." She didn't want to finish the statement. It hit her that she wasn't solving a Nancy Drew mystery. This was about the death of Henry's grandmother.

Henry got her point. He nodded and looked down. "We'll call Oak Tree Pointe and ask for Alice."

Henry called his grandmother's phone number. It rang a few times, and then he heard it roll over and start ringing again.

"Oak Tree Pointe, this is Doris. May I help you?"

"May I speak to Alice Andrews please?" Henry asked.

"May I ask who's calling?"

"This is Paul, a family friend," Henry said, looking at Paul.

"I'm sorry. Alice is lying down right now. A very close friend of hers, who was a resident here, passed away today. She was very upset, so we had to sedate her. Paul, give me your last name and phone number, and I'll tell her you called."

"Sure, uh...OK," Henry said and then hung up. He turned toward the three of them who were staring at him. "Alice was upset because her close friend, who also lives there, passed away today. So they sedated her, and now she's resting," he said to them, shaking his head.

21

The limousine pulled up the driveway to Jane's house and parked at the front entrance. Jane didn't wait for the driver to come back and open the door for her. As soon as they stopped, she opened the door and hurried to the house. Sharon and Lucy quickly followed. Jane opened the front door and ran in.

"Henry? Henry, are you here?" she called out. "Henry?"

"Mrs. Jane. I so sorry, Mrs. Jane," Esther the housekeeper said, coming from the direction of the kitchen. There were tears rolling down her cheeks. She went over to Jane and hugged her.

"Thanks, Esther. I appreciate it."

"Mr. Daniel such good man. I so sorry."

"I know, Esther. Thank you. Esther, listen—is Henry here?"

"No. He was here just before Mr. Daniel get hurt. Mr. Kepler say Henry run away after Mr. Daniel get hurt."

"He hasn't come back? Are you sure?" Jane asked, practically begging.

"I no see him," she replied.

"Maybe he came in when you were doing something else," Jane said, excited at the thought. She ran up the grand staircase to the second floor. "Henry? Henry?" she called out as she ran down the corridor toward Henry's room. She flung open the door and found it was just as he left it when he went back to school. Nothing was out of place. "Goddamn it, Henry, where are you?" she said, leaning against the door to the empty room.

She walked back downstairs like a woman defeated. "He's not up there," she said.

"You need a drink, honey," Sharon said.

"No, I need to stay focused. Where could he be?" Jane asked.

"Listen, he'll turn up. He's probably just scared," Lucy said.

Jane walked down the corridor toward Daniel's office. She stopped just outside the door that was blocked off with yellow crime tape. She turned the knob and pushed the door open. The office looked just like it always did. Fortunately there were a couple sofas in front of the fireplace blocking the view of the hearth where he had hit his head. She was glad to be spared the sight. She pulled the door shut and stood there holding her hand to her mouth, lost in thought. Sharon and Lucy stood back not knowing if they should do or say something. Jane finally pulled herself back, closed the door, and headed into the great room. Sharon and Lucy followed.

Jane sat down on one of the couches, and Lucy sat down next to her and held her hand. Sharon went to the wet bar and made some drinks. She returned with a tray of martinis.

"Here, drink this. It will calm you down."

"No thank you, Sharon."

"Just drink it. Seriously, it will calm you down."

"OK, OK," Jane said, taking the martini.

Sharon pushed the tray toward Lucy, and Lucy took a martini.

"To Daniel," Sharon said, raising her glass in a toast.

"To Daniel," both Jane and Lucy said.

Don walked into the room.

"Anything?" Jane asked.

"I was about to ask you the same question. Nothing yet on my end," Don said. He walked over to the wet bar. "Do you mind?"

"Help yourself, Don, please. I'm sorry I'm not much of a hostess this evening."

"Please, Jane, we all know the day you're having," he said. He poured himself a drink and came over and sat by the women.

Sharon's phone rang. "Excuse me," she said, getting up and walking toward the doors overlooking the backyard. "Hello? Oh, hi, Diane. Yes, we just flew back." She paused while the other person was talking then continued: "We're at Jane's house. She's doing all right considering, you know." Sharon paused, again listening.

Lucy looked over at Jane. "Is there anything I can do?" she asked.

Sharon continued her conversation in the background over by the doors.

"Could you please wake me up from this bad dream, Lucy?"

"I wish I could, sweetie. I'm so sorry you're going through this," she said.

"Thanks, Lucy."

"Jane, that was Diane Zavad," Sharon said, coming back over by them. "She said something disturbing I think you need to know."

"What is it, Sharon?" Jane asked, terrified of the answer.

"Diane said on the national news tonight, they had a report about Eleanor, Daniel, and William."

"It was on the national news?" Jane asked.

"Yes, and she said the news reported that Henry is a person of interest, and that sources say what happened to Daniel and William may have to do with who inherits Eleanor's money," Sharon said, shying away, afraid that Jane was going to shoot the messenger.

"What? Seriously?" Jane asked, looking like the wind had been knocked out of her.

"Maybe I shouldn't have said anything," Sharon said. "I'm sorry, Jane. I just thought you should know what they're saying."

"No, Sharon, don't be sorry. I'm glad you told me. Oh my God. This is proof that Henry is innocent. No one in the family inherits Eleanor's money when she dies. A few years ago, Eleanor gifted Daniel and William money and set up a trust for Henry for when he turns twenty-five. Upon her death the rest of her estate is going into trusts to be distributed to charities. Henry is aware of all of this, so he stands to gain nothing by harming Daniel or William. We have to find him."

"Are you sure he's aware of that?" Don asked Jane.

"Of course I'm sure, Don," Jane said. She looked around. "Henry knows."

With that last statement, Don thought Jane didn't sound so sure of herself. She almost seemed to question herself. Since there was a possibility that Henry didn't know, as far as Don was concerned, his plan to frame him was still in motion.

22

Jessica looked at Henry and felt great sympathy for him. His whole world had changed since that afternoon. He was a happy-go-lucky college student when he left his town house earlier in the day, and over the course of a few hours, he became a suspect in the deaths of two family members.

"Henry, what do you want to do now?" she asked.

"I've got to expose this somehow. I'm not exactly sure how one goes about doing such a thing."

"Maybe we should call Diane Sawyer," Paul said.

"Jackass, really?" Jessica asked. "Now is not the time to try to joke. That isn't funny."

"I'm serious. Henry should give the flash drive to her and show her what's on it."

"I think Paul may be on to something," Henry said. "We'll drive to New York, or wherever Diane Sawyer is located, and I'm sure security will let a guy—who happens to be a person of interest in the deaths of two family members—in to meet with her," he said sarcastically.

"It was just a suggestion. I was trying to help," Paul said.

"I know, man. I understand and thank you," Henry said.

"Hey, my cousin works for the *New York Times*. I can call him and explain the situation," Chad said.

"Seriously?" Henry asked.

"Don't sound so surprised, Henry. Not everyone in my family is a stoner, dude. Do you want me to call him?"

"Yes. Please."

Chad scrolled through the address book on his phone. "Here's his number. Let's just hope it's current," he added.

Chad dialed the number, and after a few rings his cousin answered the phone. "Hello?"

"Ben, it's me, Chad. Dude, how's it hangin'?"

"Chad, what's up, man? How have you been?" Ben asked.

"I've been good. Real good. How about you?"

"The usual. Work, lots of work. What's up?"

"Well, listen. I have a friend that's in a situation."

"Chad, I'm not lending you money. My mom told me your mom got pissed when she found out I lent you money the last time."

"Dude, seriously. I don't need to borrow money, and either way I paid you back the last time. Listen—it's a buddy of mine. Did you hear what happened to the Pendelton family today?"

"I work for a newspaper, Chad. Of course I heard."

"Well, Henry Pendelton is my roommate."

"No shit. Does he want to confess to me or something?" Ben asked.

"Ben, he didn't do it. Honestly, he's being set up. This would be easier if he could explain it. Do you mind talking with him?"

"You're there with him now?"

"Yeah."

"You realize you're now an accessory for harboring a fugitive, right?"

"Ben, seriously, the kid is innocent."

"Trouble somehow always seems to find you, Chad. All right, put him on."

Chad handed the phone to Henry.

"Hello, this is Henry."

"Henry, this is Ben Aquafen. If what Chad is telling me is true, and you're innocent, your best bet is to turn yourself in."

"I agree wholeheartedly that under normal circumstances if you're innocent you should turn yourself in, and the truth will come out. But I'm being set up by a guy who's pretty high up in the government. I witnessed him kill my father, and that's why I think he's setting me up. But I also have information that he definitely doesn't want exposed. I highly doubt that if I turn myself in that I'll live long enough to prove my innocence. Just before my dad died, he handed me a flash drive. He told me he wanted what's on the drive to be exposed. I wasn't sure what he was talking about, but the government guy and his muscle have been chasing after me. Maybe they've figured out that I have the drive."

"What's on the drive?" Ben asked.

"It's information regarding a government project to euthanize the elderly to save government money. Got to keep those health-care costs down somehow," Henry joked.

"Henry, are you sure you haven't been smoking with Chad?"

"Ben, I'm not messing with you. It's in black and white on the flash drive."

"Well, how are we going to prove that it's not just some information you made up?" Ben asked.

"There are two lists of names—a list with the people who have been euthanized and a list of people who are 'to be euthanized.'"

"Well, Henry, this isn't a story I can break right now. I'm going to have to research the hell out of this. It's probably going to take a while. Do you have a list of the government people who are involved in this?"

"It's a big file, Ben. I haven't been able to read through the whole thing. Maybe there is."

"Why don't you e-mail me the information on the flash drive, and I'll start investigating it. Plus if you come across any other information, call me at this number."

"Will do. What's your e-mail address?"

Ben gave him his e-mail address.

"I'll shoot it right over," Henry said.

"Plus, Henry, who's this government guy who's setting you up?"

"It's Donald Kepler."

"The Donald Kepler? The president's chief of staff?"

"That would be the one."

"Oh shit, Henry."

"I know."

"As soon as I get the files, I'll start working on it. Lay low, and I'll call you as soon as I think I can break the story."

"Thanks, Ben. I really appreciate it."

"No problem. Tell Chad I'll catch him later—and to stop smoking so much pot."

"I will. Take it easy," Henry said laughing. He disconnected the call.

"What did he say?" Jessica asked.

"He said it's not something he can just break immediately. He said he needs to research it first and he'll let me know when he thinks he can break it. He told me to lay low."

"So we'll wait," Jessica said.

"It's all we can do," Henry replied.

23

Jane's phone started to ring, and Sharon, Lucy, and Don all looked over at her. She looked at the screen. "It's Ava Claire," she said, sounding defeated. She sent the call to voice mail. A few moments later, the phone-message alert sounded. Jane looked at the screen. Sixty new messages. Then she remembered that she still hadn't listened to all of the messages. Maybe there was one from Henry. She called her voice mail and started listening again, skipping through the messages to see if any were from Henry.

Don's phone rang. He looked at the screen and made a little smirk. He answered while getting up out of his chair. "This is Don," he said.

"Don, it's Jim Tanner."

"What have you got?" Don asked, walking away from the women.

"Henry took money out of an ATM close to downtown a little while ago, but no other activity since then. I'm assuming his girlfriend is Jessica Barrington. She's the only Jessica whose number has been calling Henry Pendelton, and she owns a silver Audi. And she just rented a room a little while ago at the Ritz-Carlton in Georgetown."

"Thank you. Let me know if anything else comes up."

Don quickly called Tom Laurel to ask him to have the chief of police surround the Ritz until they got there.

While Don was on the phone, Jane continued to skip through her messages. Toward the end of the messages, she finally heard Henry's voice: *Mom, it's Henry. Listen, you have to stay away from Uncle Don. I didn't want to say anything to you earlier because I didn't want to get you involved. I didn't fight with Dad. I walked in on Uncle Don and Dad fighting, and I saw him inject something into Dad's neck with a needle. He killed him, Mom.* Jane looked over at Don. She tried her best not to show what she had just heard. *Now he's trying to set me up as if I did it. Before Dad died he gave me a flash drive and he said he wanted me to expose what's on it. I think Don's after me and trying to set me up because I saw him kill Dad, but he could also somehow know I have this flash drive. Just please stay away from Uncle Don. I'm not sure if he'll try to hurt you as well and try to pin it on me. Please be careful. Call me on Jessica's phone as soon as you land. I love you.*

Jane disconnected from her voice mail. She felt as if someone had just punched her in the stomach for the umpteenth time that day. She got up and started to leave the room while looking in her address book for Jessica's number so she could call Henry back. She found the number, and as soon as she started to call it, she heard footsteps behind her and looked back to find Don coming quickly toward her. She quickly hung up and dropped the phone into her purse.

"Jane, we think we may have found him," Don said.

"Where is he?" she asked.

"Possibly at the Ritz-Carlton in Georgetown. Come on let's go."

"Maybe I should stay here just in case he's not there and he comes here," Jane stammered.

Both Sharon and Lucy looked at her like she was on drugs.

Don looked at her and tilted his head like something didn't quite add up. "I think it's best if you come with us in case we need you to talk to him," he said. The thought crossed his mind: *plus you're going to be my leverage to get Henry.*

"All right," Jane said. She didn't know what to do. She couldn't think of an excuse as to why she wouldn't want to go. "Well at least you two can go home, and you can call me if you hear from him, right?" Jane asked the girls.

"Of course we will. We'll call you if we hear from him. Don't worry, Jane, he will be OK," Sharon said, sounding not too confident.

"Thank you both. I mean it," Jane said, hugging Sharon and Lucy. Don stood waiting. As Jane walked with Don toward the front entrance, she fought the urge to lunge at him and scratch his eyes out.

The limousine was still waiting for Don. He opened the back door for Jane, and she got in and slid over toward the other door. Jack got in and sat facing Jane with his back to the driver. Don slid in next to Jane. Don picked up the phone connected to the driver.

"Yes, sir?" the driver asked.

"Take us to the Ritz-Carlton in Georgetown as quickly as possible," Don said.

The driver then raced down the driveway toward the street, slowing only for the opening gates.

Jane got an idea and reached into her purse. Jack just sat staring at her, so she grabbed her lipstick and a small mirror and applied the lipstick. She looked at Jack and made a face at him, gesturing *do you mind giving me some privacy*. Jack shrugged and looked out the window. She reached back down into her purse putting her lipstick away, and while keeping her phone held down in her purse, she pressed the *Send* button. The last number she had dialed, which was Jessica's, displayed. She pressed *Send* again, keeping the phone in her purse and out of sight. The phone displayed that it was calling the number. Then it showed that it had connected. She took her hand from the bag so she wouldn't look suspicious. She waited a few seconds to make sure Jessica or Henry—whoever answered the phone—was listening.

"Don, how do you know Henry is at the Ritz-Carlton in Georgetown?" she asked.

"I got a phone call that his girlfriend rented a room on her credit card at that hotel. I'm betting that they're hiding out there. DC police are on their way to surround the hotel," Don said.

"They won't hurt him, will they?"

"They have been ordered to stand down until we get there."

"If someone hurts him, Don, I will never forgive you."

"No one there is going to hurt him, Jane. We will go to their room and talk to them," Don said.

"It's just that I know he didn't do any of these things they're accusing him of on the news. Henry knows there is no inheritance coming from the death of his grandmother. Henry knows he gets the trust money regardless of whether his father, William—or I, for that matter—are alive. Henry would never do these things, Don. I just hope he knows I love him, and I just want him to be safe. Now that we're heading toward the Ritz in Georgetown to get him and Jessica, I guess I can tell him there," she said, nodding her head at Don.

Don looked at Jane again, tilting his head and shaking it. Since Jane had a few martinis at the house, she didn't realize she was unconsciously lowering her face toward her purse to make sure that Henry could hear her. Don figured she was up to something. He quickly grabbed Jane's purse from her lap and looked in it, shaking his head. He spotted her phone and saw *Connected* displayed on the screen along with the amount of time the call had been connected.

"Don, what are you doing? Give me back my purse!" Jane shouted, grabbing at her bag on Don's lap.

Don swatted her hands away. "Jane, you're interfering with an investigation. Now sit back down. I'm trying to help you here!" he yelled at her.

She pressed herself against the side of the car, trying to get as far away from Don as she could while the limousine sped toward the hotel.

24

Jessica's phone started ringing. Henry picked it up off the table and looked at the display.

"It's my mom," he said to the group. "Hello?" There was no answer. "Hello?" he asked again, and once again there was no response. He was just about to disconnect the call when he heard his mother talking in the background. It sounded the same as when someone would accidentally "pocket dial" him.

"Mute it," he called over to Paul, who had the remote for the TV. Paul fumbled with the remote and found the mute button. The room went silent. Jessica, Chad, and Paul all stared at Henry with the phone pressed against his ear not saying anything.

Henry twisted the phone down so his mouth was away from the microphone, but he still held it pressed to his ear listening to the speaker. "They know we're here. My mom is talking to Don asking him how he knows we're at the Ritz in Georgetown," he stood up. "Come on, grab your stuff. We've got to get out of here." Keeping the phone to his ear, he went and powered down his laptop. He put the flash drive back in its case and put it in his pocket.

Everyone got up and looked around the room for things they needed to take with them. They quickly realized there really wasn't anything to gather. Henry closed his laptop, put it under his arm, and put on his baseball cap. As they all made their way toward the door, Henry stopped suddenly. "Oh no," he said. He still had the phone pressed against his ear. They could see the look of terror on his face.

"What's happening, Henry?" Jessica asked.

Henry heard Don yelling at his mother. He was terrified that Don might be adding another family member to Henry's apparent résumé of inheritance victims.

"Hello?" Don said into the phone.

Henry's heart hammered in his chest. He wasn't sure why he was so terrified of Don over the phone.

"Hello?" Don said again. "Are you there?"

"Fuck you, Don!" Henry said, surprising himself.

"Henry, is that you?" he asked. "You seem to have gotten yourself into a little bit of trouble there, my boy."

"I'm not your boy, Don. I swear to God, if you touch my mother, I will hunt you down and kill you if it's the last thing I do."

"Henry, now why don't you just stay put, and we will discuss this like adults. Your mother and I are on our way. We want to help. We will get together and formulate a plan."

When Don said stay put, Henry realized he was wasting valuable time standing there talking to him. He motioned to Jessica, Paul, and Chad, who were waiting for him by the door, and mouthed the words *let's go*. He continued talking to Don while they hurried toward the elevators. "I'm not kidding, Don. Do not touch my mother, or I will go public about the little project you're involved in."

"I'm not sure I'm following you, son," Don said, knowing exactly what Henry was talking about.

"Oh, you better follow me, Don. Dad gave me a flash drive with all of the information about the project—the one about the elderly and saving money. Does that ring a bell, Don?"

Don was intentionally silent. He had watched Daniel hand Henry the flash drive in the reflection of the glass door earlier that day. Don pretended to be surprised, giving Henry a false sense of security. Don knew Henry saw him kill Daniel. There were no two ways about it: he could not let Henry live. So if Henry thought the drive was a bargaining chip, then so be it. That would ultimately bring them together. Otherwise Henry would most likely go to the authorities to try to save his mother. Don had Jane. Henry thought he could bargain her release from Don with the drive. This was starting to go in the right direction for Don.

"The great Don has nothing to say?" Henry asked.

Don wished Jane wasn't sitting next to him so he could tell the little prick that if he tried to go public, neither he nor his mother would be alive much longer. But since Jane was sitting next to him, he had to try the diplomatic approach. "Henry, your mother is right here worried about you. She's a nervous wreck.... What? You want me to give her some sedatives to calm her down. I'm not sure that's such a good idea. She's been drinking. Why don't you just stay there, and we can negotiate an end to all of this."

"We'll get together, but I'll call you and let you know where and when. Once again, do not lay a fucking finger on my mother or I'll go public," Henry said, disconnecting the call.

25

"What just happened?" Jessica asked as they piled into the elevator.

"My mother must have secretly called me to let me know they were on to us, and Don caught her," he replied. "Come on. Come on," he said, looking up at the floor numbers ticking off on the elevator."

"Where should we go?" Paul asked.

"I don't know. We just need to get out of here. I heard Don say the police were going to surround the hotel. Let's just hope they're all stuck in line at donut shops."

"A donut sounds good; I could go for a donut," Chad said. They all laughed.

The elevator doors opened, and they hurried across the lobby toward the parking area.

"So far, so good," Henry said, taking Jessica's hand. He pulled his baseball cap lower trying to cover his face.

They went down the hallway to the door that led to the parking area. Paul opened the door and held it for Jessica, Henry, and Chad. They went cautiously out the door looking around. They turned down the aisle where Jessica's car was parked. There were two DC police cars parked by her car. Their emergency lights were off; otherwise they would have seen them as soon as they came out of the hotel.

"Oh shit!" Chad said. They quickly turned around and headed back to the hotel. One of the police officers caught their motion out of the corner of his eye.

"Hey. Stop right there!" he yelled toward them.

"Just keep going," Henry said, holding Jessica's hand tightly, pulling her faster toward the door.

"I said stop right there," the officer yelled again. "Hey, that's them," he yelled to the other officer. He started running toward them.

"Run," Henry said. They ran back to the door, quickly went inside, and hurried back toward the lobby.

They made their way across the lobby toward the front doors that led to the street. Then they saw a DC police officer quickly coming toward the doors.

"This way, this way," Henry said, heading toward another hallway that had an exit sign. He turned to look back to see if the officer was coming after them.

"Henry, watch out," Jessica yelled, grabbing Henry's arm. It was too late. Henry collided with a bellhop who was pushing a cart full of luggage out of the elevator bank. The cart tipped over, and luggage spilled all over the marble floor.

"I'm so sorry, sir," the bellhop said as he was trying to stand back up.

Henry looked back, and now the officer was running toward them talking into the radio on his shoulder.

Jessica helped pull him up and they all ran toward the exit.

26

The limousine carrying Don, Jane, and Jack pulled up to the front of the hotel. There were two police cars parked in front. A bellhop came over to the car and opened the door. More police cars came screeching into the parking area in front of the hotel.

"Stay here," Don said to Jane and Jack. He got out and stopped an officer heading into the hotel. "Excuse me. I'm Don Kepler," he said pulling out his credentials and flashing them at him. "The chief is expecting me. What's going on?" he asked the officer.

"The Pendelton kid was just spotted heading from the parking area through the lobby of the hotel."

"Thanks," Don said to him. He leaned into the car. "He's in the lobby," he said to Jack. Jack climbed out, and when he was close, Don whispered in his ear, "Take him out if you have to, and get the drive."

Jack nodded and ran toward the lobby of the hotel.

While Don was sliding back into the car, Jane was opening her door and starting to get out. Don grabbed her wrist and pulled her back in the car toward him. "Where do you think you're going?" He reached across her and closed her door.

"What are you doing, Don? I'm going in there to find Henry."

"No, Jane. You're going to sit right there and wait for the police to do their job."

"You don't tell me what to do, Don. I'm going in there to get Henry."

"This is a police investigation, and I can't let you get in the way. Now just sit there."

"I've always treated you like family. This is how you repay me?"

"Jane, this isn't personal."

"I beg your pardon? What exactly is it then, Don?"

"I'm protecting you. Now please just stop it. I understand you believe Henry knows there's no inheritance, but his actions clearly show otherwise. Now please, just humor me, and let me protect you until we get to the bottom of this. Why don't we have a drink while we wait?" he said, moving toward the stocked bar in the back of the limousine. He opened the cap on the decanter holding a clear liquid and sniffed.

"Vodka?" he asked Jane.

"Why not?" she replied. She knew he wasn't letting her out of the car. She realized it was probably best to just go along with the whole protection thing he was spinning. She didn't want to push him too far now knowing he had killed Daniel.

He put ice in both glasses and poured the vodka. "Here," he said, handing her a drink.

"I will never forgive you if they hurt Henry," she said.

"I know, Jane," he replied. A thought started forming in his head. Once they got Henry, maybe he would shoot Jane and then shoot Henry. A murder-suicide. That would wrap things up nicely. He did, however, hate to shoot Jane. He thought she was so beautiful, and it would be such a waste.

27

Motion sensors triggered the glass doors to slide open as Henry and the group ran down the walkway toward the street exit.

"Go this way. I left my grandmother's car a few blocks away."

They ran back toward where Henry left the car. A police car came down the road toward them with its lights flashing. Henry looked back and could see four police officers running after them.

"Let's cut through the mall," Henry yelled.

They cut through the side street and then over the canal on the same footbridge that Henry had crossed hours earlier.

"Stop or I'll shoot!" one of the officers shouted from behind them.

A woman screamed at the sight of the police with their guns drawn and grabbed her two small children, hurrying them back into the store they just came out of. All of the shoppers turned to see who was shouting. Henry, Jessica, Paul, and Chad also instinctively looked back to see how close they were.

"Holy shit. Look!" Paul yelled to the others pointing back at the police officer. "He's actually got his gun out, and he's aiming it at us. Look at all of these people. Is that guy crazy?"

When Paul pointed back, the officer thought he was aiming a gun at him, so he fired a shot at Paul. Thankfully it was the first time the officer had fired his gun in the line of duty, and the shot went high, hitting one of the decorative columns on the side of a storefront façade. The sound of the gunshot led to more people screaming, and suddenly there was pandemonium.

"He's got a gun!" Henry yelled toward the people who were ahead of him. Henry of course failed to mention that the *he* in question was a cop who was chasing them.

Jack came across the footbridge just as the officer fired the shot, and he could see Henry and his friends running with the cops close behind.

He ran down the path that was cleared by all of the terrified shoppers. He quickly gained on them. Henry's group turned left down a walkway heading toward the M Street exit. Jack caught up with the police officers and passed them.

Up ahead there was a huge crowd forming that was trying to exit onto M Street away from the gunfire. Henry and his friends separated and weaved their way through the crowd. Jack lost sight of them, but he pushed ahead yelling that he had been shot and needed to get through to get help. It was actually working.

Once on M Street, Henry and the others found each other. With Henry leading the way, they crossed the street and ran in the direction where the Bentley was parked a few blocks away. When Jack made it outside, he saw Henry and his friends running toward a busy intersection. He ran toward them holding his gun down at his side. Henry and his friends had stopped at the intersection waiting for the traffic to stop so they could continue. Henry looked back just as Jack finished crossing the street to their side. He saw Jack hurry down the sidewalk heading toward them. They locked eyes, Henry grabbed Jessica's hand, and—not thinking—they ran out into traffic. Chad and Paul followed.

Jack raised his gun and aimed it at Henry. He was using a silencer, so he didn't have to worry that passersby would look as the gun fired. Tires screeched as the group crossed the intersection. A car slammed on its brakes and started sliding sideways. The front end of the car hit Henry in his side, knocking his feet from under him, and he started to fall toward the pavement.

Jack took his shot.

Chad saw that the car wasn't going to stop in time, and just as it hit Henry, he lurched forward to catch him before his head hit the pavement. He felt a stinging pain in his chest just as he caught Henry. He figured he must have pulled a muscle or something when he reached for Henry. He helped Henry to his feet. "Are you OK, dude?" he asked.

A man in a suit jumped out of the car that hit Henry. "I'm so sorry. I tried to stop," he said.

"Come on. I'm OK," Henry said to his friends. He walked toward the man who had hit him, intending to ask him for a ride out of there.

The man backed up thinking Henry wanted to fight him for hitting him. "It was an accident. I'm really sorry," he said, stepping back from Henry. "Just relax, and we can get you some help. There's no need to get physical."

Henry looked at the car with its door wide open. "Hurry, get in," he said, just loud enough for Jessica, Paul, and Chad to hear. He took a couple more steps toward the man, as if he was going to fight him, and the man took a few more steps back. Then they turned and ran for the car.

Before the man knew what was happening, Henry and his friends hopped into his car. "Thank you, God," Henry said when he found the keys still in the ignition. The man who owned the car came running over. Henry quickly locked the doors.

"Hey. What do you think you're doing?" the man yelled.

"Everybody stay down. The asshole who shot at me in the river is coming at us over there," Henry said, pointing toward Jack, who was now running toward the car. They all slid down in their seats. He started the car, put it into drive, and floored it.

"How did I get blood all over me?" Chad asked, looking down at his bloodstained shirt.

Jack took aim and shot at the car Henry was pulling away in. Bullet holes formed spiderweb cracks along the rear window. The car kept moving, so he aimed lower at the tires. Smoke came from the driver-side rear tire. Then Henry turned down a side street, and the car disappeared from view. Jack holstered his gun and ran back toward the front of the hotel. He pulled out his phone while running and called Don.

"I'm heading back to you. He got away in a black sedan. He just turned onto a side street off of Wisconsin Avenue. I'm heading down Wisconsin, coming back toward the hotel."

"We're on our way," Don said.

28

"Chad, what the hell happened to you?" Paul asked. "Hey guys, something is wrong with Chad. He doesn't look too good."

"I don't know where all this blood came from," Chad said.

Paul lifted Chad's shirt revealing a bullet wound just under his right nipple.

"Uh, guys? We have a problem. Chad's been shot."

"What?" Henry and Jessica both asked turning around.

Henry tried to drive and look back to check out Chad. "Did he shoot him through the trunk?"

"I don't know. Lean forward," Paul told Chad.

He gingerly moved forward. "Oh, that hurts, that hurts, that hurts," Chad cried out.

"No, there's no hole in the seat. Here, sit back," he said to Chad, helping him slowly sit back.

"I think I was hit when I reached out to grab Henry after the car hit him. I thought I had pulled a muscle, but that fucker shot me."

"We need to get him to a hospital. There's a lot of blood back here," Paul said.

"If I don't move, the pain isn't really that bad," Chad said. "I'm OK."

"My grandmother's car is just a couple blocks away. Let's get to it, and then we'll take him to the hospital. We're not going to make it in this car with a flat tire and bullet holes all over it. Major red flags."

"Jess, look and see if there are any napkins in the glove box or center console so I can try to stop some of this bleeding," Paul said.

She opened the glove box. "There actually are napkins. What are the chances?" she asked, pulling them out and handing them back to Paul. When she reached back to close the glove box she saw that the napkins had been covering a revolver. "And then there's also this," she said, pulling out the gun. "And this," she said, pulling out a plastic placard that said *Official Business*.

"Oh shit. That guy must have been a cop or FBI or something. Dressed in a suit with a gun in the glove box," Henry said.

"You stole a cop's car," Chad said laughing. "That's great. You stole a cop's car," he said again.

"I don't think a cop or FBI agent would have backed off like that. He was probably a diplomat or something," Jessica said.

Chad started to laugh again, and then it turned into a coughing fit. Blood started spraying with each cough. "That can't be good," he said, looking at Paul.

"You'll be all right, buddy," Paul said, holding the napkins against the wound.

Henry headed back to where he left the car. He double-parked behind his grandmother's car, and they got out and went to the Bentley.

"What should I do with this?" Jessica asked, holding out the gun.

"I'll take it," Henry said, taking it from her and shoving it into his waistband.

Paul helped Chad out and over to the car.

"I can't get in. I'll get blood all over the seats," Chad said.

"Chad, believe me—even if my grandmother was alive, she wouldn't mind you getting blood on the seats. You took a bullet for me. Now get in the car so we can take you to the hospital. We've got to go,"

Chad hesitated then finally got in. "This is a really nice car," he said.

"Thanks, Chad. Let's go get you some help," Henry said. He started the Bentley and pulled out of the spot, leaving the borrowed, shot-up car double-parked in the street. He raced toward the hospital.

Five minutes later Henry pulled up to the emergency room entrance. Paul hopped out and grabbed an empty wheelchair that was up against the wall. Henry got out and helped Paul lift Chad out of the car and into the chair. "I'm so sorry I can't come in with you," Henry said.

"Thanks for taking a bullet for me, buddy. I owe you big time. I'm so sorry I dragged you into this shit."

"It's not your fault, Henry. Get out of here before someone recognizes you," Chad said.

"All right, take care, Chad," Henry said. He rubbed his shoulder. "I'm truly sorry."

"Stop," Chad said.

"OK. Paul, call us as soon as you talk to the doctor," Henry said, running back around and hopping into the car. He turned to Jessica. "Jess, why don't you go with them?"

"I'm staying with you, Henry. I'm not a doctor. There's nothing I can do for him in there."

"Jess, I'm not saying you're a doctor or that you can do anything for him. It's just…I don't want you with me."

Jessica looked at him, clearly hurt by what he had said.

"You know it's not that I don't love you. I've been putting all of your lives in danger, and now Chad's hurt bad. I can't live with myself if something bad happens to you too. Now please go with them, Jess."

"I'm staying with you, and you better start moving because there's a security guard coming this way."

Henry looked up and spotted the guard. "Jess, please."

"Just go. I'm staying with you," she replied.

Henry put the car in drive and pulled away from the hospital.

29

Don's phone rang. He looked at the caller ID, and it was the CIA director Tom Laurel.

"This is Don."

"Don, what the hell is going on down there? I've got reports that there was a shootout at The Shops at Georgetown Park and also shots fired on a busy street."

"Tom, everything is under control. We are in pursuit of Henry Pendelton right now."

"The hell you are. The chief of police just called to let me know they found the car that Henry was last seen in on a side street with blood all over the back seat. Why the hell were the police shooting at the kid in a crowded mall? He's just a person of interest at this point, for God's sake."

"Tom, hold on a second," Don said, picking up the car phone to call the driver.

"Yes?" the driver asked.

"Pull over and stop the car," he said, hanging up the phone. The driver slowed, pulled to the curb, and stopped the car.

"Well what is it, Don?"

"Just another second," he said. He didn't want to talk in front of Jane. He opened the car door and got out onto the sidewalk, shutting the door behind him. "I wasn't completely honest earlier. Daniel Pendelton was trying to expose the Health-Care Initiative."

"Why the hell would he want to do that? Wasn't it his idea in the first place?"

"Well, yes it was. But this afternoon there was a mix-up."

"What kind of mix-up, Don?"

"Eleanor Pendelton was accidentally euthanized due to the program, and Daniel figured it out. Then our IT security department notified me that Daniel was copying files onto a removable drive.

"Jesus Christ!" Tom said.

"I went to his house immediately on the pretext that I was there to offer condolences. The housekeeper let me in and told me Daniel was in his office. When I went to see him, I saw that he was out on the patio off of his office. So I looked around his computer and his desk, but I couldn't find the drive. I went out on the patio and tried to reason with him. Things got out of hand, and unfortunately his son Henry witnessed it."

"Witnessed what, Don?"

"I had to stop Daniel. He was hiding the drive and wouldn't give it up. He threatened to expose the program unless it was stopped. I had syringes on me just in case I couldn't talk him down—"

"And?" Tom prompted.

"And...Daniel had a...a heart attack."

"I get you, Don. So what's that have to do with the son?"

"When he walked in, I had Daniel pinned to the floor. He ran over to us, and I got up. I moved away pretending I was calling nine-one-one. Henry was leaning over talking to his father, and I saw Daniel hand him the drive. I called Jack in from the car so we could get the drive away from him, and Henry took off. We chased him, but he jumped into the river and got away."

"My God, Don. He still has this drive?"

"He does, and I have Jane Pendelton. I intend to swap Jane for the drive."

"This story just keeps getting better, doesn't it, Don?"

"I'm not sure it could have been handled any differently, Tom."

"We'll see about that. Have you notified the president of the compromise?" he asked.

"Not yet."

"Jesus, Don. What do you need from me? You need troops? We'll shut the city down. We'll tell the public he stole information from his father containing material vital to national security."

"I don't think that's necessary yet. If we keep this quiet, I can still fix it. I think he's scared I'm going to hurt Jane. He's supposed to call me to let me know where he wants to meet."

"You've spoken with him?"

"Yes. He said he knows about the project. I'm pretty sure I've scared him into thinking I'll harm Jane if he doesn't give me the drive. I'll tell him if he gives me the drive back, I'll make the deaths of his father and uncle prove to be accidental, and he'll get his mother back. If he goes public in the future, his mother will have an accident. That should keep him quiet." Don didn't want to tell Tom that he actually planned to get rid of Henry and Jane. Henry was an eyewitness, and Don wasn't going to let that hang over his head.

"You better hope this works, Don. Call me with updates."

"I will," Don said, ending the call. He got back into the car.

"Who was that?" Jane asked.

"Just an update," Don replied.

"Well?"

"Nothing yet."

"Why don't we go back to the house and wait for him there?" Jane asked.

"Good idea," Don said. He figured since Henry had dumped the car, he had no leads to go on. They might as well go wait it out at Jane's house.

30

"Where are we going?" Jessica asked Henry as they sped down the city streets away from the hospital.

"That's a good question. We need to lay low and let Ben do some research."

"I guess charging another hotel room isn't going to work."

"I don't think so. I have some cash, but I don't think they'll rent you a room without a credit card for deposit."

"We can go stay with Stephanie." Stephanie was Jessica's friend from Syracuse who she knew from her freshman year. She also had her own town house.

"No, I don't want to put anyone else in danger," he said, leaning his head back against the headrest. After a few minutes, he sat up straight. "I've got it. We'll go to the place they would never think we would go."

"Where?"

"My parents' house."

"I don't think that's such a good idea. There's probably police there or detectives or something."

"We'll drive by, and if it looks empty, we'll go in. Sometimes the best place to hide is the most obvious. Plus if they come back there, maybe I can somehow separate my mom from Don."

"I guess we could try it. What else is there?" Jessica asked, sounding a little scared.

Henry was angry with himself for not making Jessica stay at the hospital. He wasn't afraid for his own life; he was afraid for Jessica's.

Henry turned down his parents' road and let off the accelerator when they came up to the driveway. He could see there were no cars parked out front. He pulled, turned the headlights off, rolled his window down, and entered the code to open the gates. The gates slowly opened, and he drove up the driveway. Coming up to the house, he went right toward the garage. He put the car in park and left the engine running. "Let me go pull the golf car out, and you can pull into the garage so no one sees the car."

"OK," Jessica replied.

Henry got out and went up to the garage where there was a panel located next to one of the doors. He lifted the cover and entered a code. The garage door next to the panel opened revealing his mother's Range Rover. Henry walked into the garage, disappearing from Jessica's sight.

"Please be OK, Henry," Jessica said in the empty car. She realized she was shaking and holding her breath. She tried to concentrate by taking deep breaths to calm herself down.

The door Henry went through started to close, and the door next to it opened. Jessica waited for Henry to pull the golf car out. Instead Henry walked out and motioned for her to pull in. He went back into the garage, and Jessica pulled the car in. He motioned for her to stop when she was in far enough. She turned off the car, and he went over and pushed the button to lower the door back down.

"I thought you had to move the golf car?" Jessica asked.

"I forgot that my dad's car isn't here; he got a ride home today. This is his spot...or I guess I should say it *was* his spot," he said softly.

Jessica looked at him and frowned, not knowing what to say.

He opened the door from the garage into the house. He stopped and listened. "The alarm didn't go off, which means Esther must be home."

"Esther?"

"My parents' housekeeper. She has an apartment on the lower level. We have to be quiet. She's cool, but I don't want to get her involved," he explained. "There's a guest apartment up here above the garage. Follow me."

They went down a hallway to the right that led to a set of stairs that went up to the apartment. They went in, and Henry flipped the light switch illuminating the rooms. There was a living room to the left with a sectional sofa facing a fireplace that had a flat-screen television above it.

There were three sets of French doors on the far wall of the living room leading out to a rooftop deck. There was a full kitchen and eating area to the right with a hallway leading down to two bedrooms and a full bath.

"I could live here," Jessica said.

"Yeah, it's nice," Henry said, heading toward the bathroom. "I've had to take a major piss for the past hour. Note to self—don't drink a lot of beer when you're on the run."

"Duly noted," Jessica replied. "I'm after you."

Henry finished and came back to the kitchen, and Jessica took her turn in the bathroom. He propped a kitchen chair under the doorknob to the entry door. Even though the door was locked, at least if someone tried to force it open, the chair would slow him or her down and make enough noise to alert them. He went back to the kitchen and grabbed a bottle of Rodney Strong cabernet out of the wine rack. He opened it and poured two glasses. He found a lighter in the drawer, lit the candles on the small kitchen island, and turned the lights off.

Jessica walked out of the bathroom. "I was just about to say maybe we should turn the lights off so we don't attract attention if they come back here," she said.

"Great minds think alike," Henry said. "I guess it's being a little overcautious since the bedroom windows are the ones you can see when you pull up the driveway."

Jessica walked over to him, and Henry handed her a glass of wine. She took a drink, then set it on the counter and hugged him. "I'm so sorry for what you're going through. I wish I could do something to help you feel better," she said. She pushed back from him, and he could see she was crying. "I know that sounds cheesy," she said, "but I can't stand to see you going through this. You're such a nice guy, Henry. You don't deserve this."

"You don't deserve this, Jess," Henry said to her, pulling her back in and hugging her. "The only good part about this day is that it makes me realize just how much I really love you," he said.

They kissed.

He pushed back from her. "Jess, don't be mad, but it's been a long day, and I could really go for a cigarette right now," he said.

"OK, that was random," she said. "Henry, you're not going back out there to buy cigarettes," she said, sounding angry.

"No, I have some stashed in the cabinet over here," he said, walking over to the cabinet next to the fireplace that housed the components for the TV. He bent down and opened the glass door. He reached inside and pulled out a pack of cigarettes. "I used to sneak out here and have a smoke without my parents knowing," he said. "Grab your drink, and come on out here," he said, walking toward the French doors.

They went out on the deck. There was a gentle breeze, and the stars were blazing in the sky. They could hear the Potomac flowing down below. They sat on two lounge chairs next to each other.

"I wish you hadn't, but I'm glad you stayed. Does that make sense, Jess?"

"I understand, Henry," she said, taking a drink of wine.

Henry shook a cigarette from the pack and offered it to Jessica.

"All right," she said, taking the cigarette from him.

"Really? Look at you," Henry said. He was surprised because Jessica never smoked.

"I'm on the lam with a wanted fugitive. I'm pretty sure it would be criminal if I didn't smoke," she said. "Let's just hope this ends before I have to get a tattoo or something."

They both laughed. Henry lit Jessica's cigarette and then shook one out of the pack and lit it for himself. He went over and grabbed an ashtray that was stashed under a chair in the corner.

He lifted his glass up and Jessica did the same. "To my grandma, dad, and uncle."

Jessica nodded and they tapped glasses.

They finished their cigarettes and sat in silence finishing their wine. Henry held Jessica's hand and unconsciously rubbed it with his thumb. He pulled her hand over and gently kissed the back of it. He was completely relaxed and realized that the hand rubbing was starting to turn him on. At first he was disgusted with himself. His dad, grandmother, and uncle had died today, and he was thinking about getting laid. Then he figured that all three of those people always just wanted him to be happy. *And what would make me happier than getting lucky with Jessica?* he thought.

"You want to turn in?" he asked her.

"Sure."

They grabbed their wine glasses, and Henry hid the ashtray back in the corner. They went back inside, and Jessica went over and opened the fridge.

"Water?" she asked him.

"Sure. Grab me a couple, please."

While she grabbed the water, he grabbed one of the candles and went into the bedroom on the left. He found clean sheets in the closet, and he and Jessica made the bed by candlelight. He left the candle on the nightstand, went back to the kitchen, and blew out the other candle. When he went back in, Jessica was just finishing getting undressed. She reached back and unhooked her bra, letting it fall down to the floor. The candlelight shadows danced across her bare breasts.

Henry pulled off his shirt and looked over at her. "Very nice, Jess," he said, looking at her exposed breasts with a goofy grin.

"What are you, five?" she asked, pulling the sheet back and sliding into the bed. He dropped his pants and slid into the bed next to her.

"Interesting," Jessica said, looking at him.

"What?" he asked.

"My mother always told me to wear clean underwear in case I was ever in an accident. Apparently yours suggested no underwear in case you're ever chased by a government official."

"My underwear was wet from the river earlier, and I didn't feel comfortable wearing my uncle's."

"All I said was 'interesting,'" she said giggling.

He reached over and cupped her breast with his hand and gently kissed it. He moved on to kissing her neck under her ear. He knew it drove her crazy. She let out a soft moan and climbed on top of him as they continued to kiss. She eased herself back into Henry's lap. After they finished, she rolled off of him.

"That was great," Henry said. "I could go for another one of those cigarettes now."

They both laughed. He reached over and kissed her.

Goodnight, Jess, I love you," he said.

"I love you too, Henry. Goodnight."

Jessica spooned his side, and she gently ran her fingers across his chest until Henry finally fell into a deep sleep. She watched him sleep for a while, feeling so bad for him that she began to cry. After a while she too drifted off to sleep.

31

At the same time Henry was propping the chair under the door to the apartment above the garage, the limousine carrying Jane, Don, and Jack pulled up the driveway and parked under the porte cochere at the front entrance to the house. Henry had missed the lights that could be seen from the guest apartment windows that had lit up the trees as the limo curved up the driveway.

Once again Jane didn't wait for the driver to open her door. She got out, walked up the front walk, and disappeared through the front door. Don and Jack quickly followed. Don caught sight of her going down the hallway and into the master bedroom.

"Should we follow her in there?" Jack asked. "Or do you want me to go outside and make sure she doesn't leave?"

"No," Don replied, "just give her a minute."

They walked into the great room that was just off the hallway that led to the master bedroom.

"Do you want a drink?" Don asked Jack. "I imagine it's going to be a long night.

"Just water," Jack responded.

Esther came into the great room as Don was pouring the drinks.

"Good evening, Mr. Kepler," Esther said. "Hello," she said to Jack.

"Good evening, Esther. How are you?" Don asked.

"I fine, thanks. Is Mrs. Jane here?" she asked with her thick accent.

"Yes, she went into her bedroom to freshen up," Don said.

"Do you going to stay for dinner?" Esther asked. "I fix pot roast with potatoes and vegetables. It's cooking in slow-cooking pot in kitchen," she said.

Jane walked into the great room. She had considered making a run for it but wasn't sure if that would just make Don hurt Henry when he got him. The old saying occurred to her: *keep your friends close to you, but keep your enemies closer.* She decided she should just trust her gut, and she would know if and when the time was right to do something.

"Hello, Esther," Jane said.

"Mrs. Jane, how are you doing?" she asked, going over to her and rubbing her shoulder.

"I'm doing fine, Esther. Thanks for asking."

"I just telling Mr. Kepler I make pot roast if you hungry," she said. "I understand if you no hungry," she said, wringing her hands. It was evident that Esther didn't know what to do regarding the recent events.

"Thank you very much, Esther, but not right now—maybe later," Jane said.

"You hungry?" Esther asked Don and Jack.

Jack looked to Don not knowing how to answer. At this point he was so hungry he was ready to chew on one of the leather sofas. He hoped Don would say yes.

"That sounds delicious, Esther. Would you mind bringing a couple of servings in here for us?" he said, motioning to Jack and himself. "I don't want Jane to be alone right now."

"No problem—I bring right out," she said, clearly happy to have something to do with herself.

"Don, why don't you just go in there and eat. I'm exhausted," Jane said. "I'm going to go lay down. Just let me know if Henry comes or you hear anything."

"Jane, actually I'd rather you didn't," he said as if telling a child that unfortunately she couldn't go outside and play. "I understand you don't think Henry is behind any of this, and frankly I'm baffled myself. But I would be remiss in my duties if I left you unattended until we know the whereabouts of Henry. Why don't you just stretch out on the sofa so I can keep an eye on you and know that you're safe? That's what Daniel would want."

Jane wanted to scream. She could feel her face flush from the blood rushing to her head. She wanted to yell at him: *I know you killed my husband, you asshole.* She figured that may tip him off, so instead she made herself a drink, grabbed a blanket out of the closet, and stretched out on the sofa, turning on the TV with the remote. She prayed that there was a God in heaven who would make Don rot in hell for all of this.

32

Marcus woke up and looked at the clock on his nightstand. It was 4:43 a.m. He sat up and listened. He lived alone in his condo, so if there was a noise coming from inside his place, that definitely would not be a good thing. The building his condo was in was once an old factory. A few years back, a developer converted it into a luxury building with loft-style condominiums. He tried to think rationally that maybe the noise was just the building settling.

But he wasn't even sure whether it was a noise that woke him, or if it was just his nerves after what had happened at the nursing home. He'd dreamt about the woman Eleanor he had accidentally euthanized the day before. Maybe that was what woke him up., although he knew he should at least take a look around the condo to make sure.

He quietly eased out of bed grabbing the nine-millimeter automatic he had under the pillow. He walked over to the open bedroom door. He stood in the doorway motionless looking out into the living area to see if he was just being paranoid. His bedroom and bathroom were the only two rooms that had walls. The rest of the floor plan was open. He looked around and didn't see any movement. There were floor-to-ceiling windows along the exterior walls, interrupted by a set of French doors in the center of one of the walls. The doors led out to a patio overlooking downtown DC; that patio was what sold him on the unit.

He looked out at the twinkling city lights. The hair on the back of his neck stood up when he spotted what looked like the shape of a person standing out on his patio. It looked like someone was standing between the ficus plant growing in the corner and the table and chairs that were off to the side. Marcus watched for a minute to see if the person would move. After a couple minutes, he took a few steps toward the patio while keeping his eyes on the figure. He finally realized that the "person" was just a market-style umbrella that was standing closed. His neighbor had given him the umbrella the week before when he had moved out, and Marcus had completely forgotten about it. He let out the breath he had been unconsciously holding.

He moved toward the bathroom and looked in the open door. It was a large, open spa-like bath with no place for someone to hide, and it was empty. He walked quietly to the kitchen. There was an island that someone could possibly hide behind. He went up to it and lunged around it with his gun aimed in front of him. There was no one there. He took in a deep breath and exhaled. He smiled and relaxed a little. It was definitely paranoia getting the best of him. He looked around and determined he wouldn't be able to fall back asleep now with the amount of adrenaline surging through his body. So he decided to stay up.

He flipped the switch on the wall that turned on the low-voltage lighting under the kitchen cabinetry. It cast a soft light over the kitchen. He set his gun down on the counter and made a pot of coffee. While it brewed he went to the bathroom, relieved himself, and then washed his hands. He went back to the kitchen and poured a cup of coffee. He then walked back toward the bathroom with his coffee, looking out the windows as he walked, trying to figure out how he mistook the umbrella for a person. No matter how hard he tried, he couldn't trick his mind into seeing it again.

He went into the bathroom and set his coffee on the countertop. He brushed his teeth and shaved. He leaned up close to the mirror and smiled, checking his teeth to see if he missed anything. He glanced at the reflection behind him, and he noticed the open bathroom door. He tensed up. He didn't think there was enough room behind it for someone to hide, but it wasn't pushed back flush against the wall. He wondered if that's where the person could be who woke him up. He tried to remember when he peeked in earlier if it had been away from the wall like that, or if someone was behind it now. He reached for his gun, and it wasn't there. He glanced around the bathroom then remembered he had left it in the kitchen when he made the coffee. He turned around keeping his eyes focused on the door.

He walked toward the kitchen intentionally using loud footsteps trying not to tip anyone off that he suspected they were there. He went into the kitchen and grabbed his gun. He turned and quietly walked back to the bathroom. He slowly stepped inside the bathroom and stood back. He grabbed the door handle, and while aiming his gun, he swung the door shut, revealing an empty wall behind it. "Jesus, Marcus. Get a hold of yourself," he said to himself dropping his hands down.

He started thinking what a stretch it would be for his handler—or anyone else in the project—to have already figured out he had euthanized the wrong lady. It hadn't even been twenty-four hours. He set the gun down on the countertop and then turned the shower on so the water could warm up. He stepped back out. He pulled the bathroom door back open, peeked his head out, and looked around the condo, once again finding it empty. He closed the door again, locked it, and stepped into the shower. He showered, toweled off, and wrapped the towel around his waist. After putting on his deodorant, he picked up the empty coffee cup and his gun and walked back to the kitchen. He poured another cup of coffee and then opened a door leading out to the patio to see what the weather was like.

A warm breeze blew in from outside. A front had come through making it an unseasonably warm morning. He decided it was nice enough to go out and enjoy his coffee. He figured it was early and he didn't have to be anywhere anytime soon. He walked out, leaving the door open to air out the condo, and sat on a patio chair sinking down into the deep cushion. He set his coffee cup and gun down on the table beside him. He put his feet up on an ottoman and took a drink of coffee. He relaxed back in the chair, steadying the coffee cup on his lap, and looked out at the sleeping city. This always made him feel better. He loved to come out on the patio when it was dark and watch the city. The darkness gave him privacy, and the lights of the city put him in a kind of trance. It was like the relaxation you would get staring into a campfire.

He tilted his head back and looked up at the few stars that competed against the lights of the city. He closed his eyes and tried to think.

He needed a plan. He thought about the mistake he had made the day before. That fucking old lady questioning him. Then the flasher old fart sticking his brave nose in to help the crusty old bitch. He would definitely return to take care of those two on his own time, sooner rather than later. He didn't need them giving anyone a description of him, and he really couldn't see another option.

His mind wandered back to his employer. If they found out about the mix-up, would they just let him continue? Would they fire him and let him walk away? He pondered these questions looking out at the city lights. He took another drink of coffee and then leaned forward putting his cup back on the table. That was when he felt the cold steel barrel of a gun press against the base of his skull. He froze.

"Who sent you?" Marcus asked calmly. When he didn't feel a sharp pain in the back of his head after asking the question, he felt a little better. "Was it Brooks?" he asked, referring to his handler.

"What does it matter?" the assassin responded.

This is good. He's engaging in dialogue. There was a chance he could make it out of this alive. *Keep him talking*, he thought. "Come on. Give me that much, for Christ's sake. Who sent you?" he asked again.

The assassin was silent.

"OK, so you're not going to tell me. That's all right," Marcus said. "Well listen, we both know how these things work. Can I ask you one little favor? I just don't want to go out, umm, not wearing anything."

The guy with the gun started to laugh. "Why not? That's how you came into this world. Why not go out the same way?"

"Come on, man. As a professional courtesy toward each other? I've got a mother who's still alive. What you're about to do is going to break her heart, and I understand it's just a job to us, but to have them find me naked, it's just—" Marcus went silent for a moment. "It's just embarrassing," he finished.

"You're not completely naked; you've got your towel," the assassin said, continuing to laugh.

"Come on, please?" Marcus asked.

"Who the hell goes out on their patio at five a.m. and has their coffee with no clothes on?" he asked.

"I know, I don't know. Come on, man," Marcus pleaded.

"OK, get the fuck up, and let's go get you dressed for your mommy then, asshole," he said. "Hurry up—like I want to be here this early in the morning. Let's get this over with so I can go home and get back to sleep," he said.

Marcus realized he had a better-than-good chance of remaining alive at this point. He walked back into his condo and headed toward the bedroom.

"Let me just throw on some boxers," he said, turning around to get a look at his would-be assassin.

"Just turn around and keep moving," the assassin said from behind him.

They went into the bedroom, and Marcus went toward the walk-in closet. He stopped and started shaking his head. "That's where you were the whole time, wasn't it?" he asked, pointing toward his closet.

"That's right, Einstein," he replied. "No wonder you're getting iced. Who doesn't look in the closet?"

"That's a good question," Marcus replied. He couldn't believe he never looked in the closet. It had never occurred to him that someone could have snuck past him undetected while he slept and snuck into the closet. How could he have been so dumb? It almost made him ask the assassin guy to just shoot him right there for being so stupid. But he wasn't that stupid. Marcus flipped the switch for the closet light and went in to grab his clothes. "Why didn't you just shoot me while I slept?"

"Not my style. I'm not going to shoot a sleeping guy in the back. I thought there was a good chance that you had a gun under your pillow or nearby, so I went into the closet and pounded on the wall. Only you, the professional that you are, missed looking in the closet. Then you locked the bathroom door, and I actually fell asleep waiting for you. Now hurry up, and don't try anything, or I swear I'll desecrate your body so badly your mother won't even claim you," he said.

"I know, I know," Marcus said, reaching for a pair of boxers that were folded in a stack on the shelf. He grabbed a pair and then bent down to step into them. With his body blocking the assassin's view, he darted his hand in under a pile of sweatshirts on the shelf next to him and pulled out one of the several guns he had hidden about the place. He glanced back at his assassin, "What are you doing? Trying to sneak a peek?" he asked.

Instinctively the assassin turned away. Right then, in one fluid motion, Marcus brought the gun around and shot the would-be assassin in the hand that was holding the gun. The assassin dropped the gun from his bleeding hand and cried out. He quickly reached around his back with his other hand. Marcus assumed he was trying to go for another gun, so he shot him in that arm. Marcus shook his head looking at the assassin.

"Who doesn't keep his gun trained on the subject?" he asked him shouting. "Especially when the subject is poking around in his own shit."

The assassin looked at Marcus with fear in his eyes. "I wasn't treating you like I would a regular mark. I was giving you a professional courtesy. I wasn't going to take you out," the assassin said, shaking his head. "I promise. I was just going to scare you and let you get out of town. Come on—it's a brotherhood that we share. Look, I was letting you get dressed. Please don't kill me," he said, begging Marcus.

Marcus was disgusted by not only the ineptitude of this guy, but also by the fact that he was showing fear. "So you really weren't going to desecrate my body? You didn't really want to get this shit over with and go back to bed?" Marcus shouted at him. "Rule number one: you don't fucking talk with your subject. Rule number two: you don't fucking let the subject lead you around. Idiot!" he said with disgust. "This is who they send to take me out?" he asked, throwing one hand up in the air and shaking his head, while keeping the gun trained on him with the other. "Now I'm going to ask you again: Who sent you to do this? And don't fuck with me. This may determine whether you walk out of here alive," he said.

"It came from the top," he said in staggered breaths.

"Be more specific," Marcus demanded.

"Jesus Christ, this hurts," the assassin said, whimpering. "It really, really hurts."

He was holding his bleeding hand with his good hand, looking down at the wound in his arm that was seeping out blood. Tears rolled down his cheeks.

"How the hell did you get this job?" Marcus asked him. He tried to relax. "OK, one last time. Who sent you to take me out?" he asked calmly.

"It was Mustin. General Mustin," he said, sounding resigned.

"General Mustin sent you? General David Mustin? Really?"

"Yes, really. Why would I lie to you?" he asked, wiping his nose with his good hand.

Marcus thought about it and realized he was right. *Why would he lie about it?* he thought, tilting his head to the side while he looked at him. He raised his gun and shot the 'would be' assassin in the head. "Rule number three," he said to the lifeless body. "Don't trust anyone who says you may walk out alive. Key word there being *may*," he said, standing up.

He walked past the body and went back out into the kitchen. He poured another cup of coffee and went back out onto the patio. He sat in the same chair he had been sitting in ten minutes earlier and tried to relax and think about what to do next.

Five minutes later it came to him. He would deposit the idiot assassin on General David Mustin's doorstep. He laughed out loud when he thought of it. Apparently he was fired anyway, so what was there to lose? He drank the last of the coffee and went back inside. He went in the kitchen and poured yet another cup of coffee. He went to the bathroom and relieved himself of some of the coffee he had processed. Then he went to his bedroom and back into the closet, stepping over the assassin. He pulled off his towel and tossed it on top of the assassin, covering his face. He knew it was silly, but he honestly didn't want his dead eyes looking at him while he got dressed. He found it creepy. He slipped on the boxers he had used earlier to stay alive and then put on a dark jogging suit, which seemed to be all he ever wore, he thought.

He went out and got his Dyson vacuum, a roll of duct tape, and a trash bag from the utility closet. Then he went back to his room and vacuumed the area rug at the foot of his bed. He wasn't just being his usual anal-retentive self; he didn't want any DNA evidence left on the carpet to transfer to the body. He spent a good ten minutes going over the rug just to make sure it was clean.

He went back into the closet and shook open the trash bag. He leaned the assassin forward, crossed his arms over his chest, and put the trash bag over his upper body. He then wrapped duct tape around the bottom of the bag that was around his waist in an attempt to stop the transfer of blood onto his carpet. He bent down, picked him up under the arms, dragged him out into the bedroom, and placed him on top of the rug. He rolled him up in the carpet, exposing the restored hardwoods and wincing at the thought of how cliché this all was, rolling a body up in a carpet. He didn't care. If he had the time, he would have cut up the body and removed it in a safer manner. *Sometimes you just had to roll with it*, he thought.

He wound the tape around the carpet at both ends and in the middle, and then looked at the clock. He figured he had enough time before sunrise to pull this off. He typed a message to the general on his computer, printed it out, and then folded it and put it into his pocket. He grabbed his keys and wallet and put them in his pockets, and then bent down and hoisted the assassin burrito up on his shoulder. He almost lost his balance laughing when he thought of it as the assassin burrito. He stood up using every muscle in his body. It was incredibly heavy, but he knew he could do it. He walked out of the condo balancing the burrito on his shoulder and locked his door.

It was a ten-minute drive from Marcus's condo to the upscale neighborhood General David Mustin called home. Marcus knew the place; he had been there before with his handler on a couple occasions. He pulled up the circular drive, stopped right in front of the front door, and quickly got out and popped the trunk. He dropped the assassin burrito onto the drive. He pulled out his Cutco pocketknife and sliced through the duct tape. He kicked the carpet, sending it unfurling down the drive. He bent down and threw the assassin over his shoulder, and, using all of his strength, hurried over to the front porch. He sat the body up and leaned it against one of the columns supporting the roof over the porch. He used his knife to cut the duct tape on the trash bag and pulled it off. He scrunched up the bag, reached into his pocket, pulled out the note he had printed, and placed it in the hand of the assassin. He stood for a moment appreciating his presentation and then raced back toward the car. He threw the bag in the trunk, rolled up the carpet, tossed the carpet in the trunk, and slammed the trunk shut. He hopped in the car and quickly drove away back toward his condo. No matter how hard he tried, he couldn't wipe the grin off his face.

33

Henry and Jessica both startled awake just after 6:00 a.m. when Jessica's cell phone rang. Henry grabbed it and looked at the screen. "It's Paul," he said. He connected the call. "What's up?"

"Sorry to wake you up. These people are a pain in the ass. I sat here all night, and they wouldn't tell me how Chad was doing."

"Why not?" Henry asked.

"Even though I brought him in, they wouldn't release any information unless I was family. I finally just told them he was my gay lover, and if they didn't let me know how he was doing, I would call the ACLU and then the media to let them know the hospital was discriminating against our people."

"You didn't actually tell them that did you?" Henry asked. "That's wrong on so many levels."

"Of course I did, and it worked. They told me that Chad's out of surgery and he's in recovery. I can see him in a little bit."

"Is he going to be all right?"

"They said it was close. The bullet nicked an artery in his chest, but he made it through the surgery, and the doctor is optimistic."

"Did they figure out that you were with me?"

"No. I told them we were walking down the street by the mall and Chad just dropped. I told them some nice passerby gave us a ride so we wouldn't have to wait for an ambulance."

"Just be on your guard. I don't know what Don is trying to do. Tell Chad I'm sorry again."

"Henry, it's not your fault. Give it a rest. Don is the one who owes all of us an apology."

"I'm working on that," Henry said.

"Where's Jess?" Paul asked.

"She's right here."

"Where's here?"

"I know this sounds paranoid, but I'd rather not say."

"Times like this, I guess it's good to be paranoid. Well, sorry to wake you. I thought you'd want to know he's out of surgery. I'll text you and let you know if anything changes."

"All right. Thanks, man. I appreciate it. Hey, wait a second—do you have Chad's phone?"

"Yes. I've got all of his stuff. He's my significant other, remember?"

"Nice, Paul. Anyway, has Chad's cousin Ben called? The one who works for the *Times*?" Henry asked.

"No, he hasn't gotten any calls. Dude is a sad case with no friends besides us," Paul said laughing.

"You're such an ass. Can you look in his phone book and get Ben's number for me?"

"Sure, hold on a second," Paul said. He scrolled through Chad's address book and found the number. "Do you want me to just text it to you?"

"That would be great," Henry said.

"Anything else? I'm going to go down to the cafeteria for the seven thousandth time to get something to eat."

"Seven thousandth? Really? That many times?" Henry joked with him.

"Piss off. I'll let you know if anything changes on this end."

"All right, take it easy," Henry said. He ended the call and turned to Jessica. "Did you catch that?"

"Chad's OK?"

"Yes. The bullet hit an artery in his chest, but he's out of surgery and in recovery."

"What did Paul do that you couldn't believe?" Jessica asked.

"They wouldn't give him any info because he wasn't family. So Paul finally told them they were gay lovers, and if they didn't give him info, it was because of discrimination and he would alert the media."

"He is such a freak," Jessica said laughing. "Only Paul."

Jessica's phone beeped indicating a text message. "Paul said he would text me Ben's number," Henry said as he retrieved the text. He quickly typed up a text to Ben letting him know that he could be reached at Jessica's number and sent it to him. He didn't mention the fact that Chad was in the hospital. He didn't want to do that over a text, and it was too early to call.

"I'll go make us some coffee," Henry said, getting up out of the bed.

He started a pot of coffee in the kitchen and then walked over and looked out the doors at the Potomac down below. A shiver went through his body thinking of when he jumped into the river the previous day. He turned away and then went to the bathroom. He grabbed one of the robes his mother had hanging for guests on the back of the bathroom door. He walked back into the room and went over to the window overlooking the front lawn and driveway. "They must be here. There's a limo in the driveway," he said, turning toward Jessica.

"Do you think Don spent the night here?" Jessica asked.

"I would imagine he didn't want to leave my mother alone. He probably slept on a chair outside her room, the freak," Henry replied.

"Do you think it's OK to take a shower?" she asked.

"Let me sneak down there first and see if I hear anyone. Maybe I can get to my mother, and we can get the hell out of here and away from Don. There's a bridge that crosses the foyer and the great room on the second floor, and I can see the hallway and the door to her room from up there. I can check to see if there's anyone outside it. Plus I can get to my room and get some clothes, including some underwear, so you can relax."

"That's a step in the right direction, but I would recommend putting some clothes on for your adventure."

"Good idea," he said sarcastically. He threw his loaner clothes back on. "Listen, if I'm not back in twenty minutes, you should get out of here. Here are the keys to my car. Otherwise when I come back up, I'll knock and then I'll say it's me. Put this chair back up in case they catch me and figure out you're up here. If they do try to come through the door, climb down the lattice off the deck and run. I love you, Jess."

"This all sounds so *Mission: Impossible*. This is crazy," she said. "I love you too, Henry." They kissed and he headed down the stairs.

He got to the bottom of the stairs and listened. The house was silent. He quietly walked down the back hallway and peeked around the corner into the kitchen. It was empty. He went up the back staircase to the second floor. The hallway was empty. He walked down, went into his bedroom, and gathered some clothes and another pair of shoes and threw them into a small bag. He crept back into the hallway and headed down toward the bridge overlooking the great room. He got to the bridge and peeked down. He saw Don laid out on one of the leather sofas facing the television and his mother sleeping on another one. Jack was sitting in a chair with his back to Henry looking out back toward the Potomac. Henry couldn't tell if he was sleeping. He turned and quietly retreated back to the apartment over the garage.

He knocked on the door at the top of the stairs. "It's me, Henry," he said. He heard Jessica pull the chair back from the door.

"What happened?"

"Don's sleeping on one couch in the great room and my mother is sleeping on another nearby. Jack is in a chair facing the backyard. I couldn't tell if he was sleeping."

"They made your mother sleep on the couch?" Jessica asked.

"I'm sure Don doesn't want her out of his sight," Henry replied. "You want to hop in the shower?"

"Sure."

"You don't have to wash your hair, do you? It's just that I have a plan, and we need to get moving."

"No, I'll be five minutes." She grabbed her coffee and headed toward the bathroom.

"There should be new toothbrushes and toothpaste in the drawer. I know my mother supplies those in all the guest baths."

"Thanks," she said and went into the bathroom.

Henry heard the shower start. He grabbed some coffee and turned on the television. Thankfully in the five minutes that Jessica showered no news about him or his family came on.

"Your turn," Jessica said, coming out of the bathroom wearing the other robe that was on the back of the door.

"Thanks," Henry said. "You're looking pretty hot in that robe Jess."

"You think?" she asked, opening her robe and flashing him. She laughed covering herself back up.

"OK, definitely hotter without the robe," he said.

"Go take your shower so you can tell me your plan."

"Right," Henry said. He went and took his turn in the shower. He showered quickly, and when he came out of the bathroom, Jessica was already dressed. He got dressed and peeked back out the window. He noticed the limo was still in the driveway.

"So what's your idea?" Jessica asked.

"You'll see. Come on, let's go." They left the apartment and headed down the stairs.

34

General David Mustin rolled out of bed at precisely six thirty, just like he had every other morning since he could remember. He went down to his kitchen and poured his morning coffee. His wife, Gabby, was still sleeping upstairs in their bed, which turned out to be a very good thing. The general discovered the package that was left for him when he went out to get the morning paper. At first he thought it was a Halloween dummy that someone had left on his porch. Then on closer inspection he realized it was no dummy. He recognized the face as Steve Lentner, the guy he'd sent to rid the world of Marcus Landon per the request of that asshole Don Kepler.

He reached down and plucked the folded paper from his hands. He unfolded it and read the words printed on the paper: *Next time send a professional, you asshole!* He crumpled the paper up so tightly he drew blood from his fingernails pressing into his palm.

He walked back into his kitchen and picked up the phone. He dialed his second in command, Kevin Mavret.

"Yes sir, General. How can I help you?" Kevin asked politely.

"Get someone the fuck over to my house immediately to pick up the dead body that was left on my front porch. And do it before my wife gets up or my neighbors see it," he said curtly into the phone.

"Dead body?" Kevin asked.

"Yes, goddamn it. There is a dead body sitting on my front porch. I'm assuming from the note I'm holding in my hands that it's a present from Marcus Landon—the guy who was supposed to be disposed of by Steve Lentner, who instead is now sitting dead on my front porch."

"He's sitting, sir? Are you sure he's dead?"

"Of course I'm sure he's dead. There's a goddamn bullet hole in the middle of his forehead. Excuse me for not being more specific. He's propped up against the column on my front porch. I'm sorry I was so lackadaisical with my description. Do you have any other questions?" the general asked sarcastically. He didn't wait for an answer. "Now get your men over here right now to dispose of him, and get me Marcus Landon's head for insulting me in my home like this. My goddamn home he came to," the general said mumbling and slamming down the phone.

Kevin quickly called a couple of his guys and told them to go over to General Mustin's home immediately and pick up the person who did not belong on his front porch. Then he called his most experienced guy, Mike Kroyer, and told him to go to Marcus Landon's place and watch him until Kevin let him know what to do next.

35

On the way back to his condo after dropping off the gift for General Mustin, Marcus called the escort service he had used on occasion. Since his encounter that morning, he thought there was no better way to celebrate being alive than by getting laid. He requested a girl to meet him at his condo that morning. The service told him she should be there in forty-five minutes.

Pulling up to his building, he rolled into his assigned parking spot, threw it in park, and turned off the car. He checked to make sure no one was looking then got out, took the carpet and the trash bag out of the trunk, and brought them back up to his place. The elevator reached his floor, and he walked out and looked around making sure there was no one waiting for him. Slowly sliding the key in, he quietly unlocked his door and walked in. He put the rug and bag down and then checked every square inch of his condo, finding it to be empty. He was certain that this time he was in fact alone. Going back to the entrance, he picked the carpet and bag back up and carried them to his bedroom. He tossed the trash bag into his closet and then rolled the carpet back into place.

He went to the utility room and grabbed a fresh trash bag and some cleaning supplies out of the little tray the cleaning lady used. Stopping by the bathroom, he grabbed some towels and was now ready to clean up the mess from earlier.

He bent over the carpet and sprayed the spots of blood with Oxi-Clean, and like magic they disappeared. He blotted up the wet spots with one of the towels. Then he went into his walk-in closet. He used one of the towels to wipe off the remnants of the assassin that were left on the floor and the wall, and then he threw it in the bag. He used another towel to wipe up the remaining blood, trying to get most of it up before also throwing it into the bag.

It looked relatively clean, so he sprayed the OxiClean over the area onto the wall and the hardwood floor, and it turned the light bloodstains white. Every time he used it, he thought about buying stock in the company. He wiped up the last of the residue, throwing the last towel into the bag, then threw in the trash bag from earlier and tied it shut. He carried it into the kitchen and threw it under the sink for the time being. The building had a trash chute, but he didn't want to take the chance of bloodstained towels being found anywhere near his place. He would dispose of it later.

His intercom by the door buzzed. He walked over and pressed the talk button.

"Hello?" he asked.

"Hi, it's Lauren. I believe we have an appointment," the call girl said.

"Sure, come on up." He buzzed her in, unlocked the door, and then went into the kitchen to wash up. He was drying his hands when he heard her knock on the door.

He opened the door revealing a gorgeous woman wearing a tight black dress that left little to the imagination.

"Come on in," he said with a smile.

"Thanks. Nice place," she said, looking around.

"Thank you." He walked over toward his bar area while she took in the view. He took out two glasses, tossed ice into one of them, and poured eighteen-year-old Glenlivet into it.

"Would you care for a drink?" he asked her.

"It's a little early, don't you think?" she asked, turning from the view and looking at him with a smile.

"Suit yourself," he said, taking a sip of his drink.

"OK, I mean if you're having one, then why not?" she said, holding her hands together down in front of her waist.

"I'm having scotch. What would you like?"

"Scotch is fine."

"Straight or on the rocks?"

"On the rocks, please."

He fixed her drink and handed it to her. "Sorry to get you up so early," Marcus said, lifting his glass to her. "It's just I woke up and I have the urge. You know," he said, smiling and looking down. He didn't know why he felt the need to explain himself to her.

"No problem—that's what I'm here for," she said, tilting her head at him and smiling.

"Let's go out here and enjoy some fresh air," he said, walking out onto the patio.

He pulled a chair out for her and then sat next to her in the same chair he nearly died in hours earlier. They looked out at the city coming to life and sipped their drinks.

"Absolutely beautiful view," she said.

"I know, isn't it?" he said, not expecting a response. They sat looking out and not saying anything. After a little while, Marcus swirled the little amount of scotch left in his glass and then tilted it up and finished it.

He reached over and set his glass down. "OK then," he said sitting up and putting his hands on his knees. He looked over at her and smiled. "Do you mind blowing me?" he asked, pointing toward his lap, even though he knew she would do it whether she minded it or not.

"If that's what you'd like," she said, getting up and coming over to him.

Marcus reached over and grabbed the cushion off the ottoman to the side of him and tossed it down in front of his feet.

"Thanks," she said, sounding grateful as she knelt down on it.

"No problem," Marcus said, sliding his pants down.

She bent over his lap and started while Marcus leaned back. He closed his eyes and relaxed.

After he couldn't take it anymore and was about to finish, he pushed her head back. "Do you mind if we finish this inside?" he asked her, tilting his head toward the condo.

"No problem."

She backed away and Marcus stood, pulling up his pants. He took her hand and helped her up, then walked back into the condo. He led her into the bedroom, stopping to grab a condom from his drawer. It wasn't that she wouldn't let him do it without a condom—she would, of course, for an extra $500—and it wasn't the money. Marcus didn't know if this girl had anything he didn't want to catch; also he didn't want to take a chance on getting her pregnant. He knew he was a good-looking guy with money, and he also knew that she liked his place. That could be tempting for a girl who did this kind of thing for a living, and a paternity suit wasn't what he had in mind for the future.

He pulled the comforter off the bed and turned to her.

"Do you mind the closet?" he asked. "I know it's a little weird since there's a perfectly good bed here, but...." He couldn't come up with the right thing to say, and once again he was confused as to why he was explaining himself to her. He thought maybe it was because while he'd had good-looking call girls in the past, this one seemed especially fucking hot to him.

"It sounds like fun," she said, slipping her dress down revealing her bare breasts. She pushed it down past her hips letting the dress fall to the ground. "Wherever you'd like," she said, pulling off her black thong.

Marcus almost finished right there when he caught the full sight of her. He quickly got undressed, went into the closet, and spread the comforter out. She came in and lay down.

He put the condom on and then pressed inside her. They rocked in unison until they both groaned with relief. He figured she was probably faking it since she was a professional, but she did a damn good job of faking it. She kissed his neck and rubbed his back with her hands. Right at the moment Marcus finished, he thought of the assassin who left this earth just a while ago in this very spot, and he thought it was ironic how alive he felt just then.

"That was great," she said.

"It was, wasn't it?" he said. "Thank you." He pushed back and stood up. "Would you like to wash up or anything?" He helped her up with his hand. "You can take a shower if you'd like."

"No thanks," she said, following him out of the closet. She stopped and pulled her thong back on and then pulled her dress back up.

Marcus stepped into the bathroom and flushed his condom. He grabbed a towel and wrapped it around his waist. "Let me just grab you a little something," Marcus said, returning to his bedroom to get her a tip. The escort service charged the fee to his Black Rock corporate credit card, but he liked to give them a little cash on the side. If he got her again, he knew she would return the favor. He took the cash out of his wallet and went back out to her.

"Thanks again," he said, slipping her the cash and giving her a quick hug.

"Thank you. I hope I see you again," she said, returning the hug.

He let her out and then closed the door behind her, locking it.

He went back to the bar and fixed another drink. He took a sip and then went into his bathroom. Dropping his towel, he stepped into the shower, turned it on, and then sat on the bench against the wall waiting for the water to warm up. He sipped his drink. Once the water warmed up, he put his drink on the shelf next to the shampoo and washed himself for the second time that morning.

When he finished he toweled off and then went into his bedroom and got dressed. Then he went to the kitchen to fix breakfast. He turned on the TV, and *The Today Show* was on. Savannah Guthrie was talking with the author Dean Koontz about his latest book. Marcus watched it while his eggs fried in the bacon grease. He was buttering his toast when he heard Savannah conclude her interview.

"And thanks again to Mr. Koontz for talking with us this morning, although I do have to admit that I was a little upset to see you here—" she said.

Koontz looked at her a little offended. "OK," he said.

"You didn't let me finish," she said jokingly, slapping his leg with her notes. "Upset to see you here *alone*, I was trying to say. I was hoping you would have brought that beautiful golden retriever with you. The one that's in the pictures with you on the back covers of your books."

"Oh, you had me going there for a minute," he said with a laugh. "I promise I'll bring my dog next time."

"I'll hold you to that," she said laughing. "Now let's go out to Matt on assignment in Washington, DC, covering the latest arrivals at the zoo there, and see what's coming up next," she said, looking into the camera.

The camera panned to Matt standing outside the panda bear exhibit. "Thanks, Savannah. Coming up we'll take a look at the tiny new addition to the zoo here, but up next we'll take a look at what's happening right here in Washington, DC, regarding the deaths of the late senator Pendelton's wife, Eleanor Pendelton, and her two sons, Daniel and William," he said with a grimace. Pictures of Eleanor, Daniel, and William displayed on the screen. "Plus the search for her grandson, Henry Pendelton, who is a person of interest." Music played as a picture of Henry displayed for a few seconds, and then the station switched to a commercial.

Marcus stood over his eggs looking at the television. "That couldn't be the same Eleanor as the one from yesterday?" he asked himself in the empty kitchen. He suddenly lost his appetite, and it dawned on him that maybe this was why he was visited by an assassin this morning.

36

Jane's phone rang, and Don, Jack, and Jane all jumped. Don grabbed the phone and held it out away from him so he could see whose name was on the display. He answered it. "Hello?"

"You kept my mother's phone, you asshole?"

"She's right here, Henry, I answered because I was closer to it."

"My mother's with you?" Henry asked, trying to sound surprised.

"I didn't want her to be alone last night. I was worried about her, so I stayed over. Where are you, Henry?"

"Good one, Don. Meet me in half an hour in front of the Ritz-Carlton in Georgetown."

"Sounds very cloak-and-dagger, Henry. Why don't you just come home to your parents' house? Let's not make this complicated."

"By 'complicated' do you mean it's easier to give my mother and me shots in the neck in private?" Henry asked sarcastically. "It's going to have to be public, Don. So meet me in half an hour, and I'll call you when I see you arrive."

"Henry, don't be so dramatic," Don said into the phone, but Henry had already disconnected.

"What did he say?" Jane asked.

"He wants to meet in front of the Ritz in Georgetown in half an hour."

"Let me just freshen up," Jane said, heading down the hallway toward her bedroom.

Don followed behind her. He didn't know if she would try anything now that she knew where they were supposed to meet Henry.

"Do you mind?" Jane asked.

"I'm just trying to make sure you don't do anything rash, Jane. You've been through a lot. We don't have much time, and I thought I could help hurry you along," he said, making it up as he went.

"Did you want to wipe my ass for me too, Don?" Jane asked. She walked into the master bath and closed the door. Don quickly headed to the bathroom off the great room and relieved himself.

He came out of the bathroom just as Jane walked out of the master bedroom.

Fast enough for you?" she asked, walking past him and heading toward the main entrance.

Jack had already finished using the bathroom off the foyer and waited for the two of them to come along. Jane turned the corner and walked toward him with Don following close behind. Jack opened the front door for both of them. They walked down the sidewalk to the driveway where the limousine was waiting for them.

Jack walked over to the front passenger door and rapped on the window, clearly waking up the sleeping driver. "Unlock it," he yelled to the driver through the window.

"Sorry," the driver mumbled and then hit the button that unlocked the doors.

Jack opened the back door of the limo. They all piled in and sat in the same spots as the day before. Don picked up the phone and waited for the driver to pick up the extension.

"Yes?" the driver asked.

"We need to go to the Ritz-Carlton in Georgetown please."

"Yes, sir," the driver said and hung up.

They reached the Ritz rather quickly, and as they pulled in, Don picked up the phone to the driver again.

"Yes?"

"We're going to wait here for a minute. I'll let you know if we need anything."

"Thank you, sir," the driver responded and hung up.

After a couple minutes, Jane's phone rang.

"Yes?" Don answered.

"I'm assuming you have your goon, Jack, with you," Henry said.

"Yes. Do you want me to have him wait in the car?" Don replied.

"No, have Jack get out of the car and come into the lobby—alone."

"What? Why?" Don asked.

"Just do it," Henry replied.

Don tilted the phone away from his mouth. "Jack, get out and go into the lobby."

"Are you sure?" Jack asked.

"Yes," Don replied.

Jack got up, opened the door, and got out.

"Tell Jack to hold on," Henry instructed.

"Jack, hold on," Don said.

"Now hand him your cell phone—not my mother's that you've hijacked, but your phone," Henry said.

Don reached into his pocket and pulled out his phone. He handed it to Jack.

"Thank you," Henry said. "Now have Jack come in to the lobby."

Don was wondering what this little asshole was up to. "Head into the lobby, Jack," Don said. He was wondering why Henry wanted his phone. Maybe he wanted a list of his contacts or something.

"You can close the car door now and leave Jack here. Head over to Arlington Cemetery, and call me when you get inside the main entrance."

"Henry, come on, this is getting ridiculous. You're starting to test my patience," Don said into the phone.

Henry could tell he was really starting to piss Don off.

"I'll call you when I see you come through the main gate," he said, disconnecting the call.

Don threw the phone down into his lap and pulled the car door shut.

"What did he say?" Jane asked.

"He thinks he's James Bond," Don replied. He picked up the phone to talk to the driver.

"Yes?"

"Take us to Arlington Cemetery, and stop just inside the main gate. I'll let you know once we're there what to do next."

"Yes, sir," the driver replied.

They arrived at Arlington about twenty minutes later. Jane's phone rang.

"Yes, Henry," Don said into the phone.

"Drive up to the Kennedy plot, and I'll call you when I see you're there," Henry said, then disconnected the call.

Don picked up the phone to the driver.

"Yes?"

"Drive up to the Kennedy plot. I'll let you know where we are headed next once we get up there."

"Yes, sir."

The limousine pulled up into the cemetery, weaving around the curvy roads heading toward the Kennedy plot.

The driver pulled up to the area, stopped the car, and awaited instructions from Don.

Jane's phone rang.

"Where this time?" Don asked into the phone.

"Aren't you cute?" Henry said. "Get out of the car and head toward the eternal flame by JFK's grave, and bring my mother with you," Henry said, disconnecting the call.

"Come on, Jane," Don said, opening the car door and getting out. Jane got out. "He wants to meet by the eternal flame."

They started toward the Kennedy family plot.

"That's far enough, Don," Henry said, pressing the gun against Don's back. He was using the gun that Jessica found in the glove box of the car they had borrowed the day before.

"You're making a big mistake, Henry," Don said, turning around to face him.

"Go with Jessica, Mom," Henry said to his mother.

"Henry!" his mother said, coming up and hugging him. She kissed the side of his head repeatedly. "I was so worried about you."

"Mom, please just go with Jessica back to the car," Henry said, shaking his mother loose while keeping the gun trained on Don.

"Where's the driver?" Don asked.

"He's a little bigger than me as you can tell," Henry said, shrugging in the driver's clothes. "But I do kind of like the hat," he said, tipping the driver's hat on his head toward Don. "He's back at my parents' house—unless he got the duct tape off already. I caught him sleeping this morning behind the wheel. I do have to say that the whole driver-phone-intercom thing was a bonus. I wasn't expecting that. I was expecting a roll-down divider, and I thought I was going to have to keep my hat pulled low and just try to avoid detection. But that worked out well, huh? Plus Jessica didn't have to spend the entire time hiding down below the dash. Well, enough about me and how we got here. Let's keep walking, Don," Henry said, motioning with the gun for him to continue.

"You were calling me from the front seat the whole time? Unbelievable. Why did you have me give my phone to Jack?"

"So you wouldn't have your contact numbers to call your people and have them meet us here."

"Henry, you don't understand what you're getting yourself into."

"What I'm getting myself into?" Henry asked incredulously. "Just move," Henry said, motioning with the gun. "You murdered my father and my uncle, and you're trying to pin it on me, *Uncle* Don. You're right—I don't know what I'm getting myself into," he said, shaking his head.

"It was your father's fault, Henry. He was trying to be a hero. I begged him to try to be rational," Don said matter-of-factly.

"He was trying to stop your program to kill the elderly so the government could try and save money? What a monster, huh, Don. Thanks for trying to stop his madness—his trying to be a 'hero' as you put it," Henry said sarcastically.

Don stopped and turned toward Henry. "The Health-Care Initiative was your father's idea, sonny boy—right after your grandfather suffered through those final last months. His plan was to euthanize the elderly who were suffering. Like a Kevorkian thing only on a bigger scale with the government doing the euthanizing. Of course he knew no one would sign on to a plan like that. The government doesn't care about old people suffering. Then he saw how much money your grandmother blew through in the final months for your grandfather's care. So he came up with the idea that he could sell the project by showing that the government would ultimately save money in Medicaid and Medicare costs, as well as end suffering. To him it was a win-win situation. And we're talking about saving a lot of money here, Henry."

"It's always about the almighty dollar with you people," Henry said.

"You know your father. He was passionate about the idea. He sold it and they bought it. Fortunately for your father, one of this administration's biggest projects is reducing the deficit, and by doing so, it needs to cut health-care costs. The only problem was that once the project got running, it wasn't turning the profit it was supposed to. So in order to make it truly profitable, the project had to become automated instead of operating on a case-by-case basis. That was when the project took on a life of its own. Unfortunately once anything becomes automated, there's always the risk that mistakes can happen—collateral damage, if you will."

"Collateral damage—like my grandmother," Henry said.

"Yes, Henry, like your grandmother," Don agreed. "Listen, Henry, I'm not the bad guy here. This project goes all the way to the top. Your father was understandably upset, but you can't just stop it. Even if I wanted to stop it, I couldn't. It's no longer stoppable; it's saving too much money."

"So you killed him."

"Henry, your father knew he couldn't just try to stop this thing without consequences. It got physical, and I tried to stop him from doing something stupid."

"And my uncle?"

"He knew too much. You told him about the drive and the injection I had to give your father. Now come on. Just give me the drive and we can go back to normal. I can make it so the police understand that you're not a suspect. All you have to do is keep your mouth shut about the project, and your mother will be safe, Henry."

"I'm to believe it's that easy, Don?" Henry asked.

"It is that easy. I'm trying to tell you. Just keep your mouth shut, and we can all go back to our lives."

"You promise that if I don't say anything, you'll leave me and my mother alone? That's it?"

"I promise, Henry, that's it."

"OK. Here's the drive. I guess I have no choice but to trust you, Don," Henry said.

"You're making the right choice, Henry," Don said. He couldn't believe his luck that this kid was such an idiot.

Henry reached into his pocket and pulled out Jessica's phone. He kept the gun aimed at Don. He pressed a button on the phone. "It's a nice feature on this phone. Can yours do it?" Henry asked.

"Do what, Henry? Where's the drive?" Don asked, looking confused and pissed off.

"Can your phone record conversations like this one?" Henry asked, waving the phone up at Don with a devious grin on his face.

"Henry, you're worse than your father. I don't care what you just recorded. You really think the people above me are going to let this be exposed?"

"Keep walking, Don," Henry said, motioning with the gun.

Don turned and started walking.

"Go around this hedge here," Henry said. Don walked around the hedge and out of view of Jessica and Jane. Henry pushed the gun into Don's back. "Wait, Don, stop here and don't move." He held the gun to Don's back and patted him down with his free hand. He felt a gun in a small holster under Don's arm. He took it. Then he patted Don's back pants pocket and felt his wallet. Leaving it, he patted his front pockets. He felt his mother's phone. "I'll take this," he said. Continuing his search, he patted Don's suit coat and then found them. "What are these? Henry asked, reaching in and pulling out three syringes.

"Henry, you don't want to do this," Don said.

Henry put two of the syringes into his coat pocket and put the other one up to his mouth and pulled the cap off with his teeth. "You mean do this?" Henry asked as he jabbed the needle into Don's neck and plunged the syringe. He pushed Don forward and put the cap back on the needle. He placed the now empty syringe into his coat pocket with the other two syringes.

"What the hell have you done?" Don asked, grabbing his neck with his hand.

"That was for my family that you murdered, you asshole. I hope it hurts. I was hoping you had those on you so I wouldn't have to shoot you. Looks like my recently departed loved ones were looking out for me."

"Please get me help, Henry. Call nine-one-one. I can still get you out of all of this. You're not going to be able to do this alone. I can help you, please."

"I can take care of myself, you asshole," Henry replied. "I have your confession right here. The last thing I recorded was me giving you the drive. When the authorities ask, I can tell them that I left you here alive and well with the drive. Jessica and my mother will be my witnesses that when we drove away, you were still alive. They'll just think one of your higher-ups must have caught up with you here and got rid of you in an attempt to cover this whole thing up. Think about it, Don. You were a loose end after all," Henry said, nodding at Don grimly.

"Henry, please!" Don cried.

Henry turned, walked back to the limousine, and got behind the wheel.

Don had gotten up and was walking back toward the limousine. Henry picked up the driver's phone and called back to the passenger area. Jessica picked up the extension.

"What's going on, Henry?" she asked.

He put the car into drive and started to pull away.

"Please take note that Don is clearly alive right now. When the police ask, just be honest. The last we saw Don, he was alive," he said to Jessica. "Please ask my mother to do the same." He could hear Jessica relay the message to his mother. She took the phone from Jessica.

"Henry, are you OK?" his mother asked. "What happened with Don?"

"I'm fine, mom. Don and I came to an agreement. He confessed to the killings of Dad and Uncle Billy."

"All right, and what do you have to do as part of the agreement?" she asked.

"I had to give him a flash drive that he wanted. But now I'm going to drop you off at your house, and then Jessica and I are going to have to get out of town for a few days until the truth comes out."

"Henry, what's going on?"

"Mom, really, the less you know the better. Please just trust me on this. Listen, I'm sorry to do this, but I need to hang up. I have to make a phone call."

"Henry, please. Enough already. Let's just go to the authorities and let them sort this all out."

"Mom, I wish it was that easy. Listen, please. I know what I'm doing, and I need to make a call. I'm sorry," he said, disconnecting the intercom phone.

He played back the recording of him and Don talking at the cemetery on Jessica's phone. When he finished listening, he forwarded the recording to Chad's cousin Ben's phone. Then he called Ben.

"Hello?"

"Ben, this is Henry Pendelton."

"Henry, what the hell happened to Chad? My mother just called and said my aunt called saying Chad was shot."

"Yeah, I'm really sorry about that. We were chased and Chad took a bullet for me. Our other roommate, Paul, called me from the hospital this morning and said they think he's going to be OK. Ben, you have to believe me—I never wanted Chad to get hurt. The only reason he, my girlfriend, and our other roommate were with me was because I was more afraid that Don would do something to them in order to get to me. You have no idea how sorry I am and how much more this makes me want to expose this."

"I understand, Henry."

"The reason I'm calling is because I just sent you a recording of a conversation I had with Don Kepler. He admitted that he killed my father and uncle. Not only should this recording clear me in the murders, but he also talks about the project. I'm pretty sure this should help you expose it. I'm going into hiding until you let me know that you can run the story. So the sooner, the better, OK?"

"I'll do the best I can. I'll call you as soon as I think we can print it."

"Thanks, Ben. Please tell Chad's mom I'm really sorry I got Chad wrapped up in this."

"I will, Henry. Take care."

"You too," Henry said and ended the call.

Henry had considered telling Ben about the two syringes he still had in his possession, but the more he thought about it, the more he realized that if he was caught by the police while carrying them, he could possibly be implicated in the murders of his father and uncle. As he drove back to his parents' house, he rolled down the window, tossed the empty syringe he had used on Don, and sprayed the solution out of the others. He then tossed them into the Potomac as they crossed over it.

37

Marcus got dressed and started packing his belongings. He surmised that it had to be Eleanor Pendelton that he had accidentally taken out yesterday. It made sense. And now with that stunt he pulled with the dead assassin on the front porch, he knew he had to get out of the country as quickly as possible. He almost regretted the time he wasted with the call girl, but he was glad he couldn't change that. He raced around his apartment trying to shove anything he didn't think he could live without into two large suitcases.

He finished scurrying around, closed up his suitcases, and grabbed his shoulder bag that was packed with all of his supplies in case an event like this ever arose. It contained cash, credit cards, fake ID's, passports, disguises, and a combat first-aid kit. He took one last long look at the view of the city, realizing it would probably be the last time he saw it for a very long time. He was sad because he really liked it here. He took a deep breath, looked out the peephole in the door to make sure the hallway was clear, and walked out of his condo with his suitcases. He felt his pockets to make sure he had his keys and wallet. Once that was confirmed, he locked the door and set off toward the elevator.

The whole way down to his car, he was in full-force paranoia mode. After the stunt he pulled on Mustin's porch, it wasn't a matter of *if* they were going to send someone to take him out but when. Once he got to his car, he tossed his luggage into the trunk. He looked through the windows to make sure no one was hiding in the back seat, and then hopped in the car, started it, and threw his shoulder bag on the passenger seat. He quickly backed up and sped out of the parking area.

Mike Kroyer was sitting in his car in Marcus's parking area watching as Marcus threw his luggage into the trunk and then sped off. Mike followed him. He picked up his phone as he sped through the streets trying to keep up with Marcus's Audi.

"He's on the move," Mike said to Kevin, who had assigned him to Marcus.

"Please tell me you're following him," Kevin pleaded.

"Well, sir, you didn't tell me to follow him—you told me to watch him," he said, pausing for a couple seconds. "OK, I'm only messing with you; of course I'm following him."

"Mike, I'm seriously going to fuck you up for that the next time I see you," Kevin said.

"Relax. Now what do you want me to do with him? Mike asked.

"Keep following him, and call and tell me where he ends up going."

"Did I fail to mention the fact that he has two suitcases with him?"

"Yes, you failed to mention that little fact."

"Well?"

"Do not let him get out of the country. Take him out, but try to do it discreetly. Try to give him a heart attack. Do you have syringes on you?"

"Never leave home without them."

"OK, if you can't get close enough for an injection, then shoot him as a last resort. Just realize if you want General Mustin to let you see tomorrow, then do not let him get away."

38

Henry pulled into his parents' driveway and punched in his code. The gates swung open, and he drove up the driveway and parked in front of the house. They all got out. Henry's mother ran to him and squeezed him with a hug.

"Mom, not so tight."

"Oh, Henry. I was so worried about you. I've been sick thinking the police were going to harm you."

"I know, Mom. I was worried about you too with Don.

"He really killed your father?" she asked.

"Yes, Mom. I walked in as he was pulling a needle out of Dad's neck. Dad said to tell you that he loves you."

"I loved him so much," she said, starting to tear up. "I don't know what we're going to do without him, Henry."

"I'd love to stay and tell you everything, but I need to go untie the real driver."

"Where is he?" Jane asked.

"Just around the side of the house. He's all right. I just used a little duct tape. I promised I was just going to borrow the car and then return. I gave him all of my cash so he would know I was serious."

"Oh, Henry."

"Mom, really there was no other way," he said, walking toward the side of the house.

The driver was sitting with his back leaning against the house. Henry had hog-tied him with duct tape to a wrought-iron fence that enclosed a rose garden.

"I told you I'd be back," Henry said to him. He gently pulled the duct tape away from his mouth. "I really am sorry. You can keep the cash."

The driver just looked at him. Henry unwound the tape from his legs first and then from his hands.

"The guy you were driving—Don—was holding my mother hostage. I'm really sorry about all of this. Your car is out front, and the keys are in it," Henry said to him.

The driver looked at him. "What about my clothes?" he asked, looking at Henry. Henry had swapped clothes with him earlier in case he had to get out and open the door for Don. Fortunately it didn't have to come to that.

"Oh, I'm sorry. I forgot. Here, we'll trade back," Henry said, emptying his pockets and taking off his borrowed clothes. "Oh, and here's your phone back," he said, tossing the driver his cell phone back. "I'm really sorry." They both got dressed in their own clothes.

"Where is Mr. Kepler? Am I supposed to go pick him up?" the driver asked.

"I'm not sure if you're supposed to pick him up. Last I saw him he was at Arlington Cemetery. He said he was supposed to meet with someone," Henry said.

The driver shook his head. "I'll keep the cash, and as long as it turns out that Don was, in fact, holding your mother hostage, I won't tell the police what you did to me. But if I find out you're lying to me, I'll have no problem testifying that you abducted me," he said. He hurried away from Henry and went back to his car. Henry saw him stop and talk to his mother, and then he got in and drove away.

Jessica and Jane were standing by the sidewalk leading up to the front entrance.

"What did he say?" Henry asked his mother.

"He asked if Don really held me hostage, and I told him he absolutely did, then he drove away."

"That's great. Jess, we've got to go," he said, taking her arm and heading toward the house.

"Where are we going?" she asked.

"Not in front of my mother," he said. "I don't want her to have to lie to the police."

"Henry, tell me where you're going. I have no problem lying to the police to protect you," Jane said.

"Aw shucks, Mom, that's mighty nice of ya. Maybe we could get adjoinin' rooms in prison," Henry joked.

"They're not going to put me in prison for telling them I don't know where you went."

"Really, just…I'll call when we get where we're going. You need to get out of here. Go over to Sharon's or Lucy's. You can't stay here."

"Henry, I'm not going anywhere. I'm exhausted."

"Mom, please. I don't know who's going to come, but believe me someone will come looking for me. I don't want whoever comes to be able to use you as leverage to get to me—like Don just did."

"I guess I could go stay at Lucy's," Jane said.

"Why don't you take Esther with you? I don't know if they would go after her since neither one of us will be here."

"All right, I will, Henry."

"Please go sooner than later. I love you," he said, hugging her and kissing her cheek.

"I love you too, Henry. Please be careful. Call me as soon as you get wherever you're going."

"Oh, that's right. Here's your phone back," Henry said, reaching into his pocket and pulling her phone out that he had taken back from Don. He handed it to her.

She took it and held it in her hands. They all went inside.

"My car is in the garage. We'll take that," Henry said to Jessica. He headed through the house toward the garage leading Jessica by the hand. "Let me just go upstairs and grab some clothes." He went up the back stairs to his room and packed a small bag. He came back down after a few minutes. "Goodbye, Mom. I love you," he said, hugging her.

"I love you too, Henry. Be careful." She hugged Jessica. "Goodbye, Jess. You two be careful."

"We will. Goodbye, Mrs. Pendelton. Take care," Jessica said.

Henry and Jessica went into the garage and got into his car. He backed out of the garage and drove down the driveway toward the gates.

39

Marcus had a couple of errands to run before he left the country. The first one he was not looking forward to. He actually hated to do it because it went against his core principal of live and let live. Alice Andrews and the old flasher guy Glen were witnesses, and he had to figure out what to do about them. He decided to go visit them. If security to get into Oak Tree Pointe was more than just the stand-alone sign-in book that they had yesterday, then that would confirm that Alice and Glen had most likely told authorities about him. He would have to break his own rules and take them out. There was a little flicker deep inside him that had a problem with it, but the military did a good job of beating down his personal beliefs. So in his twisted logic, he thought that was fair enough—technically it was they who were deciding their own fate.

He pulled into the lot and parked. There were no police cars or anything suspicious by the front entrance. *Score one for Alice and Glen*, Marcus thought. He reached into the shoulder bag and pulled out his disguise. It consisted of a baseball hat, a gray wig, and a pair of big, tinted nonprescription glasses. He put his fake identification for this particular disguise into his wallet in case they were now requiring it to gain entry, which would not be good for Alice or Glen.

He looked in the mirror and approved of his disguise. He got out and headed to the front entrance. When he walked through the front door, he saw a guard sitting behind a desk who hadn't been there the day before. It brought a wave of sadness over him. Obviously Alice or Glen had talked about him, and now he was going to have to take two more innocent lives. He realized she and Glen had most likely given descriptions of him to the authorities, but those could be disputed by any good attorney. But he couldn't afford to have eyewitnesses stand there and point him out to a jury—which he was afraid might happen if he was stopped before he could get out of the country or if he was dragged back. Had he known yesterday that the woman in the bed was Eleanor Pendelton, he would have taken the three of them out, and he would already be lying on a beach in the Caribbean drinking a Corona.

As he walked over to the guard, it occurred to him that he was only going to take one innocent life since Alice was supposed to have been euthanized the day before. That thought made him feel better as he approached the desk. The security guard looked Marcus up and down.

"Can I help you?" the guard asked. He had a grim look on his face, as if the fate of national security rested on his shoulders.

Marcus wanted to punch him in the face, but instead he answered him in his best old-man voice. "My cousin Alice Andrews. I'm here to see her. She has had a terrible time since yesterday," he said, shaking his head and looking down toward the sign-in sheet.

"Sign in. And I need to see some identification," the serious guard said.

"Identification?" Marcus asked, signing the sheet.

"Driver's license, nondriver ID, passport—something to identify you," he said as if explaining it to a five-year-old.

"Oh sure, it's right here," Marcus said, reaching for his wallet. He pulled the fake ID from his wallet and handed it to the guard.

The guard gave it a cursory glance, then looked up at Marcus and handed it back. "Do you know where you're going?" the guard asked.

Marcus thought of bitch-slapping him and having him beg for his life, but instead he replied, "Oh yes, thanks." He walked through the door and into the maze of hallways.

Marcus made his way to Alice's room and found the door closed. He lightly knocked and opened it. Alice lay in bed softly snoring. He walked over and nudged her a couple times until she woke up. She looked at him, and her eyes grew wide as she realized there was a stranger in her room.

"Yes? May I help you?" she asked, trying to push herself up.

"I'm sorry to bother you, but do you know what room Glen is in?" Marcus asked in his old man voice. "The gentleman at the desk told me, but I forgot. I thought he said this room, but apparently it's not."

"Glen Black?" Alice asked, surprised that she finally remembered the old flasher's name.

"Is there more than one Glen?" Marcus asked with a grin that settled Alice's fear.

"Oh no, just the one. Let me think," she said. She eased her legs over the side of the bed and sat up, bringing her finger up to her mouth as she thought. "He's in room three twenty-four. The end of the hall and turn right," she said with a smile, pointing with her finger in the direction he should go.

"Thank you for being so kind," Marcus said, leaning down and giving her a hug.

Alice was uncomfortable with the forwardness of this stranger, but she didn't want to be rude, so she lightly patted him on the back.

As he hugged her, he intentionally stepped on her toe and pressed down with all his weight, while at the same time plunging the needle into her hip through her clothing.

"Ouch, you're hurting me," Alice cried out pushing him away.

"I'm so sorry," he said, pulling back from her. "Did I step on your foot?" he asked, pointing down at it. He was trying to redirect her attention to the pain in her toe and away from the injection site in her hip.

"Oh my gosh, that hurts," Alice said, looking at her foot. She had put one hand down rubbing at her hip, but focused her attention on the toe that Marcus was pretty sure he had broken. He really did feel bad. He didn't want to cause her any unnecessary pain, but he couldn't take any chances on screwing this one up.

"I'm so sorry. Let me take a look," he said. He held her hand and bent down to take a look. "I'm so clumsy. I hope I didn't break your toe," he said, sounding legitimately remorseful.

Alice sat there and looked down evaluating her toe, then she grabbed her hand to her chest. "Oh my gosh, my chest. My chest is killing me," she said, trying to get up.

"Oh no, I didn't hug you too hard, did I?" he asked, gently pushing her back down. "Oh gosh, look what I've done. Stay put—I'll go get help."

Alice lay back on her bed. A wave of déjà vu came over her. She looked hard at the stranger who was standing there. A silly thought crossed her mind just before she lost consciousness—that she recognized the stranger in her room.

Marcus left Alice's room and walked down the hallway following the directions she gave him to Glen's room. As luck would have it, when Marcus turned the corner, Mr. Glen the flasher was just pushing behind his walker into his room. Marcus didn't waste any time knocking; he went right in behind him.

"Glen?" he called out, walking over toward him.

Glen turned and smiled. "Yes?" he asked.

"Come on, Glen. You don't remember me?" Marcus asked.

"Oh yes, how have you been?" Glen asked with a smile, although it was clear he was lying.

"Come on, man, give me a hug; it's been too long," Marcus said, embracing Glen. He pressed the needle into Glen's thigh as he pinched his cheek really hard, trying to distract him from the shot. "Look at you," he said, as he twisted his cheek. How the hell have you been?" he asked.

"Ouch!" Glen said, grabbing his cheek with one hand and his thigh with the other.

"Oh, come on, don't be such a baby," Marcus said, slapping him a couple of times lightly on the cheek he had pinched. "You always were such a baby. So how have you been?" Marcus asked, completely ignoring the pain Glen clearly was in. He reached over and messed with his hair. "Hey, Glen, you don't look so good, maybe you should sit down," he said,

The Mercy Project

directing Glen into a seated position on his bed. "So where were we?" Marcus asked.

"I'm not sure what's happening," Glen said thoroughly confused, holding his face and his thigh with his hands.

"Wait a second—hold that thought. I need to go use the restroom," Marcus said, starting to turn away toward the door. "Bladder isn't what it used to be, huh. Either way I'll go get someone and tell them you're not feeling well. Be right back, Glen. Sit tight." He exited Glen's room, leaving Glen utterly confused and in incredible, increasing pain.

Marcus quickly walked down the hall away from Glen's room and toward the main entrance. He waved at the guard and told him to take care. He didn't want to stand out. He made his way to his car and then proceeded to leave Oak Tree Pointe, much slower this time than he did the day before.

Now he was on to his second errand before leaving the area. He drove in the direction of his self-storage unit. He needed to drop off some of his arsenal of weapons that he didn't want to fly with or leave in his condo. He was afraid that whoever was sent to look for him might plunder his weaponry stash.

40

Henry stopped the car at the end of the driveway and turned to Jessica. "Any ideas where we can go hide out until Ben can break the story? Somewhere where we won't put anyone else in danger and doesn't require a credit card?" he asked.

"What about my parents' place? They're out of town," Jessica said.

"Well, maybe, but I'm pretty sure if they've already tied you to me at the Ritz, it won't be long before they check out your parents' place."

"What about my parents' summerhouse?" Jessica asked. Her parents had a summerhouse on the beach in Delaware. She had mentioned it to him before. "They had the caretaker close it after Labor Day weekend," she said, "so I know it's empty."

"You don't think your parents would mind?" Henry asked.

"They'll never know. It will be perfect. It's secluded, and there are no neighbors, so we don't have to worry about being spotted."

"You're a thinker, Jess. That's why I love you."

"Is that the only reason?" she asked.

"Do you want me to be honest?" he asked jokingly.

Henry pulled out of his parents' driveway and headed toward the interstate.

On the way to the beach house, Henry exited off of the interstate.

"What are you doing?" Jessica asked.

"We need to pick up one of those throwaway phones so I can call my mother and tell her we're here and we're safe," Henry replied.

"But we're not there yet, and why don't you just use my phone?"

"I know I'm acting paranoid, but I don't know who else is looking for us. I can't imagine Don was the only one after us for a project that supposedly goes all the way to the top. I'm afraid if we use your phone at the beach house, maybe they can check to see what tower the signal is coming from and end up finding us. That is assuming that they have your phone number and are monitoring it."

"You're a thinker there, Mr. Pendelton. I guess it's better to be safe than sorry," she said. "Where does one pick up a throwaway phone?"

"I'm hoping at this gas station here," Henry said, pulling into a large gas station just off the exit. "Stay here. I'll go see if they sell them." He turned to Jessica and tilted his head down with embarrassment. "Jess, I hate to ask this, but I gave all my cash to the limo driver I tied up. Can I borrow some money?"

"That's something you don't say every day: 'I gave all my cash to the limo driver I tied up,'" she said laughing. "You could borrow my money if I had any on me. But since I don't and we're here—and we're not staying in this town—why don't we both just take money out of the ATM?" she asked.

"Gorgeous and smart, the lady is. How lucky am I?"

"Very lucky, I would say," Jessica responded.

They got out of the car and headed into the gas station. Henry went first and tried his card in the ATM, and it gave him cash. Jessica tried next, and she also got her cash.

"At least they haven't shut down our cards," she said.

"Not yet at least. Let's see if they sell the phones," he said, walking up toward the registers.

There was an older man with white hair standing behind the counter. He was wearing Buddy Holly glasses and a Hawaiian shirt.

"Hi," Henry said. "Do you sell the phones that you can buy the minutes for? I lost my cell and need a temporary one. I really don't want to drive on the interstate without a phone," he said. He realized he was nervously rambling, so he stopped talking.

"I have them here behind the counter. They tend to grow wings if we have them on that side, if you know what I mean," the man said.

"You mean people steal them?" Henry asked.

"You catch on quick, son. How many minutes are you looking to buy?"

"How do they come? I mean what denominations do you sell them in?"

"Thirty, sixty, or ninety minutes. You can buy as many of the cards as you'd like."

"OK, how about three ninety-minute cards?" Henry asked.

"You plan on being on the road a while, huh?" the guy asked.

"Sure. Could I also have a pack of Marlboro's please?" Henry asked.

"Will that be it?"

"Yes please," Henry said. He paid the man in cash, and he and Jessica went back out to the car. After fumbling around with the phone for a while, he finally figured out how to load the minutes onto it. He called his mother.

"Hello?" his mother said.

"Hey, Mom, we're here."

"Whose phone are you using?" she asked.

"I bought a throwaway phone, so hopefully they won't know to track it. Please tell me you're not still at the house."

"No, Henry. We're just pulling into Lucy's place now. Even though I think it's silly."

"Trust me on this, Mom. This is the best way to do it. Now I told you I'd call when we got here safe, so there you go. We're here and we're safe. Try not to call me on this number from your phone. Maybe you could use Esther's phone if you need to call me."

"OK, Henry. I'll do that. I was going to ask you where you are, but I know—the less I know, the better. Please be careful. I love you."

"I love you too, Mom. Goodbye." He disconnected the call and turned to Jessica. "Did you want to call your parents?" he asked.

"No, they're in Europe, which is a good thing. Otherwise my mother would have already freaked if she saw all of this on the news. I'll wait for them to call me on my cell. Hopefully by the time they call this will all be over."

"I can't wait for this all to be over," Henry sighed. He started the car, and they headed back onto the interstate.

41

Jack looked at the name Tom Laurel that displayed on Don's ringing phone, which he was holding in his hand. He'd been sitting in the lobby of the Ritz-Carlton since Don had ordered him out of the limousine. He'd been waiting to hear from Don to find out what to do next. He looked at the phone and decided he should answer it. "Hello, Don's phone," he said.

"Who is this?" Tom asked.

"This is Jack Mangozano, Director."

"Where the hell is Don, and why are you answering his phone?" Tom shouted into Jack's ear.

Jack figured he should just stick with the truth. "Last I knew he was with Jane Pendelton going to meet with Henry Pendelton."

"Why do you have his phone?"

"Henry told Don to give me his phone."

"You were with Henry?" Tom asked.

"No. He was talking to Don on the phone and told him to give me his phone."

"Henry wanted to talk to you?" Tom asked.

"No. He was…Don was talking to Henry on Jane Pendelton's phone. We came to the Ritz to meet with Henry. He called us when we got here and he told Don to have me go into the lobby. When I got out of the car, apparently he told Don to give me his phone. Why? I don't know. I walked into the lobby. Then when I looked out, the limo drove off with Don and Jane leaving me here in the lobby."

"How long ago was that?"

"About an hour ago."

"And you've just been sitting there for an hour?"

"Yes, sir," Jack said, wishing he had just let the call go to voice mail. Jack could feel the heat in his face. Tom was making him feel like a moron, and that really pissed him off.

"Do you have any idea where they were going?" Tom asked.

"No, sir."

"Can I ask you a question?"

"Of course," Jack replied.

"How long would you have sat there before you decided to do something if I hadn't called?"

"I'm not sure I understand your question, sir," Jack said.

"Unbelievable. Call me at this number if they show up there or if you find anything out. Got that?"

"Yes, sir," Jack said to a dead line since Tom hung up without waiting for Jack's response.

Tom picked up his office line. He called his secretary, Lara Roberts.

"Yes, Director?" She asked.

"Get the DC chief of police on the phone for me please."

"Yes, sir," she replied.

He slammed the phone down and waited. A few moments later, Lara's voice came over the intercom. "Chief Lanpher is on line one."

He picked up his phone and pressed line one. "Hello, Chief," he said.

"I was just about to call you, Director."

"Tell me you found the Pendelton kid."

"Well no, but I did find Donald Kepler."

"What do you mean?"

"One of the officers at Arlington National Cemetery just called me. They found him dead there about ten minutes ago. The officer contacted me because he remembered seeing Kepler's name on the bulletin I issued yesterday regarding the whole fiasco down at The Shops at Georgetown Park."

"How did he die?" Tom asked.

"No clue. The officer said there doesn't appear to be any trauma to him. Maybe it was a heart attack," the chief said.

Tom could feel the blood draining from his face. "Thanks, Chief. Let me know if anything turns up in the investigation or if any witnesses turn up."

"Will do," the chief said, disconnecting the call.

Tom sat staring out his window overlooking the Washington Monument. He was trying to figure out his next step. He swung back around facing his desk. "Goddamn it, Don," he said, slamming his fist down on the desk. He picked up his phone and dialed Don's cell phone, this time expecting Jack to answer.

"Yes?" Jack said, answering the phone.

"I just spoke with the chief of police. Don's dead. They found his body at Arlington Cemetery."

"Have they found the Pendelton kid yet?" Jack asked.

"No, just Don. What information have you guys uncovered since you started searching for him?"

"Well, Don had Jim Tanner—a government electronics investigation guy—looking into cell phone and credit card activity for Henry, his girlfriend Jessica, and his two roommates. Jim called and said there was activity on Jessica's credit card at the Ritz, and that's how we ended up here yesterday."

"Why didn't he just have one of our people here at the CIA investigate the activity?" Tom asked.

Jack paused for a few seconds then realized he didn't have to protect a dead guy. "Don was trying to keep things on the down-low. He thought he could contain it, and no one would know what really happened with Senator Pendelton."

"Looks like he was wrong. All right, can you put me on speaker, look in Don's address book on his phone, and give me Jim Tanner's phone number? There's no sense in me starting the investigation from scratch."

"Sure, hold on," Jack said as he pulled the phone away and looked for the speaker feature. He found it then navigated his way through the address book and found the number. He gave it to Tom.

"Anything else you can think of that may be helpful?" Tom asked.

"Not that I can think of," Jack replied.

"Take a cab, and meet me here at my office," Tom instructed and then hung up.

Tom quickly dialed Jim Tanner.

"This is Jim."

"Jim, this is Tom Laurel, the director of the CIA."

"Yes, Director, how can I help you?"

"Apparently you were doing some investigating for Don Kepler?"

"Yes?"

"Well, I just found out that Don is dead. So I need to know what you have so far."

"Oh my gosh. What happened to Don?"

"That's a good question, they found his body in Arlington National Cemetery a short while ago. There doesn't appear to be any trauma. So now that we've covered that, what have you found about the Pendelton kid and his friends?"

"Well, since I told Don about the Ritz, I haven't really found anything. I didn't know I was supposed to still be looking."

"How long before you can find current activity on them for me?"

"Since I already have all of the phone and credit card account numbers, I can find it out right now, if you have a minute."

"OK, the sooner the better," Tom said as he tapped a pen on his desk. He listened as Jim tapped away on his keyboard.

"All right, looks like Henry hasn't made any phone calls on his cell since yesterday, before Don called me."

"That's odd," Tom said. Then he remembered Don telling him that Henry jumped into the Potomac. "Unless his phone got messed up in the river," he said, talking to himself.

"What about the river?" Jim asked.

"Oh, nothing. What about the girlfriend or the roommates?"

"Let's see," Jim said, tapping away again at the keyboard. "The girlfriend has been using the phone, and she made a few calls this morning. The last one was a couple hours ago to a number with a New York area code."

"What's the girlfriend's name?" Tom asked.

"Jessica Barrington."

"Maybe she's from New York. And the roommates?" Tom asked.

"Give me a second," he said, tapping again. "His roommate Chad Turner last made a call yesterday, also to a number with a New York area code."

"Is it the same number that Ms. Barrington called?"

"Let me go back to that screen," Jim said. "Yes, same number."

"Can you find out whose number it is?"

"If it's not landline, then it will take a little bit."

"OK, work on that. What about the other roommate?"

"Let's see." He started tapping the keyboard again. "OK, I hope this guy Paul Mayer has a good plan with a lot of minutes, because who doesn't he call," Jim tried to joke.

"Did he also call the New York number?" Tom asked.

Jim looked through the call log. "Nope."

"What about credit card activity?"

"Give me a minute," Jim said. "This is interesting. Henry withdrew cash from an ATM about an hour ago."

"Where?" Tom asked.

"A gas station in Georgetown."

"He's still here in DC?" Tom asked.

"Delaware. An ATM in Georgetown, Delaware," Jim corrected. "And it looks like his girlfriend, Jessica, used the same ATM."

Tom could hear Jim tapping away at his keyboard.

"No activity for his roommate Chad, and let's see about the other one. OK, he's had five charges at Georgetown University Hospital cafeteria since last evening."

"That explains the blood in the back of the car; it must have been one of the roommates," Tom said to himself.

"Blood in the car?" Jim asked.

Tom ignored him. "Since Henry's girlfriend seems to be using her cell phone, and she and he just withdrew money together, why don't we call her phone and triangulate the position using cell towers. Then we should be able to narrow down their location."

"We could do that," Jim said.

"All right, let me know as soon as you have a location," Tom said. He disconnected the call.

Lara must have seen the light for the line Tom was using go off, because a few seconds later his office door opened, and she poked her head in. "Is everything all right, Director?" she asked.

Tom tilted his head back and took a deep breath. "Get me General Mustin on the phone," he said.

"Yes, Director. Are you sure everything is all right?" she asked. "Can I get you anything?"

"You can get me General Mustin on the phone, goddamn it," he growled.

The shock on Lara's face made Tom feel awful. He took in a deep breath. "I'm sorry, Lara. It's just one of those days," he said.

"Not a problem, Director," she said. She quickly withdrew her head and closed the door. A minute passed. "General Mustin is on line one," Lara announced over the intercom.

He picked up the phone. "General, we have a problem."

42

Marcus pulled into the self-storage parking lot and drove up to the gate. He entered his code and waited for the gate to slowly roll back. He was pretty sure this had to be the slowest-moving gate on the planet. He no longer wondered why there were several signs saying *Do not follow the car in front of you in; every vehicle must enter its own code* and *All gate activity under video surveillance—each vehicle must enter its own code*. He figured the storage company could have saved a small fortune at the sign company if they just got a faster gate. He drummed his fingers on the steering wheel waiting for the gate to open.

Once the gate finally cleared his front bumper, Marcus drove in and turned down the first aisle heading toward his storage unit. Fortunately for Mike Kroyer, the slow gate allowed him to slip in close behind Marcus, but not close enough for Marcus to spot him tailing him. Mike ducked his head down so his baseball hat would cover his face from the several cameras covering the gate.

Marcus stopped in front of his unit and got out. He opened his trunk and pulled out one of the suitcases. He went over, opened the lock, and rolled up the garage door. There were a few tall fireproof metal cabinets lining one wall, and his Harley was parked off to the side. He had just retired it there the previous week to store it for the winter. Against the back wall, there were several stacked plastic bins. They contained some of his dad's personal things that he hadn't had the heart to go through yet. His sister had asked him to take them when they sold their father's house after his death.

After seeing the bins and thinking of his sister, he had an idea. Instead of trying to take off to get out of the country right away, he thought maybe he should go hide out at his sister's summerhouse. She and her husband had been out of town for the last couple weeks, and they weren't expected back until Thanksgiving. He could lay low for a few days there, and then once everything cooled down, he could drive over and fly out of Philadelphia.

As he walked over to unlock one of the cabinets to put his guns into, he caught a glimpse of a guy sneaking up behind him in the mirror on his Harley. He bent down on one knee pretending he was going to open his suitcase, and instead he quickly swung it around. He hit the guy behind him in the knees, knocking him to the ground. The guy lunged at Marcus, and Marcus saw that he had a needle in his hand and was aiming it toward his leg. Marcus dropped and rolled away, pulled his gun from the holster under his arm, and quickly aimed it toward the guy.

Mike saw that Marcus was reaching for his gun, so he dropped the needle and went to plan B. He too grabbed for the gun in his holster, which was also under his arm. He pulled it out and they both fired at the same time. Marcus's shot went a little high, hitting Mike in the forearm, while Mike's shot hit Marcus right in the hand that was holding the gun. Marcus dropped his gun, quickly reached up with his other hand, and with all of his strength pulled one of the large cabinets down, crashing it down between the two of them.

Neither man cried out in pain from the gunshot wounds. Marcus already had the other gun pulled out from the holster down by his ankle when Mike took another shot at him just over the cabinet. It hit Marcus's side and was much more painful than the shot in the hand. He reached over the cabinet and fired blindly in the direction of his attacker.

This time Mike made a little crying noise when the bullet hit its mark.

"Let me guess—Mustin didn't like the surprise I left for him this morning," Marcus shouted over the cabinet toward Mike.

"You, sir, are correct," Mike answered.

"Listen, I'm sorry about doing that. I didn't realize who I took out yesterday. I would have left the country yesterday had I known."

"Don't have a clue what the fuck you're talking about," Mike answered sincerely.

"OK, sounds believable," Marcus responded. "I'll be honest. I was coming here to drop shit off before I get out of the country."

"That's a problem seeing as how I'm not supposed to let you leave the country," Mike said.

"Mustin doesn't have to worry about me being a loose end. I already scrubbed all of the witnesses before I came here. Next step is for me to just disappear."

"Witnesses? What witnesses? You stopped at an old people's farm before you came here."

Marcus realized this guy must not know the whole story and is just following orders to eliminate him. Marcus tried to lay it out in the simplest possible terms. "OK, maybe they didn't fill you in on why you're here to get rid of me. I made a little mistake yesterday on the job. Then next thing you know, there's a guy in my condo early this morning who tries to kill me. He tells me that Mustin sent him. So I got a little pissed at Mustin for making a big deal out of what I thought was a little mistake yesterday. After I eliminated the guy he had sent, I deposited said guy on Mustin's doorstep. Well, then I find out that the little mistake was a lot bigger than I initially realized. And now I understand leaving the guy at his house was not the right thing to do. I shouldn't have done that to General Mustin. So once I realized my mistake, I stopped at the old people's farm, as you put it, where I made the mistake yesterday, and I made a few corrections. Now there's no one to tie me to the initial mistake. If Mustin were here, he would understand my predicament. Now the way I see it, this can go down a couple of ways. We can either just keep taking pot shots at each other, and we'll both just die here, or we can just call it a day, and we'll both limp off and tend to our wounds."

There was silence.

"Hello? In a little bit of pain here. Losing a little blood. Do you think you want to just call a truce?" Marcus asked. "You can tell Mustin you killed me and dumped me in the Potomac. No one will ever know the difference. Believe me—I'm leaving the country, and I will not be returning anytime soon. If and when I do, I will not look anything like this."

Once again, silence. Marcus hoped beyond hope that the guy was dead. It took everything in him to peek his head up to look over the cabinet to check.

The bullet that grazed Marcus's scalp told him that Mike was very much alive. Marcus reached over and fired a shot in Mike's direction. He could hear Mike take in a deep breath through what sounded like clenched teeth.

"What the fuck? Do you really just want to keep shooting at each other until we're both dead?" Marcus shouted.

It was quiet for a minute before Mike finally answered. "OK, I'll call a truce. But I swear on everything holy that I am going to hunt you down and kill you if you are ever caught and found out to be alive. You need not worry about Mustin from now on; you now need to worry about me," Mike said.

Marcus heard him make his way back out to his car. It sounded like he was dragging his leg. Marcus didn't look to see because he knew if he snuck a peek that Mike would have his gun trained in Marcus's direction.

He waited until he heard Mike's car start and then pull away. Then he got up and finished the task he had started. He righted the cabinet he had pulled over and decided that maybe he should keep his weaponry suitcase with him for a little while. He could hide it in his sister's attic after he stayed there and before he headed up to Philly. After what had just happened, he decided maybe he would need them before he got out of the country. He looked around the unit and then looked out and up and down the aisle to make sure he really was alone. The aisle was empty. He decided the guy must have bought the whole idea of throwing him in the Potomac. He was glad he had thought of it.

He closed up and locked the storage unit and then headed to the car. After putting his suitcase back into the trunk, he got in and looked in the rearview mirror at his blood-covered face. He shook his head at his reflection. He reached for his shoulder bag on the passenger seat and fished around in it until he found a towel and some alcohol wipes. He wiped the blood from his face and then wrapped the towel around his bleeding hand. He then pressed his wrapped hand against the gash on his head to try to stop the bleeding. Head wounds were always big bleeders, and this one was no exception. His side burned, and his hand felt like it was on fire.

He reached into his bag and pulled out a small canister of cauterizing powder from his first-aid kit. He pulled the towel away from his head and looked in the rear view mirror as he pressed one of the alcohol wipes against the gash. After a few seconds, he quickly removed the wipe and sprinkled the powder on the wound. Thankfully the powder contained a numbing agent, but the pain was still excruciating. Then he quickly did the same to his other wounds and bandaged them as he went. When he finished, he grabbed a dark ball cap out of the bag and gingerly fitted it on his head, taking care not to brush against the throbbing gash on his scalp.

He started the car and drove down the aisle. He drove up to the gate to exit the storage complex, cursing the owners for their slow-moving gate, realizing that was how his latest assassin got in. He wanted to sue the bastards for every last cent they had for their lax security. He was on the run, however, and leaving the country. He was incensed at the thought that there was nothing he could do about it. He drove out of the complex and headed toward the interstate, making his way toward his sister's place.

43

After another hour of driving, Jessica directed him to the interstate exit for her parents' summerhouse.

"Is there a store around here so we can get some provisions?" Henry asked her as he approached the bottom of the exit.

"Sure, there's a little market just before my parents'. We're going to go right past it."

They stopped at the market and bought some provisions, again paying with cash so they wouldn't leave an electronic trail. They continued down the road. Jessica pointed for him to turn down a sand-covered lane. He slowly drove down the curvy road.

"I hope no one else comes from the other direction. It's going to be a tight squeeze if they do. This road isn't really wide enough for two cars," he said.

"This isn't a road; it's the driveway," Jessica said.

"Really?" he asked. "You weren't kidding about it being secluded, Jess."

They came to a clearing with a large two-story shingled house.

"This is really nice," Henry said.

"The property has been in the family for generations. That's why there are no neighbors," Jessica replied.

"It definitely looks closed up," Henry said, referring to all of the shuttered windows.

"Park in front of the garage," she said.

Henry pulled the car over to the garage area and parked the car. They both got out.

"I know this is a stupid question, but do you have a key to get in?"

"Oh my God. Why didn't I think of that before?" she asked, looking lost. "Of course I have a key, silly. We usually spend our summers here. I keep it on my key chain."

"Way to give a guy a scare there, Jess," Henry said.

"Oh, I'm sorry, sweetie. I was just giving you a hard time. I'll make it up to you later," she said, giving him a kiss.

She walked over to a small entrance between the main entrance and the garage. She inserted the key and unlocked the door. She twisted the knob and pushed it open. A beeping sound emitted from inside. Henry looked at her wide-eyed.

"It's the alarm," she said.

"I realize that. Please tell me you know the code," Henry said.

"Relax, Henry. Of course I do," she said, walking in and punching the code into the panel. The beeping stopped.

"Sorry, I'm a little strung out here," he said. He looked around. The house was dark since the hurricane shutters were lowered, covering all of the windows. "I was envisioning it a little bit brighter on the inside for a beach house," he joked.

"My parents were going for a Goth look when they decorated," she joked back.

She went into the utility room between the kitchen and garage and turned on the main power switch. She flipped on the light, and then, now that she could see, she opened the main water valve. She walked back into the kitchen and flipped a series of switches on the wall. They were the switches that controlled the hurricane shutters. The shutters along the back of the house slowly opened revealing the waves of the Atlantic crashing on an empty beach. "I'll leave the front and side shutters down in case someone comes down the driveway—they won't know we're here," she said.

"The car might tip them off," Henry said, smiling at her.

"Oh my God, you're right. What should we do about it?" she sarcastically replied.

"I could live here," he said, ignoring her sarcasm and looking around the place.

"I know. Wouldn't it be nice to retire here someday?" she asked. "I'll open up the garage door so you can pull the car in, thus solving the car problem. OK?"

"Sounds like a plan," Henry replied.

Henry pulled the car into the garage, and they both unloaded it, putting away the provisions. When they finished, Jessica went upstairs while Henry opened one of the doors that opened out onto the patio facing the beach. It was a beautiful sunny day. He walked out and looked around at the setting. "Beautiful," he said to the empty beach. He came back inside and went over to the refrigerator.

"Jess, you want a beer?" he called out.

"It's a little early don't you think?" Jessica yelled from upstairs.

"Why? Do you have to go somewhere?" Henry yelled back.

"Good point. OK, I'll take a beer," she said, coming back downstairs and into the kitchen.

"What were you doing upstairs?" Henry asked, handing her the beer.

"I made the bed so we don't have to later."

"You're a thinker. You want to go enjoy these out on the patio?" he asked, referring to the beers.

"Sure."

They went out and untied some lounge chairs and a table that were stacked and tied to prevent them from blowing around in a storm. They set up and sat on the chairs facing the surf. They put their beers down on the small table they had placed between them.

"Do you mind if I smoke, Jess?" Henry asked.

"I'm not your mother, Henry. You can do whatever you want. There are ashtrays over there in the cabinet under the grill."

"I know you don't like it, Jess. It's just...I've been under a little stress, and I could really go for one," he said. He went over and grabbed an ashtray. He came back and sat down in his chair. He packed the cigarettes tapping the pack against the heel of his hand, and then he opened them and shook one out. "Want one?"

"I'm definitely getting a déjà vu feeling here, Henry," Jessica said.

"I know, right?"

"You're such a bad influence. Sure, give it to me," she said, reaching for the cigarette.

He shook one out for himself, lit hers, and then lit his own. They both inhaled and blew out the pungent smoke.

"This is nice, Jess. Great suggestion." They smoked their cigarettes and sipped on their beers as they sat in silence listening to the waves crashing onto the beach.

"It's so nice out; I think I'm going to go throw a bathing suit on," Jessica said, sitting up and crushing her cigarette out in the ashtray.

"Yeah, it is getting hot out here," Henry said, pulling his shirt off.

"You didn't pack any swim trunks did you?" Jessica asked.

"That I did not. I didn't know we were coming to the beach."

"I can look in my brother's room and see if he has a swimsuit that will fit you," she offered.

"Thanks, but no thanks. It's kind of creepy. The whole wearing another guy's swimsuit. It's a little personal. I'll just go in my boxers if I go in the water."

"That's right, the whole uncle's underwear thing," she said, getting up.

"Right," Henry laughed. "Hey, if you're going inside, do you mind grabbing us a couple more beers on the way back out?"

"Sure. I'll be right back," she said, leaning down and kissing him. Then she headed into the house.

Jessica had only been gone a couple minutes when her phone rang. Henry got up, went over to it, and looked at the caller ID. The phone displayed *unknown caller*. "Hello?" he said into the phone. There was silence. "Hello? This is Jessica's phone." He threw that in just in case it was a relative of hers. The line was silent. He waited about ten seconds. "Hello?" There was still no response, so he disconnected the call. He put the phone down and went back and sat in his chair. He had started to doze off when Jessica came back out wearing a small pink bikini. She was carrying a tray with sandwiches and beers.

"You're the best, Jess. Nice bikini—you look hot," Henry said. He took a sandwich and beer that Jessica offered him. "Thanks for the sandwich and the beer," he said, holding each one up as he thanked her. "And for looking so fucking hot."

"Henry, stop. This bikini is too small. I look like a sausage popping out of its casing, but it was the only one I could find."

"Jess, trust me, you don't look anything like a sausage. You look hot. You know, though, if it's uncomfortable, you could always take it off," he said, smiling at her. "Let's just say it's a good thing Paul and Chad aren't here. They would both be sprouting wood," Henry said.

"Henry, eat your sandwich. You guys and your hormones," she said laughing. She put the tray on the little table and sat back in her chair with her sandwich and beer. "This isn't so bad having to wait here for it all to be over, huh?"

"Yeah, I just hope Ben calls soon so we can put an end to all of this running. I would enjoy this much more without everything still hanging over my head. Speaking of calling—you had a call on your phone from an unknown caller when you were in the house. I answered it and there was no one there."

"Huh. Well, if it's important, I guess they'll call back," she said.

They finished their sandwiches and lay back soaking up the rays of the sun.

44

Director Tom Laurel's phone buzzed.

"Jim Tanner is on line one for you, Director," Lara said over the intercom.

"Thank you," Tom said, pressing the intercom button. He pressed line one and picked up the receiver. "Tell me good news, Jim."

"We got a signal from a tower south of Bethany Beach in Delaware."

"Any other cell phone or credit card activity?" Tom asked.

"Nothing. But I did find out who that New York number belongs to."

"And?" Tom asked.

"Well, it belongs to a Benjamin Aquafen. When I Google the name, there's a Benjamin Aquafen who's a reporter for the *New York Times*."

Tom was silent.

"Are you still there, Director?" Jim asked.

"I'm here. Do you have an address for Mr. Aquafen?" Tom asked.

"Yes." He gave Tom an address in New York City.

"Thanks, Jim," Tom said, jotting down the information on a piece of paper. Please keep monitoring Henry and the roommates for me, and let me know if anything pops up."

"Will do," Jim said, ending the call.

Tom pressed the intercom button. "Lara, please get me Justin Pier on the line." Justin was one of his top investigators who had been briefed earlier.

Lara buzzed him back alerting him that Justin was on the line. Tom picked up the phone.

"Mr. Pier."

"Good afternoon, Director. What can I do for you?" Justin asked.

"We just found out Henry Pendelton is possibly in the Bethany Beach, Delaware area. I need you to find out if there are any hotels in the area or if the Pendelton family—or his girlfriend's family, the Barringtons—have homes there," Tom said.

"All right, let me look into it, and I'll call you right back."

Tom ended the call and pressed the intercom button again for Lara to get Jim Sidney, the head of the CIA New York City division, on the line. Lara alerted him once he was on, and Tom picked up the phone.

"Good afternoon, Jim."

"Good afternoon, Director," Jim said.

"We have a problem and I need your help."

"What's up?"

"We believe we have the suspect Henry Pendelton in Delaware, and General Mustin is assembling a special ops team—once we have confirmation of his location."

"Did you say Delaware?" Jim asked.

Tom could tell Jim was questioning why he was bothering him with a problem in Delaware.

"Yes, Delaware. However, there may have been a leak regarding material vital to national security, and it seems that Mr. Pendelton may have shared this information with a reporter who's with the *New York Times*."

"I see."

Tom continued. "It's imperative that this information is shut down. We cannot afford to have this information released to the public." He gave him the address. "His name is Benjamin Aquafen. Send someone there to see if they can find him. I need him brought in to find out what he knows and who he shared it with. If he's not there, then let me know and I'll call the *Times* and speak with the publisher to make sure he shuts it down. But let's start by going to his place. I'd rather keep it quiet from the publisher. I don't want to tip him off to a story unless we have to get them involved."

"I'll send some agents there right now. I'll let you know what they find as soon as they get there."

"Thanks, Jim," Tom said. He disconnected the call and once again tilted his head up and stared at the ceiling. He placed his elbows on his desk and dropped his head down into his hands. "I need a goddamn drink," he said, getting up and going over to the wet bar in the corner of his office. He poured himself a Jack and Coke and then went back to his desk. As soon as he sat, Lara's voice came over the intercom.

"Director, Justin Pier is on line one."

"Thanks, Lara," he said, releasing the intercom button.

He picked up the phone and pressed line one. "What's up, Justin?"

"The Barringtons have a large property on the beach in South Bethany. It's surrounded on both sides by a state park, so it's pretty secluded."

"Good work, Justin. Forward the information to General Mustin, and I'll call him right now," Tom said.

He quickly hung up and alerted Lara to get General Mustin on the line. Lara indicated when he was on, and Tom picked up the phone.

"General."

"Yes, Tom?" the general asked.

"The family of Mr. Pendelton's girlfriend apparently has property on the beach in South Bethany, Delaware, and we believe that is where Henry Pendelton and the girlfriend are now. Agent Pier said it's a secluded property bordered on both sides by a state park."

"OK. Do you have an exact address?"

"Agent Pier should be sending it to you as we speak. To be clear, Henry Pendelton is in possession of a flash drive that contains top secret classified information and is wanted for questioning in at least two deaths. If Mr. Pendelton shows any sign of aggression—such as pointing a weapon at you, for example—then you have permission from the president to obtain that drive by any means necessary. In other words if they resist, and you have to take him and the girlfriend out in order to recover the drive, then I'm interpreting that as fulfilling the president's wishes," Tom said. "Just make sure any weapons they point at you when you arrive to question them are found near their bodies. You copy?"

"That's a copy, Tom. And since you're saying it's secluded, we'll take the Blackhawk. That should cut our time considerably, and we can land on the beach. In and out," he said.

"Whatever works. You're the expert," Tom replied.

45

"You want to go for a swim?" Henry asked.

"Sure," Jessica replied, sitting up in her chair. "Let me grab some towels. You want another beer?"

"Yes, please," he replied. "Do you have any koozies so they stay cold for down by the water?"

"I'll look by the bar."

A couple minutes later, Jessica returned wearing a beach cover-up over her bikini. She had towels and two beers in koozies. He dropped his shorts and threw them back on his lounge chair. He grabbed his beer, cigarettes, and lighter. "You sure there are no neighbors? I'm not going to freak anyone out or offend anyone by swimming in my boxers?"

"No neighbors, and your boxers look just like shorts, so relax. I'll take off my cover-up so you feel more comfortable. Plus the only one you can offend is me, Henry, and the only thing I would find offensive is if you wore one of those little Speedo suits," she said, walking down the path off the patio that led down to the beach.

"Wait a minute—now that you mention it, I just remembered that I did pack my mustard-colored thong Speedo swimsuit. Let me go grab it," he said laughing. He turned pretending he was heading back to the house.

"You're so gross. I'm pretty sure I wouldn't be with you if you wore, or owned for that matter, a mustard-colored thong swimsuit," she said, giggling and making a gagging gesture.

"That's all it would take to get rid of you?" Henry teased.

"You're quickly ruining any chance of getting lucky with me later on, Mr. Pendelton."

"Jess, have I mentioned how attractive and intelligent you are?" he asked, trying to save himself.

"Nice try."

He came up beside her and took her hand while they walked down to the water's edge. They laid the towels down, and Henry tossed the cigarettes and lighter on top of his towel.

"You're starting to worry me with these cigarettes, Henry. You're going to become a regular smoker."

"Jess, relax. When this thing is over, I promise I'll go back to just having one occasionally when we're out drinking."

They put their beers down by the towels and stepped into the water.

"Jesus, that's cold," Henry said.

"Come on, you baby. It's like bathwater," she said, wading into the waves. She went in up to her knees and then turned and splashed some water back at Henry, who had made it in only up to his ankles.

"Cut it out—it's freezing," Henry called to her.

"You're such a girl," Jessica called back.

"I'm a girl, huh?" Henry said, charging toward her in the water.

"No, no, you're right—it's cold," she cried out laughing. "You're not a girl."

"Too late," he said, grabbing her and diving into the water. The cold water took their breath away.

"OK, you're right—it's a little chilly," Jessica said.

"We'll get used to it," Henry said, staying in the water up to his neck. Jessica swam over and kissed him. They wrapped their arms around each other.

"You're warm," Jessica said, resting her head on his shoulder. She could feel his chest heaving in a funny way. She pushed back from him. "Henry, are you OK?"

"Apparently I'm just having another manly-man cry, Jess. I'm such a pussy," he said, with tears rolling down his face. He looked away from her. "I don't know why—I mean, I know why, but I've been pretty good today. Every time I thought of my dad today, I tried to pretend that he and my mom are just doing their regular thing. I guess this time I didn't do such a good job pretending."

"Henry, we're not going to let him die in vain. We're going to expose this, and he would be so proud of you."

"For some reason that doesn't make me feel better. Then the whole bringing Don to Gammy's house and...if I didn't go there, Uncle Billy would still be alive."

"Henry, you didn't kill your uncle—that fuckhead Don did. Give yourself a break," she said, leaning in hugging him and kissing his forehead.

Henry started to laugh.

"What?" Jessica asked.

"Wow, Jess, you called Don a fuckhead. I'm impressed."

"You're a bad influence, Henry. Seriously, though, give yourself a break. You have done nothing wrong. You are a great person, and that is because of your parents. You are a tribute to your father just by being the good guy you are," she said, holding his face and looking him in the eyes.

"You're making the pussy cry again, Jess," Henry said as tears rolled down his cheeks. He hugged her tightly to his body. They stayed that way a little while bobbing with the waves.

"OK, I'm pretty sure that we've unofficially joined some kind of polar bear club just now," he said. "Let's go lie on the towels and warm up."

"Great idea."

They walked out of the water and lay down on the towels. They drank their beers and Henry smoked another cigarette.

"It's like we're the only people left in the world," Henry said, looking around the empty beach.

"I know. It's nice isn't it? We should make it a point to come here once a month," she said.

"Good idea. Maybe we could head to the Caribbean though for some of those months. I'm not sure if what we're wearing would be ideal here in January. Plus the water is a smidge warmer there."

"You have a point," she said.

Henry put out his cigarette. He set the filter aside so he could bring it back up when they leave and throw it in the trash. He thought there was nothing cheesier than leaving your filters in the sand. He took a drink of beer and looked out at the waves.

46

Ben was in a meeting with legal trying to push his story through. He felt like he was in a dream ever since Henry forwarded him the audio of Don Kepler admitting everything about the project.

"If we can get voice confirmation that it is indeed Don Kepler, then I don't have a problem giving the go-ahead," Austin Templer, the senior attorney for the *Times*, said.

"Obviously if you had confirmation, you wouldn't have a problem running the story. Honestly, time is of the essence. I would be willing to bet money the president is going to try and shut this whole thing down sooner rather than later. What more do we need?" Ben begged. "We've listened to the recording a hundred times. We've asked ourselves what Henry Pendelton would have to gain by making it up. What are we waiting for? We either get the story out before we get the call from the president saying it's interfering with national security, or the whole thing is going to be buried. I'm not asking to print the entire file that Henry sent. I understand that the file contains a lot of information that needs to be verified. At this point I just want to release the transcript of the audio recording. I think once that's out, the president can't shut the whole thing down. What's the worst thing that happens? We have to post a correction on page two?" Ben wasn't sure where he was getting the balls to talk like this in front of the publisher. He thought maybe it was because the more he had read on the files of the Health-Care Initiative, the more pissed off he became.

"Ben, I appreciate your vigor," the publisher said. "Although we both know that if the audio does prove to be false, and we run a story that implicates the president's chief of staff in committing murder and orchestrating a conspiracy to euthanize people, it's going to be a lot more than posting a correction on page two."

Ben's phone started to ring. He pulled his phone from his pocket to see who it was. It was his neighbor Ally who lived across from him. They had dated when Ben first moved in and stayed friends after it didn't work out. He made a gesture, shrugging his shoulders to the publisher and the attorneys, pretending he didn't know who it was so he could answer the call.

"This is Ben Aquafen," he said.

"Benny, it's Ally. I'm sorry to bother you, but I didn't know what to do. I just came in from walking Molly, and there were two guys standing outside your door. So I watched them through the peephole after I came inside, and I just saw them pick your lock and go into your apartment," she said.

"Really?" he asked. He tilted the phone away from his mouth and spoke to the publisher and attorneys. "It's my neighbor saying two guys just broke into my place."

"Yes, but the weird part is they aren't your usual criminals," Ally continued. "They were wearing suits. Do you want me to call the police? I just wanted to make sure you didn't have anything lying out that you didn't want the police to see—like Dino."

Dino was a dinosaur bong that Ben had from college, and he knew it was sitting on his coffee table. His college roommate Cary had given it to him, and he would occasionally have a smoke.

"That won't be necessary, Ally. I'm pretty sure I know who they are," he said. "Maybe you should get out of there and take Molly for a walk until they leave. Just to be safe."

The publisher and attorneys were looking at him with quizzical looks on their faces.

"OK. But I'll just go down to the corner, and I'll call you when I see them leave," she said.

'Thanks, Ally. Be careful."

Ben turned to the publisher and attorneys sitting around the conference table. "It seems as though the thieves in my neighborhood are going upscale. My neighbor said the men she saw breaking in were wearing suits."

The publisher looked at Ben. "You think it's government agents?"

"Well, I don't know too many robbers who wear suits. I think it's a little more than coincidence," Ben said. "I think they're trying to shut it down. They tried to reach me first. Once again I'd be willing to bet Lenore is going to come in here and tell you some higher up in the government is calling to talk to you." Lenore was the publisher's secretary. "We both know if they pull the national security card, we're going to have to scrub the whole story," Ben said, praying that the publisher would give the go-ahead.

"I'd bet my left nut that's Don Kepler's voice on that recording," the publisher said. He leaned forward on the coffee table, took a deep breath, and then let it out. "Go ahead, Ben—post the transcript of the audio online."

"Sir, this could get ugly. Are you sure you want to take the chance?" Templer asked.

"Austin, it could only get uglier if it's true and we have to bury it. My gut is telling me to get this out to the public."

"Thank you, sir. I know it doesn't mean anything coming from me, but you're doing the right thing," Ben said. He quickly left the conference room before Austin could change the publisher's mind.

As he ran down the hall toward his editor's office, he pulled out his phone and brought up the number Henry had called him from earlier. He pressed *Send* and called him back. After several rings it went to voice mail. It was a woman's voice, and Ben remembered Henry saying it was his girlfriend's phone. "Hi. This message is for Henry," he said. "It's Ben Aquafen, Chad's cousin. I just got the go-ahead to post the transcript of your conversation with Don. It should be online shortly. I know it's not print, but it's better than nothing. Hopefully with some more research, we can break more of it in print by tomorrow. By the way, I think someone from the government is trying to shut the story down. My neighbor just informed me that apparently some guys in suits—who I would imagine are from the government—just broke into my place. The funny thing is that was what pushed my publisher over the edge to let me post this online. Give me a call as soon as you get this. Take care and be careful, Henry," he said, ending the call.

47

Jessica lay back stretching out on her towel. Henry looked at her toned body glistening with the saltwater. He leaned over onto his side and kissed her on the lips. She kissed him back. He slid his hand under her neck and pulled her bikini's top string loose. He slowly slid his hand further down her back and pulled the lower string loose as well. He slid her top off exposing her breasts.

"Henry?" she said, leaning forward covering herself with her hands and looking around the beach.

"Jess, there's no one around—look," he said, waving around with his hand. "You said so yourself. Plus even if there were people, it's almost criminal to not let them see these breasts. Look at them, Jess," he said, gently pushing her back down. She shook her head at him smiling and closing her eyes in embarrassment. He cupped her breast with his hand and softly kissed it. "You're doing a great job taking my mind off things, Jess," he said, kissing her and running his hand down from her breasts toward her belly button.

Suddenly there was a loud thumping sound in the distance that grew louder. At first Henry thought it was somebody with a boom box with the bass cranked up. They both sat up. Jessica instinctively covered her bare breasts with her arm while reaching behind her for her bikini top.

"What is that?" Jessica asked.

"I think it's maybe a helicopter," Henry said. He started to get up and offered Jessica his hand. "Come on—maybe we ought to go back up to the house." He could feel his heart pounding in his chest. He grabbed her hand and pulled her up. As she rose she dropped her other hand that had been covering her breasts and snatched her bikini top off of the sand.

Just then a large military Blackhawk helicopter came up over the dune about twenty-five feet off the ground.

"Shit! Run, Jess," Henry said, pulling her by the hand.

"Henry, I don't have my top on," Jessica yelled as they ran.

"Worry about that once we get inside," Henry yelled back, hoping they would in fact make it inside.

Henry felt the bullet hit him in the shoulder before he even heard the gunshot. Jessica was looking down trying to not trip on a piece of driftwood in the sea grass and missed him being shot.

"Run in a zigzag motion, Jess," Henry said, dodging to the left and right as they ran.

They made it up the little sandy path that cut through the sea grass when Henry heard Jessica cry out behind him. He turned and saw that she was bleeding under her right breast. He was horrified by the look of terror on her face. He would never forgive himself for putting her in this danger.

"Just keep going, Henry," Jessica said, hurrying along behind him. "We can make it."

Henry held her hand tight and ran up the path. Just as they were coming up to the patio, Henry spotted a man standing in one of the open patio doors of the house aiming a gun at them.

"Get down, Jess," Henry said, diving into the sea grass and dragging Jessica along with him.

Jessica looked in the direction of the house to see why they were no longer moving forward, and she was incredibly confused by who she saw standing in the doorway.

48

Marcus drove down the driveway that led to his sister's place. He pulled his car around the circle and parked in front of the front door. He opened the car door, and when he stood up, he started to black out. He bent down between the open door and the car and held his hands to his knees. He took in a few deep breaths, and after a few moments he slowly stood back up.

Going to the back of the car and popping the trunk, he pulled out his two suitcases one at a time and placed them on the ground. Grabbing the telescoping handles of each one, he tried pulling them behind him, wincing at the pain in his hand that had been shot. He went back to the passenger side, opened the door, and pulled out his shoulder bag, throwing it over his shoulder. Starting toward the door again, he realized he couldn't pull with his hand that was shot, so he left one by the car and brought a suitcase and his shoulder bag up and dropped them by the door. Then he went back, grabbed the other suitcase, and went back up to the front door with it.

Just to be safe he rang the bell, although the house appeared to be empty with all of the shutters pulled down. He flipped through his keys, found the right one, and inserted it into the deadbolt. He tried to twist the key clockwise, and it wouldn't turn.

"Seriously?" Marcus said to the empty entranceway. He tried again twisting it clockwise and then counterclockwise with no results. "Son of a bitch," he said, kicking the door.

Pulling the key from the lock, he inspected it. Then he looked through the other keys on his ring, but he knew all of the others belonged to other locks. He slid the key into his mouth to lubricate it with his saliva. Since he was already feeling nauseated from all the pain he was in, the metal taste in his mouth reminded him of blood and he gagged. He bent down again with his hands on his knees, took in deep breaths, and tried not to vomit all over the welcome mat.

Once the nausea passed, he slowly stood up, waited for his dizziness to clear, and then inserted the key once again. At first he got the same results, but then he backed the key out of the lock a little bit, and this time when he twisted it back and forth, the key turned and the deadbolt clicked open. He contemplated shouting *hallelujah*, but he was afraid he would vomit in the process. He wiped away the sweat that had formed on his forehead with his good arm.

Pushing the door open he called out, "Hello? Anybody home?" Thankfully for him no one responded. Bringing his suitcases in far enough for the door to clear, he then closed the door and locked the deadbolt. Leaving his suitcases by the door, he walked down the hallway toward the kitchen and family room areas along the back of the house. He hung his shoulder bag on a bar stool and prayed there was a Coke in the fridge to help settle his stomach.

As luck would have it, there was a can of Coke in the fridge. He popped it open and took a few sips. The crisp taste of the cold soda soothed his parched throat. He walked over and found some crackers in the pantry and brought them over to the counter. After fumbling with the packaging with his good hand, he finally ripped the sleeve open with his teeth. He ate a couple crackers and washed them down with Coke. He was trying to get food in his stomach and keep it down so he could pop some pain pills.

He pulled out one of the stools at the breakfast bar and sat at the counter. He ate a few more crackers and followed them down with the rest of the Coke. When he was convinced he wasn't going to vomit, he went to his bag and retrieved his bottle of pain pills. He tapped a couple out and went over to the refrigerator to grab a bottled water to take them with. On the way to the refrigerator, he stepped on the trash can pedal lifting the lid and dropped the empty Coke can in. He heard it drop down and hit glass. He winced at the noise since it seemed deafening in the silent house.

He opened the fridge, grabbed a bottled water, and washed down the pills. Then a thought crossed his mind, and he cocked his head to the side and went back over to the trash can. He had a feeling, but he couldn't quite put his finger on it. He pressed the pedal and peeked inside the trash can. There was his empty can lying on top of a few beer bottles, some used paper towels, and a portion of a sandwich. He was puzzled as to why there was perishable trash in the can when his sister and her husband had been gone for a while and weren't expected back until Thanksgiving.

He looked around the kitchen and walked over to the sink. There were a couple of plates with some used silverware sitting on top of them, and there was mustard on one of the plates that looked fresh. Marcus looked around the kitchen and family room. Then it dawned on him—all of the hurricane shutters were up along the back of the house. He realized that someone was there but apparently didn't want anyone to know since all of the shutters were still closed along the front of the house. He couldn't believe he had missed such an obvious thing.

He walked toward the doors that led out to the patio. Then he heard the sound of a helicopter that seemed to come out of nowhere and was getting louder by the second. "Oh shit," Marcus said. He figured the guy from the storage unit must have followed him and notified General Mustin of his location. Quickly racing back to the front entrance, he opened his suitcase containing his weaponry. He grabbed the case that contained his rifle, quickly opened it, and assembled the rifle. He also pulled out a Ruger and a nine millimeter and shoved them into his waist band. Closing and righting the suitcase, he dragged it back with him into the family room in case he needed more firepower.

He looked out the doors toward the beach. The helicopter came into view and confirmed Marcus's suspicion that it was indeed a Blackhawk military helicopter. There was a gunman with a rifle leaning out the open back door of the helicopter. Marcus stepped over and gripped the handle on the patio door with his wounded hand while holding the rifle with his good one. He was definitely not going down without a fight.

As he started to open the door, he saw white puffs of smoke coming out of the gunman's rifle. But it didn't make sense because he wasn't aiming toward Marcus. It looked like he was shooting at something down on the beach. Marcus didn't understand.

Movement caught Marcus's attention in the sea grass by the path that led down to the beach. He decided they must also be coming at him on the ground. He couldn't believe Mustin was going to all of this trouble over a dead guy on his porch. He pulled open the door and lowered his rifle in the direction of the movement. He was about to shoot when a young man dressed only in his boxers and bleeding from the shoulder came running up the path pulling a topless girl behind him. Just then the girl was hit in the back by the gunman on the Blackhawk. The bullet exited her chest just below her breast. For a second Marcus thought he was hallucinating the whole scene. The girl looked familiar, and then it dawned on him that the topless girl being dragged by the underwear guy was in fact his niece Jessica.

Marcus watched as the underwear guy spotted him in the doorway and dove into the sea grass pulling Jessica down with him. From the look on her face, he was pretty sure Jessica recognized him.

"Jessica!" he yelled out to her. He then lifted his rifle and took aim at the gunman in the Blackhawk. He was mortified that he had brought these assassins to his sister's house and that now they had shot his niece. The blood surged to his head and he went into autopilot, becoming the trained assassin he was.

Once Marcus had the helicopter gunman in his sights, he took his shot and successfully hit him in the side of the head. He saw the spray of blood coat the door jamb on the chopper. The gunman slumped forward and hung suspended halfway out of the helicopter by his safety strap. Another gunman came up behind the slumped one and aimed at Marcus. Marcus was already aiming in his direction and shot him, hitting him in the face. He dropped like a lead weight. Marcus aimed at the rotor of the helicopter and fired repeatedly at it. Black smoke started to pour from the rear of the helicopter as it jerked out of control.

Marcus aimed and fired repeatedly at the pilot until the glass protecting him finally shattered. He knew he had successfully hit the pilot when the helicopter flew in a lazy circle downward, crashing into the Atlantic.

49

When there was a lull in the gunfire, Henry turned to Jessica. "Is it me, or did it sound like the gunman in the house just called out your name?"

"He did call me—that's my uncle," she said, struggling to put her bikini top back on.

"Can you tie it please?" she asked him.

"Of course," Henry said, tying her top back on. He was sick looking at the torn flesh in her back where the bullet had entered. There was a slow flow of blood coming from the wound. They heard the helicopter whining, and then they heard a splash in the water. "Well, I think he just saved us from the killers in the helicopter," he said.

Jessica slowly stood up and started to move back toward the house.

"Are you sure it's him, Jess?" Henry asked, trying to pull her back down so they could think first.

She shrugged him off and started to go back up the path toward the patio. Henry popped up and followed right behind her.

"Jessica, I'm so sorry. I didn't know you were here," Marcus said, hurrying down to her.

"What are you doing here, Uncle Marcus?" Jessica asked. "What happened to you?" she asked, looking at his wounds.

"It's a long story. We need to get you to a hospital, Jess. You're bleeding and so is your friend here," he said, nodding toward Henry.

"This is my boyfriend, Henry Pendelton. Henry, this is my mom's brother, Marcus."

"Pendelton?" Marcus asked as his eyes grew large.

Jessica gently pulled on her beach cover-up while Henry put on his shorts. He gingerly pulled his T-shirt on over his wounded shoulder.

"Yes, Henry Pendelton," Jessica said. "But listen, Uncle Marcus. I know what you're thinking, but he's innocent. He didn't kill anyone.

He's being set up by the government. We came here to hide out until our friend's cousin who works at the *New York Times* can break the story and clear Henry's name." She took in a deep breath and then grabbed onto Henry and started to pass out.

Henry caught her as she collapsed. She took in another deep breath and shook her head trying to clear it. Marcus helped Henry place her down on one of the lounge chairs.

"I'm OK. I'll be fine," she said, brushing them both away. "The bullet exited, so I'll be fine. I saw this same thing happen a zillion times on that show *ER*," she said. "It still pisses me off that it's no longer on." A red spot on the front of her white cover-up began to bloom from the wound.

"We have to get you two to a hospital right now. You're in shock," Marcus said.

Henry picked up Jessica's phone and the throwaway phone and dropped them into the pocket of his cargo shorts. Henry and Marcus lifted Jessica under her arms and acted as crutches for her as they walked her back toward the house. She remained conscious and tried to help move herself along.

"We're so lucky you showed up, Uncle Marcus," she said, smiling at him. "I don't think we would have made it if you weren't here."

The smile made Marcus feel even worse than he already did. He knew he had brought this on. "Oh, Jess, I'm so sorry. I'll get them for doing this to you. Just hold on, and we'll get you help," he said, easing her through the patio door and back into the house.

"Where's your car?" Marcus asked Henry.

"It's in the garage. We hid it in there in case someone showed up."

"OK, let's take that."

"I should go find our shoes," Henry said.

"There isn't time. We have to go," Marcus said, glancing down at Jessica then back at Henry.

As they passed by the counter, Henry reached in and grabbed Jessica's purse off the kitchen stool. Marcus reached over and grabbed a dish

The Mercy Project 235

towel off the counter and handed it to Henry. "Use this to compress the wound and try to stop the bleeding."

"OK," he said as they hurried out into the garage.

Marcus pressed the garage door button on the wall. "I'll drive," he said to Henry. Henry tossed him the keys and he caught them.

Henry opened the back door and sat in the back seat, pulling Jessica in on top of him and cradling her upper body in his lap. Marcus shut the door behind them, hopped in the driver seat, and started the car. Before Henry knew it, they were already turning out of the driveway and onto the main road. *Jessica was right*, Henry thought, *thank God for Uncle Marcus showing up.*

50

"General Mustin is on line two," Lara Roberts said over the intercom to Tom Laurel.

Tom was already on line one talking to his wife. "All right, thank you, Lara," Tom said, pressing the intercom button.

"Heather, I need to take this call," Tom said to his wife. "Just keep watching the news, and tell me if anything pops up about Don Kepler. Love you too," he said, disconnecting the call and then pressing the flashing button for line two.

"Give me good news, General."

"If good news is the fact that the Blackhawk we sent to take out your harmless boy is now floating in the Atlantic and boy wonder got away, then consider it good news delivered," General Mustin said sarcastically.

"What the hell happened?" Tom asked.

"The copilot of the helicopter said they came upon the two of them on the beach. You were right—they were there. However, as the men in the chopper overtook them and began firing, someone up in the house started firing at the chopper. The copilot said it appeared the guy in the house knew what he was doing. He took out both gunmen in the back, fired at the tail rotor until they lost control, and then fired at the pilot until he broke through the glass and took him out. The copilot and the navigator were able to call it in on the radio and then exit. I should have another chopper there in about twenty minutes."

"Jesus Christ. Can anything else go wrong with this?" Tom asked. He was repeatedly refreshing the *New York Times* website trying to see if their boy Ben was going to sign his death warrant and post something about the Health-Care Initiative. "Call me as soon as the other chopper gets there, and alert the local police that it's a military matter and not to interfere. Have the local police shut down the roads leading away from the Barrington's house as soon as possible."

"I've already alerted the local police, and they said they'll do the best they can with the little resources they have. The chief actually started bitching about budget cuts to me. He was a little prick, if you want to know the truth."

"Thanks, General. Let's get this thing contained so we can both laugh about this someday."

"Will do, Tom," he said, ending the call.

51

"How do you work this thing?" Marcus asked, pointing toward the navigation system on the dash of Henry's BMW.

"Press the button on the screen by the word *Navigation*," Henry said.

Marcus pressed it. A menu displayed with different options.

"Right there. Press the button by *Emergency*," Henry said.

Marcus pressed it. Then when the option for *Hospital* displayed, Marcus pressed the button by that. An hourglass displayed, and a voice told him to *please wait while a route is calculated*.

"I'm so cold, Henry," Jessica said.

Henry leaned forward and adjusted the rear climate controls turning the heat on. "I turned the heat up. You'll be OK, Jess," Henry said, rubbing her arm trying to warm her. He continued to press down on her wound with the dish towel, trying to slow down the bleeding.

"I'm so happy we met, Henry," Jessica said, looking up at him with a smile.

"Me too," he replied.

"You've made me so happy these last few months."

"You've made me so happy too, Jess. Now hang in there. We have a lot more time to be happy together."

"Henry, it really hurts," she said, almost panting with pain.

"Could you please go faster?" he begged Marcus from the back.

"I'm going as fast as I can, Henry. We both want her to get better. Hang in there, Jess," Marcus said from the front looking at Henry in the rearview mirror.

"Can't you make it warmer?" Jessica asked shivering.

Henry reached forward and rotated the dial to the maximum heat setting. "Could you please turn the heat up in the front?" Henry asked Marcus. "Jess is shivering back here."

"Got it," he replied, reaching over and turning the dials in the front toward maximum heat.

Jessica continued shivering in Henry's arms.

"Remember that little inn we stayed in when we took the train to Zurich?" Henry asked, trying to keep her conscious with conversation about their summer in Europe.

"Yes," she responded.

"And how foggy it was when we got there?" he asked.

"Yes, and that lady?" Jessica said. "The old lady at the inn," she said with ragged breaths. "She was so sweet. She made us have some of her homemade pie. Remember, Henry? Do you remember what she said?"

"No, what did she say?" Henry asked with tears rolling down his face. He was terrified they weren't going to make it to the hospital in time. The dishtowel was completely soaked with her blood. After all he'd lost in the last two days, he didn't think he could go on if he lost her too.

"She said, 'Sit, you must eat this old lady's pie.'" Jessica said it in the same accent the woman had used. "Remember? I don't think I've ever seen your face turn that red since," she said, grinning and closing her eyes as she turned her head toward Henry's chest.

"Yes, I remember," Henry said, grinning through the tears.

"Uncle Marcus?" Jessica asked, turning her head toward the front.

"Yeah, Jess?"

"I love you. Thank you for saving us," she said.

"I love you too, Jess. Now just hang on. Just a little longer and we'll be there."

She turned back and looked up into Henry's face. She smiled. "I love you, Henry."

"I love you too, Jess," he said. He bent down and kissed her. "Now just hang in there."

She smiled and then closed her eyes turning her head back into Henry's chest. He gently rocked her.

"Please hurry. Please, please hurry. We have to get her help," Henry said to Marcus. The tears fell into his mouth as he begged Marcus to hurry. He felt the salty taste of the tears in his mouth, and it reminded him of when he used to cry like this when he was a little boy.

Marcus didn't respond; he just sped down the road listening to the navigational instructions. As they reached the hospital, he raced the car onto the hospital grounds and followed the signs leading to the emergency room. The guard sitting by the emergency entrance didn't think Marcus was going to be able to stop in time and that they were going to crash through the doors straight into the ER. But Marcus slowed to a stop, driving right up onto the sidewalk and parking just outside of the doors. He hopped out of the driver's seat and then swung Henry's door open.

The look on Henry's face told Marcus everything.

"Don't leave me, Jess," Henry was saying through his sobs. "Don't leave. I'm so sorry I dragged you into this. I love you."

Marcus could see that Jessica was still, her eyes were half open, and she was gone. He didn't want to admit it to himself, so he ran up to the glass doors ignoring the guard getting up and telling him he couldn't park there. Once the doors opened, he screamed inside at the woman behind the admissions partition. "We need help. A girl's been shot," he yelled. He went back to the car and bent down stroking her hair. "Oh no, Jessica. No. This wasn't supposed to happen. I remember the day you were born, Jess. You made your parents so happy. They love you, Jess. I love you, Jess," he said while crying and holding his head in his hand.

A nurse and two orderlies came running out with a stretcher. Marcus got up out of the way and Henry slid out holding her. The orderlies lifted her up and put her on a stretcher. The nurse climbed up, straddling Jessica on top of the stretcher, and started chest compressions. The orderlies rushed her into the emergency room, and Henry and Marcus followed.

The orderlies ran rolling her on the stretcher down the corridor. They went through a set of double doors and kept running. They came to another set of doors, rushed through those, and then turned left into a room.

Henry and Marcus stood out in the hall watching as hospital staff swarmed around her.

"I have no pulse," a nurse said.

"I'm sorry, you can't wait here," another nurse said, coming over to Henry and Marcus.

"But—" Henry said.

"We need to do our job," she said, walking them back the way they came. "I'll come get you when we're finished."

They walked back out of the last set of double doors they had come through and found some chairs against the wall in the hallway. They both sat down.

"Did you hear that nurse say, 'I'll come get you when we're finished'? That doesn't sound too promising," Henry said.

"Let them do their jobs," Marcus said, patting Henry on the leg.

Henry dropped his head into his hands and started to cry. "This is all my fault. I should have insisted that Jessica not come with me. It's my fault that she's gone," he said. He sat there slumped over and crying.

Marcus dropped his head down. He couldn't let Henry think this was his fault. He sat there listening to Henry cry and finally couldn't take it anymore. He was the one who got Jessica killed; he couldn't let this kid think it was his fault. "No, Henry, it's not your fault. I brought them to you. I'm the one they want."

"What are you talking about?" Henry asked, completely confused.

"They were there for me. I work for the government on the Health-Care Initiative. It was me, Henry. I was the one who euthanized your grandmother and started this whole nightmare. It was a mistake—I swear to God. I was sent there to euthanize another woman."

Henry looked up. "What are you talking about?"

"I was sent to the nursing home. It was supposed to be a different woman—Alice."

"Alice?" Henry said. He couldn't believe what Marcus was saying.

"Yes, Alice. But your grandmother was lying down in Alice's bed for some reason. I thought I was taking out Alice, when it was actually your grandmother. I'm so sorry. I was the one who started this whole thing."

"What the fuck? Who are you? Was Jessica a part of this?" Henry asked.

"No. Jessica has no idea what I do for a living."

"I'm supposed to believe that my girlfriend's uncle coincidentally turns out to be my grandmother's killer?" Henry asked.

"I don't know what to tell you, Henry. I'm sorry. It's a small world. I couldn't believe my eyes when I saw Jessica behind you coming up the path, and then I couldn't believe my ears when she said your last name was Pendelton. I don't know what to tell you. I'm so sorry. I couldn't sit here and let you think this was because of you. What's happened to Jessica isn't your fault. It's clearly mine," he said.

Henry was speechless. He wanted to start punching him, but he was afraid he wouldn't be able to stop. He couldn't process the thought that this monster was somehow related to Jessica. *How fucked up is this*, he thought. He looked down at his shoes and tried to control himself.

"Honestly? You fucking killed my grandmother, and you're my girlfriend's uncle. What are the odds?" Henry finally responded. "How could you possibly be related to Jessica's mother? I've met her, and she's a classy, elegant woman. Were you adopted or something?"

"No. Fortunately for my sister, my father didn't believe in women in the military, so he just made me enlist. That's where I was trained to do what I do."

"So you kill people for a living?" Henry asked, looking down shaking his head. He was thinking this had to be a dream or that maybe he was hallucinating.

"Well, yes, but it's not like that. They sold the program to me as a mercy thing. It was to euthanize the sick. I've never killed someone who wasn't trying to kill me or was about to kill others," he said and then remembered Alice and Glen from earlier that day. He quickly brushed that thought away telling himself he would deal with it later. He continued, "It was supposed to be like when you put your dog down," he said. "You hate to take away its life, but you ask yourself, what's important? Quality or quantity?"

"Quality," Henry said numbly, although he couldn't believe he was having this conversation with the guy who killed his grandmother.

"Exactly—quality. That's where I came in. If quality wasn't there, I would relieve them of their earthly duties."

"But who are you to judge what quality is?" Henry asked.

Marcus was silent.

Henry too was silent.

They sat there both looking down at their feet, waiting for the nurse to come out and tell them what they already knew.

"You can make this right," Henry said.

"How?" Marcus asked.

"You can come clean. I already forwarded the file with all of the information pertaining to your project. I even have Don Kepler on audio admitting what the project was about. You could seal the deal. Talk to our guy Ben at the *New York Times* who's working on exposing the story and confess."

"Henry, I—" Marcus started to say and then stopped.

"I guess you have to look at your life in terms of quality or quantity," Henry said. "Do you want to live out the rest of your life just counting out the days until you're busted, or do you want to set the record straight and right this wrong? You said you were sorry—now prove it. If you're wavering at all, think of doing it in Jessica's memory—or for killing my grandmother, you asshole."

Henry looked Marcus in the eyes and waited for him to answer.

52

The computer screen refreshed, and Tom's stomach dropped.

President's Chief of Staff Allegedly Admits Government Conspiracy
By Benjamin Aquafen
The New York Times received an audio recording allegedly of the president's chief of staff, Donald Kepler, admitting to a government conspiracy to euthanize the elderly in an attempt to save money for Medicare and Medicaid. The audio is currently being verified for authenticity whether it is in fact the voice of Donald Kepler.
The New York Times received this audio from Henry Pendelton, the son of the late senator Daniel Pendelton and the grandson of the late Eleanor Pendelton. He is currently a person of interest in the deaths of several family members. Henry Pendelton stated that he taped the conversation with Donald Kepler this morning while meeting with him, and he also went on to claim that Donald Kepler was the person responsible for the deaths of Senator Daniel Pendelton, Eleanor Pendelton, and William Pendelton.

The story continued but Tom stopped reading it and called his secretary.

"Yes?"

"Get me General Mustin on the phone, and then get me the publisher of the *New York Times*," Tom said.

"Yes, sir," Lara said.

Tom sat back wishing he hadn't come to the office that day. After a few minutes, Lara came over the intercom.

"General Mustin on line one."

He picked up the phone. "Anything yet, General?" Tom asked, sounding desperate.

"My guys are five minutes out. I said I'd call as soon as I know anything," he said.

"Just make sure you do. I'm waiting," Tom said, ending the call.

He pressed the intercom button again. "Do you have the publisher yet?" he asked Lara.

"I'm on hold," Lara replied.

"Did you tell them it was me who was calling?" Tom asked.

"Of course, Director."

"And they have you on hold?"

"Yes, sir."

"If they won't put the publisher on, then insist they put on the editor or whoever it is that's in charge of the bullshit they put up on their website that needs to come down. Tell them it's a matter of national security and a directive of the president of the United States."

"Yes, sir," Lara said.

"Get me Jim Sidney in the New York City division while you're holding."

"Yes, Director."

Lara came over the intercom. "Jim Sidney is on line one."

Tom picked up the phone. "Apparently you didn't find the reporter you were supposed to," Tom said.

"I'm sorry, Director. We had a situation in Washington Square regarding a suspicious backpack next to a school yard, so I got tied up," he said. "And unfortunately, no, we did not find the reporter."

"Did I not mention this was a matter of national security?" Tom asked in disbelief.

"You did, sir."

"Then get your men over to the *New York Times* right now, and find me this reporter for questioning. If I can't shut this thing down, I'm going to hang you myself," Tom said, slamming down the phone.

53

"Henry, it's not that simple," Marcus said. "Even if I want to come clean, there's no way I'm going to live long enough to have it make a difference."

"Are you sick?" Henry asked.

"No. What I'm trying to say is that people in the government aren't going to let me live long enough to ever testify to what I've done and what they are doing."

"Don't you understand?" Henry asked. "This is the same predicament I'm in right now. I put a lot of thought into it. The more public we go with our stories, the better chance we have that they can't get rid of us."

"But, Henry, I've ended a lot of lives."

"But you were told to by our government. Right?"

"In a roundabout way, yes."

"Then just talk to Ben at the *New York Times*," Henry said.

"How about this? I'll talk to your guy and confess, but then I'm leaving the country. I'm sorry I don't have the faith you do, but I've seen the way things can be twisted by this government. I'll give him the names of everyone I know who's involved."

Henry reached down into his pocket and pulled out Jessica's phone. When he pulled it out he saw there was one new voice message from Ben. He called voice mail and listened to the message.

"He did it," Henry said, slumping down in his seat. Tears rolled down his cheeks. "Ben's posting the story online," he said, turning to Marcus.

"No shit."

"Yes shit. Are we good? Are you ready to help shut this thing down?" Henry asked him.

"OK, give him a call," Marcus said.

Henry called Ben.

"Henry. You got my message?"

"Yes. Thanks, Ben. I owe you more than you'll ever know."

"Not a problem. My buddy just called me from the office and told me Reuters picked up the story and it's going global. It's going to be pretty hard to put a lid on this thing now."

"You're not in the office?"

"No, the director of the CIA called looking for the publisher, so he and I are hiding out over at Starbucks."

"Ben, I've got someone here who I think could help with shutting this whole thing down."

"You have more?" Ben asked.

"Yes, I've got one of the guys that did the euthanizing. He's willing to talk, but then he's heading out of the country," Henry said.

"He's legit?" Ben asked.

"Of course. Hold on a second—I'll let you two talk," Henry said, passing the phone to Marcus.

Marcus got on the phone with Ben and started to tell him all of the information he knew about the project, including the names of everyone he could think of who were involved.

Exhaustion came over Henry, and he leaned forward putting his head into his hands. Marcus noticed the stain of blood that coated his back from the gunshot wound in his shoulder. He also noticed a pool of blood on Henry's seat.

"Ben, I'm going to have to call you back. Henry isn't looking too good." He hung up the phone and went to Henry.

"Henry, are you feeling all right?" Marcus asked. He could see the sweat on Henry's forehead, and his color wasn't good.

Henry just nodded his head.

"I'm such a jackass. You've been shot in the shoulder. Come on. I'm not going to let you die too," he said, lifting Henry up. He dragged him back through the double doors where they had Jessica, and as soon as they made it across the threshold, Henry collapsed.

54

"General Mustin is on line one," Lara said over the intercom.

Don picked up the phone. "Well?"

"House is clear, and local police are saying they didn't stop anyone."

"Goddamn it," Tom said, slamming his fist down on the desk. "Now what?" he asked.

"You might want to have your men track down local hospitals. There's blood here, and the copilot confirmed that they hit both the boy and the girl."

"Well, now you tell me some good news," Tom said.

General Mustin actually belly laughed. "You're one sick son of a bitch, Tom."

Tom laughed. "Now we just have to find him and recover that drive."

"Director?" Lara called on the intercom.

"Excuse me, General. Yes, Lara?" Tom asked.

"Director, the secretary for the president is on line two saying the president would like to speak with you."

"Did she just say the president?" General Mustin asked.

"I'll call you back," Tom said, disconnecting the call. He pressed the button connecting line two.

"This is Director Laurel."

"Please hold for the president," the secretary said.

Tom wasn't immediately sure if this was a good thing or a bad thing. He held the phone to his ear and waited.

"Director, what the hell is going on?" the president asked.

This was a bad thing, Tom decided. "What do you mean, Mr. President?"

"My chief of staff is admitting there's a government conspiracy? Is this true, Tom?"

Tom knew the president was completely aware of the project, but he also knew that all calls going through his office were recorded. This call was an attempt to prove that the president was clean and that he didn't know anything about the project. The question was, would Tom let him off the hook or hold his feet to the fire? They both knew that the president was the one who signed off on this, after all.

"Mr. President?" Tom answered. He paused letting the president sweat a little. "Unfortunately Mr. Kepler's body was discovered a short time ago at Arlington National Cemetery. I'm sorry to have to be the one to deliver the news. So your guess is as good as mine," Tom answered.

"Oh my gosh, Tom. What happened?" the president asked.

"There were no signs of trauma, so they think maybe it was a heart attack."

"What a shame. So we'll never know if he went rogue and tried to actually develop some plan, like they're saying in the *New York Times*. Is that right?"

"I would imagine so, Mr. President."

"Well, either way, look into this thing, and for God's sake if there's any truth at all to this story, shut down anything you come across and alert me as soon as you do. Although I would have to imagine that, if for some reason there ever was such a project, that by now anyone involved would have deleted any evidence that it ever existed," the president said, sighing. "Just bring it to my attention immediately if anything surfaces. Are we clear?"

"Perfectly clear, sir."

"By the way, that poor Pendelton kid," the president said. "Sad story. I hope his story in the *Times* isn't true about Don actually taking out his father and uncle and trying to pin it on him. Although now that Don is gone, I guess at least he's safe now, and once he's found we can apologize for what Don has done to the poor kid. I'm completely blindsided over Don's behavior. You think you know a person. I'll have to have Jane and Henry over to dinner once he's found so I can personally apologize for Don's behavior. Let everyone out there looking for Henry know that I want him found and in good condition. If Don had anyone working with him, and they harm Henry in any way, I will make it my mission to have them brought to justice. Are we clear, Tom?"

"Perfectly clear, Mr. President," Tom said.

"OK, Tom, we'll talk soon. Say hello to Heather for me."

"I sure will, Mr. President. Please tell the First Lady I said hello."

"Will do, Tom. Take care," the president said, ending the call.

Tom slammed his fists down on his desk. He pushed the intercom button.

"Yes?" Lara asked.

"Get me Mustin," Tom said.

"Yes, sir," she replied. A few moments passed. "General Mustin on line one, Director."

"General, I need you to stand down," Tom said. "Have your men get out of there, and get someone out there to clean up the Blackhawk in the water."

"What's going on, Tom?" the General asked.

"We're shutting down the project. Call your men in and debrief them. Send them back to whatever unit we got them from," Tom said.

"Are you sure you have the authority to do this, Tom?"

"I just spoke with the president. In an indirect way, he said he wants it shut down and we're to lay off Mr. Pendelton. The president is going to have him at the White House to apologize about what Don did to them."

"He's just going to pin it all on Don?"

"It looks that way," Tom responded.

"I just wish he was alive to enjoy that fact," the general said laughing.

"No love lost there, huh?" Tom asked.

"Not even a little. That guy was a prick."

55

"Would you stop crying? Now I am starting to think you're a pussy," Jessica said.

"I thought you were gone, Jess. I can't tell you how happy I am right now," Henry said with tears pouring down his face. He wiped his eyes and nose with his arm.

"I told you the bullet exited and I would be fine. I said I saw it all the time on *ER*. You were the one I was concerned about," she said, sitting up in her wheelchair.

"Oh, me? You were concerned about me?"

"You're the one who's laying in that hospital bed still."

"Oh, Jess. You really don't know how happy I am right now that you're alive. What happened?" he asked.

"They said I was DOA. Dead on arrival. Pretty creepy, huh?" she said, making a face.

"You could say that."

"Well, they performed CPR, pumped me full of blood, and got my heart beating again. Fortunately for me, they used some sort of robot to repair the artery that was torn by the bullet. So no big scar on my chest. So those plans I had to be a stripper are still on course," she said joking.

"You're such a freak, but I truly love you," he said, squeezing her hand.

She gently eased herself up from the wheel chair and leaned over to kiss him. "I know I'm a freak—that's why I love you too," she said. "Kidding aside, you apparently were in just as bad of shape as I was, Henry. You too lost a lot of blood and you've been out for two days. But Uncle Marcus stayed with me until they said you were going to be OK."

"Where is Marcus?" Henry asked.

"He said he had to leave, but he spent some time talking to Ben from the *Times*. He said to let you know that. He said you would know what he was talking about."

"How's Chad?"

"The doctor released him this morning, and he's out in the waiting room with Paul. I think they were both terrified you were going to die and they wouldn't have such a sweet place to live."

Henry smiled.

"All right Jessica, we need to get back to your room before the doctor discovers I snuck you out," her nurse said.

Jessica rolled her eyes. "They think I need my rest. If your mom wasn't waiting outside I would put up a fight," she said, sitting back down in the wheelchair. "Oh, I almost forgot. The president called here to ask about you."

"The president?" Henry asked.

"Yes, the president. He said once you have recovered, he wants you and your mom—and of course me—to come to the White House for dinner and an apology. But he said you have to wear underwear," she said laughing.

"You don't give up, do you?" Henry said. "Hey, where's the thing to turn this up?" Henry asked, pointing to the television.

"It's here on the nurse buzzer thing," she said, picking it up and turning up the volume. She sat in her wheelchair next to him and watched the television. Diane Sawyer was on, and there was a picture of Don up on the screen next to her.

In what some are now calling the biggest scandal in US history, more information is coming out regarding the president's chief of staff and his attempt to lower Medicare and Medicaid costs by using military assassins to euthanize the elderly.

Henry turned it off. "I know already. I don't need to hear it all over again."

"It's over, Henry," Jessica said, combing his hair across his forehead with her fingers.

"I know, Jess. Thank God," he said, closing his eyes and laying back.

❧

Made in the USA
Charleston, SC
11 December 2012